KAREN FRANCES

SECRETS AND LIES

Cover Design by
Kari March, Kari March Designs

Editing by
Karen Sanders

Proofread by
The Word Fairy

Interior Design and Formatting by
Clydeside Publishing

My Mum

I'd like to think I get my strength and determination from you.
I love you more than words could ever say.

PROLOGUE

THUD.

Whack.

My body shakes and winces in sympathy with each harrowing thud.

Screaming. There's lots and lots of screaming. The hairs on the back of my neck stand up. I hate this. I'm scared, and for a change, I'm not scared for myself.

"You fucking owe me," Tony hisses, walking around the room in circles. He's making me dizzy as I secretly watch on. At six-foot-two, Tony has always commanded every room he's ever walked into. Bile rises in my throat and disgust flows freely through my veins. "You can't expect to do what you've done and get away with it. I won't stand back and allow you to trample all over my turf. Better men than you have tried and failed. You're weak and useless. What makes you think you've got what it takes to bring me down?" Tony's voice sounds calm; too calm considering the situation before me. He's angry and that makes me more nervous.

I'm hiding behind a stack of boxes; my stomach is in

knots just from hearing the tone of his voice. So much anger and hatred, but there's something else… power. And the one thing Tony thrives on is having power over everyone and anyone. If he didn't have power, his life would be non-existent, and as I watch him, I come to the conclusion that it wouldn't be such a bad thing.

I've always known what my husband does for a living. It's not pretty. But there's something different about seeing it first-hand instead of just imagining what he does.

Tonight, after all these years we've been together, I'm seeing it for the very first time, and I hate the scene before me. My eyes are damp and I'm struggling to stop my tears from falling.

Upstairs, alcohol is flowing and the clubbers are enjoying the beat of the music. But down here in the cellar it's a completely different picture. It looks like something from a horror movie. *One I wouldn't watch.*

Pete, Tony's right-hand man, is torturing a guy. He has what looks like a hot poker stick in one hand and a police baton in the other. There's a table nearby and I have no idea what's on it; a range of torture instruments by the looks of it. I cover my mouth. The poor guy sits in a chair with his hands tied behind him, his face covered in blood. Whatever he's done, he's not talking. My attention changes from the guy in the chair as a young girl screams over and over.

The sound of her screams earlier hid my footsteps coming down the stairs. She's standing with her back to a wall, her whole body trembling in fear.

This is wrong. So wrong.

Tony, *my* Tony, is now turning from the guy in the chair and is skulking toward her, removing his black suit jacket. He loosens his tie. I stand frozen to the spot as he undoes the belt on his trousers. *No. Please not that. Spare her that. She's too young.* The words almost roll from my mouth as I take in what he's going to do.

"Please, no!" she screams.

Bile rises in my throat and I cover my mouth once more to stop myself from screaming out. There's a tingling in my chest and the tears filling my own eyes threaten to fall. My knees feel weak. I have to grip onto the boxes I'm hiding behind to stop me from falling to the ground. *How can he do this?* My eyes follow Tony and I finally see him for what he really is; a complete monster. A man who will stop at nothing to get what he wants. He's a man seeking revenge and he's about to destroy this poor girl. All I can do is pray that once he's finished using her, he'll end her life quickly because she's too young to get over whatever hell my husband decides to put her through.

Pete hits the guy once more across his face. My own head reels backward just watching the force of the blow.

Blood. There's so much blood.

"You won't talk or fucking pay up, so you'll have to watch as we both take something from you," Pete says, lifting the guy's chin, ensuring he has a front row seat to the show that is about to be put on. Even from here I can see his eyes widen. I don't think the guy is capable of speaking up now even if he wanted to; he's been battered so much around his face. I'm no doctor, but it looks as though his jaw is broken. "And after we make you watch, if you're lucky… very lucky, we'll kill you quickly."

The girl's screams get louder and she tries to run, but Tony already has her body pinned in place. He pulls up her dress and rips the underwear clean from her body. "You might not enjoy this, but I know I will," he sneers, leaning in to take what isn't on offer.

I can't watch. I'm defenceless to do anything to help

her. I know if I do try to help her, I'll end up in the same position as she's in now to teach me a lesson.

Slipping my shoes from my feet, I turn from my hiding spot and run up the stairs. Laughter rings loudly as I reach the top stair and then there's one final pitiful scream from the girl downstairs before there's nothing but silence.

Up until then, I knew she was still fighting against him with all the strength she could muster, but with the silence, that poor girl has accepted her fate. A fate I wouldn't want even my worst enemy to go through.

I rush out of the club without talking to anyone. Everyone is too busy dancing and having a good time to even notice me, the distraught wife of the owner. I shouldn't have come here tonight. There was a time I worshipped my husband; he was everything to me. But tonight, I've finally seen past the handsome man I'm married to and seen the ugliest part of him.

He's a monster. I'm married to a monster of a man and it's only a matter of time before he turns on me. *Again.*

My life can't go on like this.

I can't and won't be his next victim.

I grab my phone from my bag and dial the one number I know off by heart, hoping that I'm doing the right thing. "Fratello, ho bisogno di aiuto. Mi aiuti per favore? Non posso farlo più."

CHAPTER ONE

Maria

IT's FUNNY. One minute you can be riding along on the rollercoaster that is your life, feeling content, and then all of a sudden…

Crash.

Bang.

Wallop.

You're forced to stop and take in the chaos that surrounds you. Our lives are so busy, so full, that when this happens we truly don't know what to do.

I'm at this stage. Currently reflecting on my life. On all the mistakes I've made and wondering how on Earth I ended up where I am today.

Do I know the answers? I suppose, deep down I do. My life has been full of turbulence and violence, all because I fell for the wrong man. I've made plenty of mistakes in my thirty-two years, but falling for him has been *the* biggest mistake of my life and it's only the last few months that I've been able to see it clearly. I took a step back, disposed of the rose-tinted glasses, and finally saw the destruction that was happening right before my eyes.

And I hated what I saw.

The beeping of the machine to my right is giving me a sore head. I can't bear to listen to it another moment longer, but yet I know if I leave this room, questions will be asked of me. Assumptions will be made.

And I'm not ready for that. Not yet.

I pull the wires from my body and silence the damn machine then slowly step toward the window. My eyes focus on the darkness outside, and for the first time in a very long time, I don't feel so afraid. Darkness never used to scare me, but over time, something changed. Or maybe it was me. I no longer know.

There's nothing wrong with me. There's no need for me to be here, and especially not wired to some damn monitor. A hospital is a place for sick people, and I'm not sick. I'm very much fighting fit and alive. For that, I'm eternally grateful. And I'll pray to God for that every damn day.

To everyone who knows me, it looks as though I have the perfect life; a beautiful and very expensive home. A husband who ensures I want for nothing. Nice cars. Holidays several times a year. You name it, I've had it. To my husband's friends and acquaintances, it would appear he has the perfect wife. The one who has put up with the life he wants. No questions asked, *ever*.

I might not have asked the questions out loud, but they've been swirling around in my head, questioning my own sanity over the last few months. Why the hell have I put up with all his crap; the life of crime, the lies, the girls, the drinking, the threats against not just his but my life too? The living in constant fear and having protection with me wherever I go. The list is endless.

Glasgow is no different to any big city; the gangsters think they rule it, while others fight tooth and nail to claim a title that shouldn't belong to any of them. A title my husband believes he owns. Gangland wars; Glasgow is notorious for them. Tony is always slap, bang in the middle of it, pissing someone off. But he always comes out with a smile on his face.

The grey sky outside in the world beyond this room is very much like my mood as I stare out the window, wishing I was anywhere but here, waiting.

Waiting and hoping.

Hoping that the doctors finally come in and tell me what I already know. I'm sure even the detective that stands outside the room knows this as well. A smile comes easily to my lips. I'm certain his job would be easier without the likes of my husband and his cronies. They should all be behind bars instead of causing havoc around the city.

Maybe that's where I belong for playing my own silent part. I'm not exactly an innocent party in all this.

The detective has been in a few times in an attempt to question me, but I've played my role of the distressed and in-shock wife well. After all, it comes naturally to me. I've had plenty of practice over the years of acting. My mask has been firmly in place and the tears that fell were fake, even though I'm sure they looked real. Or at least I hope he thought they were real.

For the life of me, I can't remember the detective's name and I know he's told me. The only thing I remember vividly is all the details from last night, and I know they will stay with me and haunt me for the rest of my life. It's playing in my mind like a damn record stuck on repeat, going over and over.

From the minute my husband walked through the front

door of our beautiful home in what's known as the G12 village in a posh part of Glasgow, I knew my life would change. Tony was slurring his words and staggering around the house, calling my name, until he reached our bedroom door.

I had clenched my eyes tight together, pretending I was asleep, saying a silent prayer that when he climbed into bed beside me, he would fall fast asleep.

Still. I need to be still. So why won't my heart stop pounding? Please don't fail me.

I hear him move around the room. I'm sure he's taking off his suit jacket. He's always in a suit. Always immaculately dressed. To the outside world, he looks like the perfect gentleman, but those who know him know he is anything but. He's a criminal mastermind. A thug. A bully. Some would say a dead man walking.

He's breathing hard, and I try not to react when I hear him placing his gun on the bedside cabinet. He sleeps with it within reach every single night. When I was younger and naïve, I always thought the gun was just for show. Now that I'm meant to be older and wiser, I know differently.

He kicks off his shoes. I hear them landing on the floor with a thud. Next, he's loosening his belt, the zipper on his trousers, and he'll let them fall to the floor as he always does.

He's a stickler for routine, even in a drunken state. One of these nights he might surprise even me and be in a such a state that he forgets his routine.

I feel the bed dip beneath me as he gets in beside me. "My gorgeous wife," he says, running his fingers roughly through my hair. The stench of alcohol and sex fills my nostrils and I'm struggling not to react. "Come on, Maria. Time to make your man happy." Bile rises in my throat as I think about what he wants. He's come home to me, yet stinks of some whore. I'm not stupid.

He tugs on my hair, my neck jerking back. His other hand slides down my thigh before tugging on the silk of my nightdress, pulling it up around my waist.

I cringe, opening my eyes. "Please, Tony. Not tonight."

"But I want you. I always want you. Everyone wants you, but you're mine. No one else can ever have you." His voice is soft but his body is rigid and he's holding me firmly exactly where he wants me. This isn't what I want. I don't want him. I've not wanted him for months, but that hasn't stopped him from taking what he believes is owed to him.

"Tony, I'm tired."

"Tired? Too tired for your husband?" He pulls me roughly around and I don't have the energy to fight against him. I wish I did. "There you are. Now I'm sure we can both enjoy this."

I won't. "Tony, I'm really tired."

"You have a duty and I don't care how tired you are. It's your job to satisfy your husband's needs. And my need for you is strong."

"Did your whore not keep you satisfied tonight?" The words are out of my mouth before I realise what I've said. I don't see his reaction to my bitter words until his hand connects with my face, slapping me hard. Tears fill my eyes. It's not the first time I've had a slap in the face from him, but it's certainly the hardest.

He moves position until his naked body is above me, and this time I see the fist before it hits me. "You bitch. You ungrateful and selfish little bitch. It's you I come home to night after night. I could have anyone, and yet I still keep you around." Pain radiates through me as his fist repeatedly lands on my face.

"Tony, stop. Please," I cry out, but he laughs. He rips my knickers away from me and I know I should just let him get on with it in the hope that it will be over soon. Holding me tight below him, I close my eyes as he thrusts deep inside me. My tears fall as I cry out. Each time he thrusts, he lets out what sounds like a full belly laugh as he's clearly happy with what he's taking from me. Impossible as that sounds, it's true.

In between his laughter and my cries I hear a noise, like a door closing somewhere in the house. Did he bring someone home with him? No, surely not. I push my hands against his chest, hoping I have the strength to push him off me. A noise startles him and he turns his attention to our bedroom door.

Silence fills the air, and after a few moments, his attention returns to me. "Now, where were we?"

"You were going to fuck off and leave me alone."

"Oh, sweetheart. I don't think so. Not until I get what I want," he says loudly as he thrusts hard into me again, sending me into a panic. I don't want this. Not like this. His eyes close and I slowly slide my hand across the bed.

I almost gasp when I feel the bedside cabinet, but I don't. I don't want to alert him to what I'm doing. The tips of my fingers feel the gun and I pull it across, finally having it right where I need it.

My hand shakes uncontrollably as I hold it. I wrap my other hand around it and lift my arms up, slowly pushing the gun to his chest. This is it. His life is in my hands. But if I pull the trigger, will that make me as bad as him? Or can I justify it by saying I was saving myself? His eyes fly wide open, and for the first time since I've known him, a strange expression passes over him. Panic.

A noise in the hallway has us both turning toward the bedroom door. I breathe in deeply. He pulls the gun from my hands and points it at the door. Crashing and banging rings loudly throughout the house before the shattering of our bedroom window has us both turning our attention there.

Tony doesn't move.

He's just waiting and watching. Right now, my husband taking what he wants from me seems the safest option as my body shakes in fear of the unknown.

Whoever is in our home hasn't been invited. And as panic sets in about what's about to happen, there's a part of me that is also relieved that he's stopped forcing himself onto me. Tony has always been able to handle himself and keep me safe from others.

Something else flies through the window. I scream loudly when I see the bottle. Red flames spread quickly. The door bursts open and two masked men enter the bedroom with guns in their hands, pointing at us.

"I'll fucking kill you!" Tony shouts.

Everything happens so quickly yet seems to be in slow motion. One gunshot, two, then three. The men move and another shot is fired from one of their guns. "You bastards…" Tony's body falls to the side of me and I close my eyes, waiting for them to shoot again.

Waiting for my life to be taken. Waiting for the end.

"Che mi dici di lei?" a voice asks. I gasp, hearing not only the language, but the strong Italian accent that I probably wasn't meant to hear.

"Leave her. She has five minutes to get herself out of there."

"If you want her out then why not help?"

"Look, don't question me. We came here to do one thing. Now it's done. She can take care of herself. She's not our problem. Our problem is dealt with. Now! Out!"

The two men leave the room but I hear other voices shouting through the house. I need to move. I need to get out of here before I… I can't think about the what ifs. I push the rest of Tony's body away from me and scramble from the bed. I pause for a moment and look at him. Even in death destruction follows him.

His lifeless body lies on the floor, blood staining the carpet. The fire is spreading quickly through the room. I run in a panic and don't stop until I'm downstairs and outside in the garden, screaming for help.

One car speeds off while another car sits in the road, its engine revving, and three people get inside, slamming the doors closed behind them. It races off into the distance and there's nothing I can do but watch on as the flames take hold and burn throughout my home.

Tony's body is in there.

I sink to my knees and cry. It should never have come to this but, ultimately, I knew it would.

Two sets of hands grab my shoulders, pulling me to my feet and leading me away from the fire. I don't even know who it is. Sirens and flashing lights are all I see and hear. A blanket is wrapped around me and a woman's voice filters through the air. She now has me, and when I look at her and see sorrow in her eyes, I glance down at myself.

Blood.

Lots and lots of blood splattered all over my white silk nightdress.

"Come on, lovely. Let's get you checked over." I nod because, in this moment, there is nothing else I can do.

CHAPTER TWO

Jack

MARIA FRASER IS LED into the ambulance, her eyes wide and her body shaking. The paramedic has wrapped a blanket around her to keep her warm. All I know at this moment is that she fled the fire in only a blood-stained white silk nightie. I caught a glimpse of her as soon as I arrived here on the scene. The mask she's had in place for years was down, and for the first time, I saw the real woman. Not the one her husband presented to the world.

Not the one I've seen a million times before in pictures that have graced the boards back in the station, or in newspaper articles, but the real woman. A woman I'm sure has suffered because of her choice of husband. I saw her vulnerability, but I also saw her beauty along with her bruises. What the hell happened in that house tonight? Someone has beaten her, and badly.

I take a minute to clear my head. Fire crews are dealing with the fire that has spread quickly through her home. The siren of the first ambulance fades into the distance and another ambulance with paramedics is waiting. Tony Fraser is still inside, and from what I've been told, he's dead. Mrs Fraser told the paramedic he had been shot.

I want confirmation of that. I need to see his body.

The neighbours that were gathered on the street have gone back inside. Not even a curtain is bloody twitching. It's funny, now that I have officers on the scene to get information, they all disappear. No one wants to talk.

It seems even in death Tony Fraser is still feared. But why? He can't hurt anyone now.

"When can I get in?" I ask.

"Not until my lads have put the fire out and secured the building. But I'll say this, I think we'll be sifting through the rubble for evidence. I'm surprised the woman made it out."

"What about him?"

"If he's in there, we'll find him, but it won't be pretty."

"I need to see the body. I don't care what condition it's in."

"Detective, I wouldn't recommend it."

I want to remind him that I'm the DCI, detective chief inspector, but I don't see the point. I do hear what he's saying, but I have to know tonight if it is him or if this has all been some greater plan to fake his own death. Elaborate, I know, but the lengths some criminals will go to never ceases to amaze me. And if it is, how much does the wife know? He wouldn't be the first gangster to fake his own death.

I stand on the street, some of my own men still in their cars, because until the fire is out, there isn't a lot they or I can do. A few officers have already started door-to-door enquiries, although, as I look around I can see they're not having much joy.

It's always the same in cases like this. No-one wants to give out information. A nice neighbourhood like this, you'd think someone would want to see some sort of justice.

"Coffee, sir," Craig, my partner, says handing me a cup. It's funny hearing him call me sir. He only ever does that around other officers or when we're out on cases like this. When you work as hard as I do, friends are few and far between, but Craig is the closest friend I have. "What do you think?" He nods toward the house.

"I don't know. At the moment, I'm trying to keep an open mind. What facts do we know?"

"Okay, two cars pulled up at the house shortly after Mr Fraser arrived home. About six men got out. A neighbour, who doesn't want to be named and won't give an official statement, has told us that they heard what sounded like a window being broken. Then, the next minute, gunshots. The men all fled the scene and, at that point, Mrs Fraser came staggering from the house looking somewhat shocked."

"Is that it?" I ask, even though it's more than I expected. And now I believe this hasn't been some plan to fake his own death. Although, I won't rule it out until I can prove anything or see his body.

"Yes. Do we think someone has had enough of Fraser running the city?"

"Maybe. But truthfully, this could be anyone. Although, the timing all seems wrong. From our point of view, everything has been too quiet lately. No-one connected to him has been pulled in for questioning lately. Can you send an officer to the hospital? I want someone there at all times and I don't want anyone seeing Mrs Fraser until we've spoken to her. No family or any of his men, especially Pete Jamieson."

"What about you?"

"I'll go to the hospital and question Mrs Fraser once I've seen his body."

"You never could resist a damsel in distress, and let's face it, she's a mighty fine damsel."

"I'll pretend you didn't just say that, Craig. We have an investigation to run, and at the moment, she's a key witness."

"If she gives us a statement." He's right; there's no guarantee she'll give a statement.

I clear my head of all thoughts and focus on the here and now. There's always so much to do at scenes like this, even though it may appear to others that I'm doing very little.

"All clear." The paramedics that were waiting go in with a fireman. *This part is hard. Having to stand and wait for them to come back out. Everywhere I look there's a buzz of activity.*

It's ten long minutes before I see the paramedics coming toward me. A body on the trolley, fully covered. The fire chief walks beside them. I step forward.

"Are you sure?" he asks me.

"Yes." The cover is pulled back and it might not be the first time I've seen a dead man, but it's the first time I've seen a man so badly burned. There's not much of him left to recognise. I flinch. But it's him. Same body shape and size. It's Tony Fraser. The shape and style of the ring on his left hand. It's the only one of its kind I've ever seen. It's not a plain gold band, but a fine, interconnecting design.

There's bound to be some fallout from this. Whoever killed him is either very smart or very stupid, and I may end up with more than one dead body in the coming weeks.

"Two gunshot wounds," one of the paramedics tells me. "He was dead before the fire took hold."

"Where was his body found?"

"Bedroom, or what's left of it."

I rub my head. The visions and conversations of the last few hours are giving me a headache. "This is fucking ridiculous. Surely someone must've seen or heard something!" I shout at the officer before me, gathering the interest of the nursing staff that are standing talking. "What?" I'm not sure who my *what* is for, but the staff go back to doing what they were doing only moments before.

"McKenzie, you and I both know that, even if anyone saw anything, they won't talk to us. Fuck, I wouldn't want to talk to us if I was the one who witnessed last night's events. Let's face it, I'd be constantly looking over my shoulder, waiting for one of his goons to come after me," Craig tells me, looking at the young officer I've just shouted at.

He's got a point. I start pacing the hospital corridor, my

eyes drifting to the room door that is firmly closed. She might be able to give me some answers if she would only fucking talk to me.

All the work my team and I have put in over the last few months to try and pin something on Tony Fraser so he could be brought to justice for all the crimes *I know* he's committed, and this is how it ends. With him being shot dead while in bed with his wife. And the weird thing is, she's still alive, unharmed.

She has extensive bruising to her face and I know that wasn't caused by the fire. No, she was beaten before. But by who; the intruders or her husband?

That leads me to the question that is running around my head; why would someone leave behind an eye-witness to a murder? It just doesn't make any sense to me.

This is so fucking frustrating. I stare ahead rubbing my head. "I need in that fucking room! She needs to talk." I've been in a few times but she's not even so much as looked at me. She looks lost. Is she really a grieving widow?

"I'm sure as soon as the doctor has spoken with her, you'll be allowed in."

A doctor approaches me. "Detective."

"When can I talk to her?" I ask, impatient now that I'm being kept waiting for no apparent reason.

"Shortly! Now, I'm not sure if this will help with your investigation or not, and I probably shouldn't be mentioning it."

"Spit it out!" I demand, getting more annoyed by the minute that this bloody doctor is wasting precious time.

"Mrs Fraser has a lot of bruising to not just her face, as I'm sure you've seen, but also her arms and between her legs. I just thought you should know," he tells me before walking away.

All I'd wanted was a peaceful night.

Bloody hell.

I stare ahead and watch as the doctor and a nurse walk into the room.

Now I need to wait, *patiently*. And when it comes to cases like this, I'm not a patient man. I need answers.

And quickly.

And Maria Fraser is the only person who has them, but will she tell me what I need to know?

CHAPTER THREE

Maria

TIME HAS STOOD STILL as I look at the clock on the wall in this private, sterile room. I swear it's said the same time for the past hour. The sound of the door closing brings me back to reality. I wipe away the tears that have fallen and turn to face the same doctor and nurse that treated me when I arrived. They're both wearing the same expression, and it tells me all I need to know. I take a deep breath and wait for the words to flow.

My stomach tightens as silence fills the room.

"Mrs Fraser, we need to talk to you."

"Please, just Maria."

"Take a seat."

I sit down in the chair by the bed and the nurse sits down in the other chair beside me and takes my hand. I know what the doctor is going to say. I knew when the last shot was fired and his body fell.

"I'm so sorry…"

"You don't have to say it. I already know. He was gone

when the bullet hit him." The doctor studies me closely and I'm not sure what, if anything, he's looking for, but he doesn't speak. He picks up the chart from the bottom of the bed and starts reading it and taking notes. I wish he would hurry up and just discharge me. I've already been here long enough.

"Would you like to see your husband?"

The question hits me with the same force as a slap across the face. "No!" I exclaim instantly. I don't want to see him. He's caused me enough pain alive. I don't want to live with the vision of his dead, burned body in my head.

The nurse squeezes my hand, reassuring me that everything is okay. "Maria, the detective really would like to speak to you now. I've put him off long enough. If you want, I can stay," she says in the sweetest of voices.

Everyone has tiptoed around me since I was brought in. I suppose everyone who has treated me knows who I am and what my husband did.

I wish I knew who I was. I feel so lost. I have no idea who or what I've become over the years.

Maria Fraser, wife of the notorious gang lord. The woman who has turned a blind eye to many crimes over the years. The woman who has lost herself. Drowned in a relationship that was never going to end well. Although, in recent months, I didn't see this as the outcome. I thought I would be the one to end up dead given how bad things had got at home.

At this moment in time, I'm so grateful that we were never blessed with children.

A strange thought, but one that brings me back to reality. It means there's no line of succession, for want of a better term. No heirs to carry on the Fraser family name. No one to take over the running of the empire he's built

up. Now I'm hoping it will all come crumbling down with
his death, much like our home.

But, I'm sure that won't happen. No, there'll be
someone else waiting in the wings to take matters into their
own hands and keep the gangland members feuding in
Glasgow. It's their way of life; they don't know or want
anything else. But I want more. I want out. I never saw a
way before, but now there is.

"Maria?"

"Sorry, I was…

"It's okay, dear. We understand."

"I'll see the detective now, and if you could stay with
me, I'd appreciate that," I say to the nurse, taking note that
her name is Sam. She smiles warmly and squeezes my
hand. I don't really want to speak to him, but I know I
have to. I need to get it over with.

"Is there anyone I can call for you?" the doctor asks.

"Not really," I say, and my thoughts drift to my brother.
I want to call him, but I'm not sure how a conversation
between us would go. I'd love nothing more than to feel the
comfort of my brother's arms around me, holding me
close. But given the circumstances, he shouldn't be here.

And as for Lou, Tony's sister, I want to speak to her
myself. Although, I'm sure she's already been told about
what happened at our home.

The doctor leaves the room and I can see him speaking
to the detective.

"Why don't we get you back into bed before he comes
in?" Sam says, pulling down the bed sheets. "Then he
doesn't have to stay long. We can tell him you're tired."

She's lovely and can obviously read my mind. I don't
want to be having a long conversation with the detective. I
just want to get out of here.

I climb into the bed, taking note of every single ache

and pain I feel as I sit down. Sam tucks me into bed, sorting the bed sheets the same way my mother would when I was a little girl. I can't help but smile at the memory that fills my mind. I wish she was here to support me. My father too. But they're gone, and even if they were still alive, I'm not so sure they would be here for me when I needed them the most. Especially not my dad; he always said I picked a man from the wrong side of the city.

The door opens and the detective pauses in the doorway for a moment. A strange look passes quickly across his face, but it's gone before I can decipher what's wrong.

"Mrs Fraser, I'm DCI McKenzie. Jack McKenzie. I was in earlier. I'm so sorry for your loss."

I want to laugh at his choice of words. Of everything he could've said, he chose that. I study him for a moment. He's not sorry my husband is dead, and I'm sure there are many more who feel that way too. Me included. Even I know more people wanted him dead than alive. He was a man with many enemies; it came with the title and territory.

Jack McKenzie looks too young to be a DCI. I expected someone older, someone with more experience to be dealing with this case. Not some new recruit who might even be younger than me. Sam sits on the edge of my bed, freeing up the seat to my right.

"May I?" he asks, indicating his intention of sitting down. Looks like he plans on staying a while.

Not if I get my way.

"Of course," I answer, my eyes lingering on the curve of his lips.

"I'd like to talk to you about what happened."

I'm not sure that's what I want to do. Funny, now that I've focused on him, I don't want to talk. It's the furthest thing from my mind. My eyes roam his face, taking in his features. His green eyes scan the room before they quickly settle on me. The stubble around his jawline gives him a rough edge. He might be sitting down, but his presence certainly commands this room. Shivers run down my spine as I drink him in *slowly*.

These aren't the thoughts that should be in my head. Not for a woman who is supposed to be grieving for her dead husband. Christ, he's only been dead a few hours, but for me, it's been longer.

"I'm not sure what I can tell you, DCI," I say. "Everything happened so quickly." As I hear my last sentence, it sounds so practiced, so forced. Fake. And if I can hear that, I'm sure the man before me can.

"Detective is fine, and I appreciate that, but even the smallest bit of information will help. This is, after all, a murder investigation. Your husband was murdered right in front of you."

His words linger in the air.

Murdered. Images of the night flash through my mind, and all of a sudden, I want to escape. To get away from the questions. My chest tightens and my heart beats loudly within it. My eyes roam the room and Sam, as if sensing how I'm feeling, gently strokes her hand against mine, soothing me. I take a deep breath in an attempt to settle my anxiety.

"I'll do my best to help." I try to sound convincing, but I know it's not. The last thing I want to do is help the police with an investigation. It's been drummed into my head over the years to avoid the police at all costs. Now more than ever I should remember this.

"Start at the beginning and tell me what you remember."

I nod and wait, expecting him to take out a notebook

and pen or whatever it is he writes things down on, but he doesn't.

"What I remember? Well, we were in bed. I heard a noise from somewhere within the house but didn't think too much about it. Next thing, something came crashing through the bedroom window. At the same time, two masked men entered our bedroom with guns in their hands. Shots were fired and, well, you know the rest."

That's my short version. He frowns.

"There has to be more. What about the bruising you have?"

I try to think about what he's talking about. I forgot. My eyes fall to the bed and I see the bruising around my wrists, and I know there's bruising on my face. I feel the pain between my legs and on my thighs, and I can only imagine the damage Tony has caused. The marks he's left behind on my skin.

Bruising will fade through time, but the mental scars will stay with me.

"It's nothing," I say.

"That's not what I've been told. Not just your face or wrists. The doctor has told me…."

"It doesn't matter what the doctor has told you! I'm telling you it's nothing. It's personal!" I shout at him.

Sam rubs my arm, trying to calm me, but it's not helping. I just want to leave here. I don't want to stay and answer his questions. I want to go home.

But, I can't go home. I don't have a home to return to. It's gone. Everything I cherished and held close will be gone, forever. All I'll have is memories, and some of those I wish had died in the fire that engulfed my home.

"Mrs Fraser, I'll need your help in bringing your husband's murderer to trial. But I also need to know what took place between you and your husband. Did he do this to you? Why? No woman deserves this."

Should I tell him what caused Tony to strike me? No. It doesn't matter now. It has nothing to do with his murder and is something I'd like to try and forget. "I've told you all I know. Now, if you don't mind, I'm tired." I'm emotionally drained and I've not spoken to any of our family yet.

"Of course. I'll let you rest. There will be an officer outside the room for your protection. When the doctor discharges you, if you don't have family or friends that you want to stay with, I can arrange for accommodation."

"Do you think my life is in danger?" I ask him as he stands, and I want him to give me a straight answer. I want to hear what he thinks.

"No. If they wanted you dead, then I don't believe you'd be alive now. All these years your husband has been a marked man. To end his days shot dead in his own home is not what I expected."

Him and me both.

With that, he leaves the room, leaving me to ponder over his words.

I sigh and close my eyes. "Maria, I'll go and let you rest. But just so you know, I'm here if you want to talk, and not just about your husband's death. About what happened before," Sam says.

"Thank you, but I'm not ready to talk. Not yet," I say sincerely before she exits the room and, once again, I'm left with my own thoughts, fears, and regrets.

CHAPTER FOUR

Jack

THE WINDOW of my office looks out across the city centre. The noise from outside, car horns and people shouting, does nothing for my sombre mood. I need a distraction and a sleep.

I fucking hate shifts like this. So many things happening but none of it gets done quickly enough.

No sleep all night has me in a pissed off mood, and that isn't good for anyone, least of all my team who don't have any leads on this case.

Leaning back in my chair, I sigh and close my eyes. I'm tired. Too tired to deal with the shit storm that is bound to come my way. The fallout from last night's shooting and fire is going to rattle a few cages. There's bound to be someone waiting, just ready to take over where Tony left off. And that someone will be his right-hand man, Pete Jamieson. He's almost as violent as his predecessor.

Tony Fraser.

The vision in my head isn't a pretty one. All I see is his

dead and badly burnt body before me on the trolley. A completely different version of the Tony Fraser everyone knew.

He was born into gangland Glasgow, and from an early age his father started to teach him everything he knew. When his father passed away, Tony took the reins, and unlike his father, he didn't have any morals where people were concerned. His father was old school, a man of principle, and his word was a promise. Or so I'm led to believe.

Am I glad I don't need to deal with him anymore? Of course. I just wish it was an open and shut case. TV crews and journalists are already outside the station waiting for an update on this high profile murder investigation.

Anyone would think he was some sort of fucking celebrity.

Around here, I suppose he was to some.

I need to get some coffee and get myself together. Speak to my team and find out where we are with the investigation and then have a press meeting, giving out as few details as I can. This investigation is on a need to know basis, and the press don't need to know shit.

Loud knocking on my door brings me back to now. Craig pushes open the door slowly and stares at me. He has two mugs in his hand. "Thanks," I say as he enters, grateful for the gift he brings.

"Nothing to do with me. Jenny thought we might need these," he says, taking a seat. Everyone needs a Jenny in their office. She's an absolute star. Always seems to know what we need and when.

"She's right," I reply, taking a mug from his hand. "It's going to be a long day."

"No fucking kidding, Sherlock. I want my bed and you look as though you haven't slept in days."

"It feels like that," I say, taking a sip of the strong black coffee. Jenny got this right as she usually does. I take milk in my coffee unless I'm tired and stressed. And today, I am both. "What's made news?"

"Oh, boy. The shooting. The fire. That's the only factual things they've got right. They mention that Mrs Fraser was caught in the cross-fire and state she's currently undergoing life-saving treatment in hospital."

What the fuck. "The only reason she's still in hospital is because I asked the doctor to come up with a reason to keep her there for a bit. To give us some time."

"I know that, but come on. The press will print whatever the hell they want. They're in business to sell papers, and if they don't have facts, they'll make up shit. It's what they do."

"I know that, but what they don't realise is when they do that, it messes with our fucking investigation. Has anyone, family, friends, been to the hospital to see Mrs Fraser?"

"Pete Jamieson has been in but our officer wouldn't let him see her. I know her sister-in-law, Lou, is going to collect her. She called the hospital to find out when she was being discharged."

"That's fine. I'm going to go over there in the next twenty minutes. I'll speak with the team first."

"That's a good idea. Also, there's a lot of rumbling in the streets."

"From Tony's men?"

"A bit, but more from rival gangs."

"We don't need this." I stand, taking my mug of coffee with me. Craig follows. Most of the team are in the main office. "Glad you're all here," I say, walking to the front of the incident room. Craig stops and leans against his own desk.

My eyes drift along the board on the wall. It's already

filled with pictures of leading gang members from our previous investigation. "I think this board needs a change. Okay, for the time being, we need eyes on all of Fraser's businesses. I think they might well be targeted next. I also think we need to bring in and question his own men, along with rival gang members."

"What about the wife?" one of the lads shouts out.

"We need to keep an eye on her. She's a witness, after all. Although, I doubt she'll consider police protection, given who she is. And I don't think she's in any danger or she would already be dead."

"Does that put her on the suspect list?"

"Anyone and their granny could be on a suspect list. I think for the time being, no, she won't be on the list, but she is a witness and I'd like to get her to give us a statement."

"I'd like to get her to give me more than a statement," Neil, a younger officer calls out. "Have you seen those lips?"

Oh, bloody hell. I've got a bunch of men who all look as though they could come in their pants at Neil's comment. I can already picture the wet dreams they're going to have about a certain Italian woman.

"She's too old for you, Neil, and way out of your league," Craig shouts.

The men all start laughing and talking amongst themselves. "Oh, come on. Let's not get side-tracked."

There are grumbles of, "Yes, boss," around the room.

"Now, back to business." I proceed to tell them what I need from them before my press statement later today. They all listen up before I leave Craig to give them the last few instructions. I need to get over to the hospital.

I leave the building to a shower of questions thrown my way from the waiting press. I don't give them anything to feed on. There's no way I'm putting my investigation at risk by fuelling their growing appetite. This afternoon, I'll throw them a few scraps; just enough to cool things down a bit.

Jumping in my car, I drive off, away from the madness that surrounds the station. I laugh out loud thinking about the men's reaction to Maria Fraser, or Maria DeLuca. She is a gorgeous woman and she knows it. Everything about her is sexy, from her long dark hair, her Mediterranean skin, to her long slender legs. And then there's the dangerous, sexy smile she has, although it was noticeably missing when I last spoke to her.

I've read various reports about her over the years, but how the hell does a woman like her end up with someone like Tony Fraser? He was scum. Lowest of the low. He was definitely punching way above his grade.

'Wake me up when this is over.' I find myself singing to the radio, and when I realise the words, I stop and laugh. Very appropriate. I wish I could sleep through this investigation and wake up when it's over.

But, I don't think I'll get a proper sleep until I get to the bottom of who killed Tony Fraser and why.

Pulling into the hospital grounds, I look around for a space. I park the car and walk toward the main entrance. Fuck. There are more reporters here than at the station.

During my statement today, they'll be told to stay away from everyone connected to this investigation. I can't have them fucking this up. Not this time. I want whoever murdered Tony Fraser brought to justice. Although, maybe I should be thanking them for getting him off the streets of Glasgow and stopping him from committing more crimes.

I walk through the crowd with questions being thrown at me. I stop in the doorway and turn around. "I'll be giving a brief statement this afternoon at the station. Now, could you remember this is a hospital? At the moment, you are all causing an obstruction. So, if you don't want to find yourself on the wrong side of the law and in a police cell, I suggest you all move along. If you contact the station, you will be granted passes for the briefing."

"Is it true Mrs Fraser is in a critical condition?" The question is shouted from a reporter standing at the back of the crowd.

"As I've said, I will give you an update later today."

I turn and walk inside. Two security men who have been standing by the entrance acknowledge me as I pass them.

Maria Fraser is being released soon, and she can't walk through that. I'll need to speak to someone and see what other way she can exit.

I don't want her walking into the lions' den. They'd eat her alive, and right now, she doesn't need that.

I stop.

My concerning thoughts for a dead man's wife have grabbed my attention. Why am I thinking about her?

CHAPTER FIVE

Maria

"Come on. Let's get you out of here," Lou says, grabbing the bag from the hospital bed.

She cried the minute she saw me only a few short hours ago. We both sat huddled on the bed while she wept for the loss of her brother. I couldn't bring myself to shed a tear for him. Lou says I'm in shock. I'll go with that. It will do for now.

She was shocked when she first saw me and questioned all the bruising on my face and the other parts of my body she could see. What could I say? She's grieving. I couldn't add to her upset by telling her that all the bruising is her brother's handy work. I tried to play it down, but I could tell she wasn't listening to me. "You're coming to my house. My brother would want you with family and you are part of *my* family. Always have been and always will be."

The smile on my face is fake as she leads the way from the room I've been in for the last fourteen hours. I'm grateful she's here and wants to help me, but that means

I'll be seeing the same familiar faces I want to avoid. I don't want to be in company. Especially all the men. I could really do with time on my own. Time to think about what the future holds.

Uncertainty lays heavily on my mind and an emptiness fills my soul.

"I'm only staying for a day or so. Just until I can think about what I'm going to do."

"Whatever you say, but my home is yours for as long as you need it. We can go shopping. I only managed to pick up a few things for you this morning." She's trying to sound chirpy but it's not really working.

"Thank you, and yes, I suppose I'll need to go on a shopping trip."

I need new clothes; I can't walk about every day wearing the same things. There's so much I need to do. So many things to sort out.

"Maria, I should warn you. My house is busy. Some of Tony's men are there. They all want answers because, well, you know why."

Of course they are. They want someone to blame and they'll want to take matters into their own hands.

"I bet they do. But at the moment, I don't have answers to give them," I say, closing my eyes and hoping that my pain is hidden. The thought of more fighting and death turns my stomach, but I know that's how they will all react because it's what they know and live for.

"It's okay. Things will be hard for both of us, but we'll get through this together," she says, her voice full of kindness.

"I hope so."

"Mrs Fraser." I sigh hearing his voice, but still turn around to see Detective McKenzie walking toward us. "I'm so glad I caught you."

I bet he is. "What can I do for you?"

He stops before us in the corridor. He stands confident and tall. I'd go with a guess and say he's six-foot-two. He looks around the same height as Tony. I feel small standing next to him. "I need you to confirm where you'll be staying, but you'll also need to come into the station and make your statement."

"Surely not now? I want to be with family and, as you are aware, I have a funeral to arrange."

"Not now, and yes I'm aware you have a funeral to arrange, but that will have to wait until your husband's body has been released."

He's got a point. I forgot about that.

"So, where will you be staying?"

"With Lou and her family," I tell him. I'm sure it will do me good to be around the kids for a few days. The girls are at a nice age, three and five, and I adore them. "I'm sure you know where that is," I add.

"Yes, I do."

Of course he does. I'm sure everyone in the police force wouldn't even have to look at their computer system to find out any of our addresses. They've been to each of our homes too many times in recent years.

"I'll be in touch in a few days. Oh, and please could you see the nurse? She's arranged for you to leave through another exit. It's a bit congested at the main entrance," he tells me before walking away.

A few days is good; gives me some time. I don't have to worry or think about what to say to him. *Not yet.*

"Well, if he wasn't a detective and I wasn't married…."

"Lou!" I chastise her.

"Come on. Look at him." She smiles warmly, watching him walk away.

I look. "Not appropriate," I say my eyes following him.

But now that she's mentioned it, he is easy on the eye and I thought so when I spoke to him. That was before he pissed me off by wanting to know more about what happened with Tony before his death. That's not any of his business.

"I don't suppose it is, but at least I've made you smile, and this time it's a proper smile. Let's get home. The girls can't wait to see Auntie Maria."

Lou has taken the long drive home, purposely to avoid driving past my house. Or what's left of it. I know I'll have to go there in the next few days, or maybe I'll be able to avoid it. What is there left for me to go back for? She's told me fire investigation officers are still on the scene and there's been a heavy police presence, which doesn't come as a great surprise to me.

She and Mark went there during the early hours of the morning. I'm not sure what she hoped to achieve from doing that. I'm sure she only upset herself.

I sigh as we pull into her street, taking note of all the cars in her driveway and parked along the street that I recognise. She wasn't kidding when she said some of the men were here. I have nothing I want to tell them.

As soon as we exit the car, the front door opens and two gorgeous little girls come running out. "Auntie Maria," Rebecca calls out. "We've missed you."

They both stare at my face and I hope the bruising isn't scaring them. I lower myself and wrap my arms around Rebecca and Daisy. Holding them close, it's so easy to forget about everything else going on. Tony loved these two like his own. My eyes fill with tears at what they've lost, and regret rushes through my veins. Maybe he would've changed his ways if we'd have had kids of our own. Lou and I saw how he was with them. We saw his softer side. He would've done anything for Rebecca and Daisy.

"I've missed you both so much," I say, squeezing them tighter, scared to let them go. Scared that Lou might be able to read my face.

"I wanted to make you a cake," Rebecca says, pulling out of my hold. Her big green eyes stare at me. "But Daddy said you'd be too sad to eat cake."

"Maybe Daddy is right. But, I think, later on before your bedtime, we should get some cakes and I'll make us some hot chocolate and we can have that before we go to sleep. Maybe even watch a movie or cartoon. What do you both think?"

"Yes, please," they both squeal. It's easy to be around them and I can't help but smile at the two little girls who don't have a care in the world. If only I felt like that. *Maybe someday I will.*

"Come on, girls. Let's get Auntie Maria into the house," Lou says, picking up Daisy. She cuddles into her mother's arms, Rebecca takes my hand, and we walk into the house.

Even though Lou's house is big, I can hear the rabble of the men talking in the family meeting room at the back of the house. I know I need to see the men, but there's a huge part of me that wishes I could put it off. *Forever.*

I follow Lou through to the kitchen and she switches on the kettle. "Tea or coffee?" she asks.

"Tea."

I sit down at the kitchen table and rest my head in my hands. The girls' footsteps run out of the kitchen and I hear them going up the stairs. The noise from the family room has quietened down. All I hear are hushed voices now.

Lou is moving slowly around the kitchen making tea

for us both. This, staying here, is going to be harder than I thought. A door opens and closes and I hear footsteps walking through the house toward us. I take a deep breath because I know it will be Lou's husband, Mark. He'll want to check on his wife.

"Babe, are you okay?" he asks her. I don't look up. I give them a moment to themselves.

"Yes. I'm okay. I have our girls to keep me occupied, but Mar…"

I lift my head, not wanting her to continue what she was saying. "Lou, don't you dare start worrying about me. I'll be fine."

Lou nods her head, even though I can see in her eyes she's not convinced by my words. Mark stares at me and I wait to hear what he has to say. "Maria, you look tired."

"I feel it," I tell him as Lou hands me a cup of tea.

"The men would like to see you, but if you're not up to it, I can tell them."

I think about his words for a moment as I take a drink from my tea. He's given me the option, but I know the longer I leave it, the harder it will be. "No. I'll see them, but only for a moment. Then, if it's okay with you both, I'll go and lie down for a bit."

"Of course that's fine with us," Lou says, sitting down opposite me. "You don't need to ask permission for anything. We're family and we're here for you."

"Let's get this over with," I say to Mark, standing with my cup of tea in my hands. He offers me a small smile before leaving the kitchen. He hates this life as much as I do, he's just never voiced his opinions on it to anyone. Lou takes my free hand and we walk through the house to the family room. In my mind, this room should be used for the girls to play in, not house crime world meetings.

Everyone stops talking as Lou and I enter. There's at

least twenty of my dead husband's closest associates here. I'm sure they'll all be chomping at the bit to make those who murdered Tony pay.

I gulp hard at my thought.

"Gentlemen," I say, my voice wavering and somewhat quieter than usual. "I know you're all angry and looking for someone to blame. For someone to pay the price. But I don't have any answers for you."

"You must know something." I look over to where Pete is standing by the window. His stance is relaxed but his facial expression is full of anger. Unlike Tony, Pete doesn't stand out or command a room full of people. He can usually, like now, be quietly watching the goings on from a corner, taking stock. Pete is the only person Tony ever really trusted. Even before the death of his younger brother, Gary, a few years ago in a street shooting, Pete was the one he turned to. Pete might not have been related by blood to Tony, but as far as he was concerned, he was family. "You were in the same room."

"Yes, I was, and if I'm honest, I'm still in shock. Everything happened so quickly. Pete, if there was anything to tell you, you'd be the first to know," I say, hating that I'm now saying the same words over again. I wipe my eye, pretending this is all too much, hoping my reply is enough for him at the moment. "I'll need to talk to you later about the funeral when I hear back from the police." There's a few grumbles in the room at the mention of the police, but surely they know I'll have to wait before we can organise the funeral.

"I'll be here when you need me. Until then, do you want everything else ticking over as normal?" he asks.

I want to say no, to hell with the lot of it, but I know I can't. There's men in this room with families who rely on the income. "Just do what you think is for the best," I say, hating that I'm now playing a part in their criminal paths.

"No problem. I'll see to it."

I'm sure he will.

I leave the room with Lou. "I want you all to go about what you'd usually be doing for the next few days," I hear Pete say to the men.

"Everything?" someone asks.

"Yes. No exceptions. We carry on. It's what Tony would want. If anyone hears anything about last night, you come to me and I'll deal with it. No one has to rush in. No blood has to be shed, *yet*. Do I make myself clear?"

The girls thunder back down the stairs. "Stop running," Lou tells them.

"Mum, we want to go to the park."

"No. Sorry, girls…"

"Lou, spend time with them. I'm just going to rest."

"Are you sure?"

"Yes. You can't put your life on hold, not for them. They are too young to understand. They need you."

"I know, but it's hard." She kisses me on the cheek, takes the cup from my hand, and walks back through to the kitchen with the girls skipping behind her. I watch on until I can't see them before climbing the steps.

"Maria," Pete calls after me, his voice sending shivers through my body.

"Yes," I answer tiredly.

"I will find out who did this and I'll make them pay. They won't get a quick death."

"I know you'll find them and take revenge." Because that is what he does. That's all they've ever done; one life taken for another. It's a vicious cycle. A cycle I had hoped would be broken, but that was wishful thinking on my part.

I turn my back on him and walk up the stairs, his

words playing over in my head. 'They won't get a quick death.' I shiver as I make my way along the hallway to the guest bedroom at the back of the house.

Entering the bedroom, my mask finally slips. I close the door and my tears fall. Not for the man I've lost, but for everything that I could lose.

CHAPTER SIX

Jack

HER EYES ARE wide and she's terrified. Terrified from all the abuse he's inflicted on her. The bruising; I've never seen so much bruising. Her beautiful, perfect, kissable lips are all marked and cut. There's a slash mark across her cheek from a blade of some sort; a knife perhaps. It might fade but she'll always have a scar as a reminder of this night. She sits on the bed, a nurse trying to soothe her. The doctor stands taking notes, and I stand watching her, feeling so fucking helpless.

Her dark eyes drift to me and I see the hurt. She blames me.

This is my fault.

She turned to me in her hour of need for protection and I've failed her.

I was meant to protect her from that monster of a husband and I couldn't.

And now he's disappeared. My men can't find him. Tony Fraser always gets away. Shivers run down my spine as she weeps before me. I reach out to comfort her but she turns away.

What the fuck?

I bolt upright in bed, sweat running from my body, the sheets sticking to me. It was just a dream. A fucking dream. Yet everything felt so real. I take a deep breath and allow my eyes to adjust to the bright light shining through the bedroom window. I glance around. It's all pink. Everywhere. There's even pink fluffy cushions scattered on the floor.

This isn't my room.

Shit.

I've fucked up.

I shouldn't be here.

I rub my temples, trying to ease the headache that I've woken up with. Self-inflicted. I consumed way too much whiskey last night. Throwing my legs out of the bed, I grab my phone and look at all the messages I have. Not a good start to the day. I need to get into the office and catch up with any over-night developments.

"Jack, come on," the voice at the side of me says, pulling my hand to her. I turn my head and, what the hell was I thinking? "Stay. I can make it worth your while." She almost purrs the words at me.

I cast my eyes over her body, and in all fairness, it's a hot body. But it doesn't matter how hot the body is when you wake up to someone looking like a fucking panda with mascara all over her face.

She's already had too much attention from me. I pull away from her, my eyes darting around the room. I find what I'm looking for. Picking up my clothes from the floor, I start to get dressed. I must look a state. I need to get home, grab a quick shower, and get into the office.

It's only six a.m. so I have plenty of time.

"Jack, come back to bed?"

"Sorry, sweetheart," I say, because I'm that much of an arsehole I don't even remember her name. "I have a busy day ahead of me and I need to get home." I slide my feet into my shoes.

"Can I see you again?" she asks as she sits up in the bed, her naked body there for me to see. Desire fills her eyes as she looks at me.

"I'll give you a call," I say, walking out of her room and closing the door behind me. I sigh. There's not a hope in hell I'll be calling her.

"But I never gave…" her voice trails off.

I walk away, not even feeling guilty that I didn't get her name or number. In my line of work, I have no time for a woman. They're too much of a distraction and I've worked too fucking hard on my career to allow a woman into my life, especially when… I shake my head, not allowing my thoughts to drift off to the past.

But what I want to know is, why the hell was I dreaming about Maria Fraser?

I STAND STARING AT THE BOARD IN FRONT OF ME, POTENTIAL suspects filling the wall, and the strange thing is, I don't think any of them killed Tony. All familiar faces. All men I want behind bars because the streets would be far safer without them. Yes, they all benefit from him no longer being around, but my gut instinct is telling me it wasn't someone I'd expect it to be. Or maybe it was and I'm just being thrown off the scent. There's a newer picture added; Maria Fraser's.

Now, is she just a witness or should she be a suspect?

She intrigues me. Always has. But I think it's meeting her in person that has invaded my thoughts. She's different from what I expected and I'm not entirely sure why. This is a rare picture on her own. She's walking toward a waiting car. Her long, dark hair looks as though it flows in the wind. In this picture, everything about her screams confident and happy, but that's not the woman I saw.

Her mask had well and truly slipped in hospital. I don't think she was happy with Tony Fraser. In fact, from what the doctor said, he was abusing his wife and she has the bruising to back up the doctor's claims. This should make her a suspect, but she didn't do it. She's not capable of murder.

She's a victim.

I stare at the board for a long few minutes, hoping that something shows up, but when I can no longer think straight and my team start arriving, I walk into my own office to escape the noise.

The preliminary reports from the fire investigation are sitting on my desk and I'm to expect the first forensic report back later today, hopefully by lunchtime, the message on my phone said. That should at least give us a starting place for this investigation.

"Morning, boss," Craig says, entering my office. "Where did you end up last night?" He was sensible; one drink at the pub and then straight home. I'm now wishing I had done that because I have very little recollection of the night.

"You don't want to know," I tell him, hoping he doesn't question me any further. "Has there been any developments?"

"No, and everything has been exceptionally quiet. It's like the calm before the storm."

"I hope not." But, deep down, I know he's right. The death of Tony Fraser is bound to set off a war. A deadly war that our city hasn't seen for a number of years. Call it instinct or whatever the hell you want, but I know we're waiting to see who kicks off first.

If I was a betting man, I'd say Tony's right-hand man, Pete, will make the first move. He'll be wanting to prove his worth to the rest of the men. And if he was to deal with Tony's killer personally, he would prove how capable he is at taking over, and I'm sure that would be enough to give him the territory and title Tony had.

I give Craig a few tasks and tell him to get in touch if he needs me.

"Where will you be?"

"I have a house call to make."

"Oh. A certain Italian lady?"

"Yes. I still need to convince her to make a statement."

"I'm sure you of all people can charm her into finally making her statement," he says, laughing at me. "And if that doesn't work, well, I'll think you've lost it."

"If we weren't friends, I'd be finding you some crappy job to do today."

"Seeing as you're the one going to pay Mrs Fraser a visit, any job I do today will pale into insignificance." He leaves my office still laughing, shaking his head.

If he keeps it up with his fucking cheek, I'll have him on boring desk duties for the foreseeable future. But even I can't be angry at him for his very accurate response. Charming women is what I do best.

Now, it's time for me to go and charm Maria Fraser. *What a hardship.* It's a tough job, but someone has to do it.

I smile, gathering up a few documents from my desk, looking forward to seeing her again, even though I shouldn't.

CHAPTER SEVEN

Maria

THE HOUSE IS QUIET, too quiet, and I'm not sure I like it. I've gotten used to the noise level of the girls over the last few days. They've been a welcome distraction to the chaos that is going on around me. Lou has taken the girls to school and nursery today, she wants to try and keep things normal for them both, and I can't say I blame her. They are too young to understand everything.

So innocent and pure.

My wish for Rebecca and Daisy is that they stay that way. That they grow up having a normal childhood, not one surrounded with pain and trauma.

The house has been so busy, with men coming and going, all trying to go about their duties, whatever they are. I've not asked what, although I probably should. In all fairness, I couldn't care less. I just wish I didn't have to see any of them. Pete has been here most of the time; he and Mark are always whispering between themselves. I'm not sure where Mark is. I've not seen him this morning, which is unusual, and now that I think about it, Pete hasn't been here either. If he has, I haven't heard him.

There's a selection of newspapers sitting on the kitchen table. Lou had already told me that most of the papers had the same front page headline: *Tony Fraser dead*. Glasgow's most notorious gangster shot dead in his own home.

I know I shouldn't, but I find myself flicking through the papers as curiosity gets the better of me, to see what has been written. Not that much about his death but lots on his criminal lifestyle. Drug dealing, money laundering, prostitution, murder; it's all before me in black and white.

My stomach turns at many of the stories. All these accusations. This is what I've turned a blind eye to. This is what paid for our nice house, expensive cars, clothes, and jewellery. All this is why my husband has been one of the most feared men in Glasgow in the last decade.

I've always known, but seeing it printed makes it all seem so real.

Tony was always being hauled into the police station to be questioned over one crime or another, but he was never arrested for any. He never even had so much as a parking ticket to his name. Why is that? Was he paying everyone off?

Of course he was. Tony Fraser always believed he was untouchable. Thought he was one step ahead of the game. Although, he learned the hard way he wasn't. Some would say he's finally paid the price for his life of crime and destruction. Me included.

I slam the newspaper down. I can't read any more of what is written.

"This is all wrong," I say out loud. The story is about a young lad who was gunned down on the doorstep of his mother's home, in what the papers described as a drive-by shooting. The boy, who was only twenty-one, was shot dead after, supposedly dealing drugs on a patch that Tony had control over.

This is wrong. A young life taken so brutally.

Loud banging on the front door grabs my attention. I stand up and walk through the house. The front door opens and it's one of Tony's men, Joe. "Mrs Fraser, there is someone here to see you," he says, stepping aside. That's when I see him. Detective McKenzie. "Pete is on his way," Joe tells me.

"Thank you. Come on in, Detective." I knew he would be here sooner rather than later. I did hope I would get a few more days before he appeared. A few more days to sort myself out, decide what information he needs to know.

He smiles, passing Joe, and closes the front door, shutting Joe out. He'll be pissed off, and I know Pete will be too when he arrives and sees the detective in the house without supervision.

"Mrs Fraser."

"Hello. I wasn't expecting to see you so soon," I say, leading the way into the kitchen. "Tea or coffee?"

"Nothing for me," he says, taking a seat at the table, his eyes pondering over the newspapers. "Papers."

"Yes. I've had a read through some of them. I wanted to see with my own eyes what was printed," I tell him, sitting opposite him.

He's studying me closely, watching every move I make. I should feel nervous, but for whatever reason, I don't. I'm at ease around him and I know I shouldn't be. I can't let my guard down, which, right now, would be so easy to do.

"As you should." He leans back in the chair, taking a quick glance around the room. Seemingly happy with what he sees, he turns his attention back to me. "Maria, what are your plans?"

Maria? Should he not be calling me Mrs Fraser?

"Excuse me?" The hairs on the back of my neck stand up, and not in a good way.

"This empire your husband has built up… what do you plan on doing with it?"

"Detective McKenzie, I've not given it any thought. Why would I? Should I remind you my husband was shot dead in our home? In our bed."

"About that. How are you? I can get you some counselling. You've witnessed a traumatic event and it's bound to be upsetting."

"I have family and friends, and if at a later stage I decide I need counselling, I'm sure I can organise that for myself. Believe it or not, I can be an independent woman."

He sits tapping his fingers on the table. All the while, his eyes stay on me. "I still need an official statement on what happened that night, including the events before the shooting. The bruising on your body indicates…."

"Indicates what?" asks Pete, his voice raised and his eyes wide as he stares at me. I never even heard the front door open or him walking toward the kitchen, too busy concentrating on the man before me. "Carry on, Detective." He leans against the doorframe, his eyes surveying the room.

My gaze falls to the floor. I don't want to look at either of them. "The bruising on Mrs Fraser's body indicates someone forced themselves onto her, and I believe that someone was her husband."

"Maria." It's the softest I've ever heard Pete's voice. He's by my side, kneeling in front of me. "What happened?"

I take a deep breath, lifting my head and squaring my shoulders. "My business is no concern for either of you," I state. "Detective McKenzie, I can make my statement this afternoon at the station, if that suits?"

"Yes. I'll make myself available, Mrs Fraser, and hopefully, I'll be able to find out when Mr Fraser's body will be released."

I stand, making it clear he is no longer welcome here. I can be strong and confident when I need to be; that's something I should remember.

"Thank you for your time, Mrs Fraser. I'll see myself out." He pauses as though about to say something else, but one look at Pete and he walks away.

"Maria, if you're going to the station, you should call your lawyer and have him with you," Pete says, reminding me that I need to watch what I'm saying. I wish everyone would stop it. I'm not fucking stupid.

"You're right." I sigh and wonder when this craziness will stop being my life.

"Are you going to tell me what happened between you and Tony?"

"What's to tell? My husband didn't get his excitement from whichever whore he was with before he came home and thought it was my duty to make him a happy man. When I refused and tried to put up a fight, he used me as a punch bag before taking what he thought was his given right."

"So he...."

"Don't say it. Don't you dare. If I don't hear the words, then I can pretend it didn't happen like everything else. Our marriage was a farce."

"Maria, I'm sorry."

I wonder if he said sorry to the young girl he and my husband raped months ago in the cellar of the nightclub.

Tears fill my eyes as I think about her, about what she went through. This is all so fucked up.

"You've nothing to be sorry for when it comes to me and my marriage. I blame myself for putting up with all his shit for so long." There comes a point in everyone's life when they think to themselves, 'I wish I had listened to my family.' I reached that point months ago. My parents hated Tony when we first got together fourteen years ago. Mamma DeLuca will be turning in her grave. God rest her soul. And as for my dad, I lost count of the number of times he said, 'Lo uccidero.' I'll kill him. It's just as well they've not witnessed everything over the past few years.

"You don't mean that."

"I loved him, but these past few months, the way he's treated me, it was very easy to feel nothing but anger toward him."

"I can understand that. Especially knowing what I know now. I won't make excuses for him, but these past few months have been hard."

"Hard? Oh, yes. I know all about that. Shooting a young lad on his doorstep for what? Dealing drugs on his patch? Do you know how fucking petty this sounds?" I shout at him. "So what else has happened the last few months? Will there be more stories about dead men or women? Let's face it, *my* husband wouldn't care who it was that crossed him, he would deal with it in the only way he knew. With violence and killing."

Pete puts his hand on my shoulder. I shiver from his touch and he pulls away. "Sorry. I'll go and leave you. I'll send a car for you to go to the station. Just drop me a text of the time."

I nod and he leaves.

Silence fills the house, and yet again, I'm alone. Although, now my mind is filled with visions. Visions of death and destruction, and all of it caused by Tony.

I hate that man with everything in me. I hope he rots in hell for all he's done.

CHAPTER EIGHT

Jack

"DETECTIVE," says the man standing guard at the front door as I walk out. I don't bother looking at him. I walk straight to my car, every muscle in my body tense. Anger flows through my veins. My heart is pounding hard against my chest.

Why?

That fucking man, Pete Jamieson.

I want to kill him *so badly*.

I saw the longing look of desire in his eyes as he knelt before her, his soothing voice offering her comfort. *Fucking hypocrite*. He feels sorry that Tony raped her. He and Tony have done worse to others. So what makes Maria so different in his eyes?

I wish I knew the answer to that.

But she is different. *So bloody different*. So damn different to any woman I've ever known, and I don't know her, not really.

My blood is boiling. I want to march back up the path,

straight into the house and punch that fucker for the thoughts I know are running through his head. He wants her. The thing is, he already thinks he can have her and that alone makes him a very dangerous man. Pete Jamieson thinks he can step into Tony's shoes in all aspects of his life. I hope I'm wrong.

Pete Jamieson is a man who should be behind bars, and for a very long time. He'll trip himself up sooner or later, and when he does, I'll be the man to make sure he goes where he belongs.

Gripping my car door handle, I pause for a moment and look back toward the house, taking several deep breaths. The man standing guard at the door stares at me. He must be wondering what the hell is wrong with me.

I need to take back control of all the emotions sweeping through me. I have no right to be angry and frustrated. Yet I am.

I drive off quickly.

The roads are quiet, but I take the wrong street, or maybe not, as I find myself outside the destroyed home of the Frasers. I park my car and get out. There's still an officer standing guard outside the sealed off area. There are no fire officers here, so I'm presuming they've removed everything they need to finish the investigation and that they've made the building safe.

"Officer."

"McKenzie."

"Has there been anyone hanging around?" I ask.

"No. Everything has been quiet, although the neighbours to the right, the wee old dear, has brought me out coffee. She's lovely," he tells me.

"Has she spoken about the Frasers?"

"Only that she hopes Mrs Fraser is okay. She has a lot of time for her and asked if she was still in hospital. She smiled when I told her no. I didn't really want to ask her any questions because of her age."

I nod, accepting what he says. I wouldn't want someone that age to come forward. I'd hate to think of them living in fear of the consequences. See, this is what is wrong with our society. Criminals have been able to rule the city for far too long, putting everyone else's life in danger because they are too scared to speak out.

Dipping under the blue and white tape, I walk toward the building. From the front, it all looks normal, but as I wander around the side of the building, I can see the extent of the damage. The roof is completely off and the walls that remain are so badly damaged that I expect the whole building will need to be demolished. I wander through the dirt and ashes and it's hard to imagine the rooms that would've been here on the ground floor, or even the bedrooms that would've been upstairs. From what I know of Maria, I'd imagine her home was spotless and well-furnished. Like a showroom. She comes across as the type of woman to keep most aspects of her life in order.

Walking around this building in daylight is completely different from all the activity from the other night. It's quiet and that surprises me. I had thought that there might be a few reporters hanging around, hoping to get another angle on the story. But, nothing. Maybe they took my warning from my press statement about not interfering with this case.

What reporters don't understand is that our job is hard enough without their constant meddling, but they don't see it that way. They see it as their duty to give the public the facts as they see them.

My eyes search the rubble and remains, but I'm not sure what for. A clue that's been left behind? Who am I kidding? The fire investigation team will have removed everything they need for their investigation, and forensics would have taken anything that was left behind.

I stand, staring upwards. "How many times did you hurt your wife, Tony?" Why I'm even asking this question I don't know, but I do want the answer, and I want Maria to be the one to tell me. It's really bothering me.

It's only been a few days, but I already sense this is going to be a long, drawn out investigation. I also think with every stone we turn over, I'll learn something new about Tony Fraser. I had him down for a lot of things. I believed he was an evil man, but I honestly didn't expect him to abuse his wife. Always thought he respected family values.

I was wrong about that. So what else have I been wrong about?

Enough. Time to leave, and I'm taking the officer with me. I'm sure Maria or Pete will organise their own security this afternoon. I don't need to be wasting tax-payers' money when they can look after things themselves.

Time to be back in the station. To find out if anyone has a new piece of information. Even the tiniest piece could be the biggest clue and give us the breakthrough we need.

———

ENTERING THE INCIDENT ROOM, THE FIRST THING I NOTICE is that the phones are going crazy. Has something happened today that I don't know about? It sure seems that way with the high level of activity in this room. Craig walks toward me, a pile of papers in his hand. "What's going on?" I ask, my eyes still taking in how busy it is.

"Well, it seems everyone in Glasgow wants to report a crime that Tony Fraser has committed."

"Why?"

"According to one man I had on the phone today, he hopes to get some sort of compensation."

"What the fuck?" I say, taking the papers from Craig's hand.

"That's what I thought."

I look around the room. All of my officers are on the phones, frantically scribbling down whatever they are being told. This isn't right.

"Everyone, I need your attention. Now. I don't care who is on the other end of your call, hang up." My voice bellows around the incident room.

It takes a minute or so, but my officers all hurry up and end their conversations. "These calls are all well and good, but has anyone taken a call that relates to the murder of Tony Fraser?" I ask, and watch on as every officer in the room shakes their head. "Okay then. We have to ask ourselves why these people didn't come forward with their allegations when he was alive. We don't have the time or the manpower for all my officers to be taking phone calls. I'm not saying they aren't important, but we are in the middle of a murder investigation and that has to take priority over crimes Tony Fraser committed in the past."

Everyone stays silent but nods in agreement. "Jenny." My eyes search the room and find her. "Jenny, can you find out if there are any uniformed officers on desk duty within the station, and if there are, ask their superior if we can have them. They can help you man the phones today. You know what to do. Write everything down and Craig and I will see if there are any we need to follow up. Now that we've cleared that up, Craig will allocate jobs for the rest of you." We might actually get some bloody work done.

I walk to my office as the noise levels start to increase. I need some time to myself before I have to deal with Maria and her statement. I also need to give the superintendent an update on the case. He'll want this investigation dealt with as quickly and efficiently as possible.

He's not the only one, but somehow, I don't think either of us will get our way on this case.

CHAPTER NINE

Maria

I CATCH my reflection in a window as I walk toward the station with Pete and my lawyer, James Stevenson, on either side of me. For someone who is meant to be grieving, I don't look too bad. I smooth down the front of my black dress. My dark sunglasses hide the black circles under my eyes that not even my make-up could hide. Although, the bruising on my face doesn't look too bad today.

Not sleeping and over-thinking is taking its toll on me.

Too much on my mind.

Joe sits in the black car just farther down the road. He'll wait there until we're finished. I don't want to be surrounded by my husband's heavies wherever I go. I want a normal life, if I even remember what that is.

I really could've done this on my own. But, oh no, here I am about to walk into the lions' den with my minders in tow. I hadn't given much thought to what I would put in my statement and I was nervous about coming here. But, now that I'm facing the entrance, there's a bubbling in my stomach, and that alone has me on edge. And not because of what I'm about to do. A certain detective springs to mind.

It's wrong and I know it is, but I can't help the warm feeling that spreads through my veins as I think about seeing him again.

"How long will this take?" I ask.

"We shouldn't be long. It's only a formality," James tells me. His voice is soft and reassuring, yet I don't take any comfort from it.

We walk inside. James gives my name to the officer at the front desk. He casts his eyes in my direction and smirks. I fold my arms across my chest, suddenly not wanting to be here, but knowing I need to get this over with.

"Everything will be fine," Pete says, resting his hand on my shoulder. I nod as I try to internally convince myself that everything will be okay. He offers me a smile, one that seems warm yet cautious at the same time.

Pete being touchy feely with me… I don't like it. He's never been like this with me before, so why now? He reminds me of Tony on a good day. I know I should be on my guard around him. Be wary of him because I know deep down he's as bad, if not worse, than my husband.

James joins us, offering me a seat, but I don't want to sit down. It will only make me more agitated than I already am, and right now, I want to try and stay composed.

James and Pete stand whispering to each other, but I'm taking no notice of them. My eyes are scanning around the unwelcoming area I'm in. In all the years Tony and I were together, this is the first time I've ever been inside the police station and I don't like it.

After a few minutes, the door to my right opens. "Mrs Fraser." Detective McKenzie says my name and his voice sounds smooth and commanding in this small space. "Mr

Stevenson. Mr Jamieson." I stare at him and I'm trying not to smile as I think of Lou's words in the hospital. *If only she could see him now.* A few days ago, he looked good but tired, but today, he's something else. He's standing there in his tailored dark grey suit looking mighty fine. His hair is combed back and there's something about his eyes. Something dark and dangerous, yet intriguing. His presence is really felt. I wonder if the others notice, or is it just me?

Why did I not notice this earlier when he was at the house? Is it because he's in his own environment?

I think it is.

"Detective," they both say in unison while I stand watching him. I must be a callous bitch. I'm as bad as my husband. He's only been dead a few days, and here I am wondering how McKenzie would look like out of the suit. I can only imagine he looks as perfect out the suit as he does in it.

"Mr Jamieson, I'm afraid you'll have to wait here," McKenzie tells Pete. I knew he wouldn't be allowed in the interview room, but I'm thankful to have it confirmed. My tense body relaxes a little.

"That's fine," Pete says, taking a seat. "I'll be right here, waiting." James nods his head. Detective McKenzie holds the door open, waiting for me. I step toward him and smile as I pass him when I see the corner of his mouth curl. He looks smug, as though he has the upper hand. I suppose, today, in a way he does. But is it because he has the upper hand with Pete?

I think that's it.

I stop in the corridor and wait, trying to compose myself because I have no idea of the direction we will be going. James looks very professional, and that un-nerves me. Thoughts of all the times he's been here with Tony beside him enter my head and I'm suddenly wondering how many times James has got him off the hook. I take a deep breath before calling on my inner strength and putting my mask back firmly where it belongs.

McKenzie walks past with only a quick glance in my direction; James and I follow. The only noise that can be heard is the clipping of my shoes along the corridor. He stops at the end, opening a door, and we all go in. James and I take seats at the table. McKenzie takes his seat opposite me.

Even with the light on overhead, the room still feels small and dark. Intimidating. A police officer in full uniform enters the room and takes a seat beside McKenzie. He introduces himself, but I'm not listening to him, although he does tell me that he will be recording our conversation. I'm trying to stay focused on what's about to happen, the questions I'm bound to be asked, and not on the man before me that has captured my attention.

"Mrs Fraser, thank you for coming in at this very difficult time. I'll try not to keep you too long," McKenzie says. "I do have a few questions but I'd like you to tell me in your own words what happened on the night of Friday thirteenth of March."

Funny, I hadn't even thought about the date, but now it all makes sense. I glance at James. "Maria, take your time," he says.

"Tony had been out. Where he was is anyone's guess. You might have a better idea on that than me. I had been at home all evening and decided to go to bed. I was tired. Tony came home around twelve-thirty. Well, I think that was the time." I pause, and I know McKenzie has his suspicions of what happened, but I'm not sure I want to tell him that my husband forced himself on me.

"Mrs Fraser, can you tell me about all the bruising on you?"

I straighten my back, squaring my shoulders, finally removing my sunglasses. "I'm sure you already know, Detective, but if you need to hear it. My husband forced himself on me. He came home drunk and looking for me to satisfy his needs. When I refused, he pinned me down on the bed. The bruising on my face is a result of his handy work, and, well, I'm sure you can work out what happened next. You are an intelligent man."

"Mrs Fraser, for the record, your husband raped you?" he asks. I hate that word. It makes me think of weakness and victims, and I wouldn't say I'm a weak woman. I certainly don't want to be a victim, although I suppose that's what I am.

"Yes." James flinches at my side, but I don't turn to him. Instead, I carry on talking. "I heard a noise in the house and I thought he had brought people home. I decide not to put up a fight, thinking it would be over sooner, then I'd get to sleep. Tony closed his eyes, enjoying everything he was taking from me. His body relaxed along with his grip on me and I grabbed his gun from the bedside cabinet and pointed it against him. His eyes widened in shock. Was I prepared to use it? I don't know, probably, but the next thing I know, the window was smashed, the door burst open, and two men with their faces covered came into our bedroom with guns in their hands. Then there was burning. Tony pulled the gun from my hands, and several shots were fired before his body fell on top of me. That was it. The men left."

"Mrs Fraser, was that the first time?" McKenzie asks, and I hear the sorrow in his voice.

I close my eyes and gather some strength. "No," I answer, looking at James, and from his facial expression, my answer comes as no surprise to him. Of course it wouldn't. He knows, like we all do in this room, what Tony was capable of.

My husband was capable of murder.

Although, I'm certain he justified to himself everything that happened in our marriage these last few months because I was his wife.

"The men… did they say anything?"

"No." It's a lie, but one I need to keep to myself for the time being.

"So, they left you, a witness, alive and what? Just left you there?"

"I know that must sound strange, but that's exactly what happened."

"It doesn't matter what I think. I'm only interested in finding out the truth and bringing your husband's killers to trial."

I laugh a little. "You don't have to pretend. I'm sure you are one of many who is secretly relieved my husband is no longer alive." As the words leave me, I realise I've left myself open to be questioned.

"What about you, Mrs Fraser? Are you glad he's dead?" He asks the question I hoped he would stay clear of.

"Mrs Fraser has come in to help with your investigation," James states. "She's not here to be interrogated."

"Of course." The two men stare at each other across the table and, suddenly, this room feels even smaller, if that's at all possible. "Mrs Fraser, your husband's body will be released today so you're free to make funeral arrangements."

"Thank you," I say. As James stands, so do I. The officer switches off the recording and McKenzie stands too, walking toward the door. We follow him, and I'm pleased this is over with for the time being.

I'd be kidding myself to think this would be the last time I'd be inside a police station. For some reason, I think this will turn out to be the first visit of many. I hope I'm wrong, but I also hope I'm right because it would give me an excuse to see McKenzie.

We walk in silence along the corridor until McKenzie opens the door to the front area. Pete stands and steps quickly toward me. He wraps his arms around me, pulling my body to his. "Are you okay?" he asks. His actions are totally out of character. Even James eyes him suspiciously.

I pull out of his hold and smooth down my dress. "I'm fine. There's no reason I wouldn't be," I say, looking at him.

I'm conscious that McKenzie is still standing beside us and watching on. No doubt wondering, like I am, what the hell is going on. "Mrs Fraser, I'd ask that you give us all the arrangements for your husband's funeral as soon as you have them."

"Why?" I ask.

"Because it's my job to keep you safe as I continue my investigation, and as I've said, you are a witness in a high profile murder."

"I'll be in touch as soon as arrangements are made," James tells him, shaking his hand.

"Thank you." McKenzie holds out his hand to me and I reluctantly take it. His grip is as strong as I expected when I shake his hand. His eyes stay on me and my guard is down. All my vulnerability is on show and I know he can see me.

The real me. And that scares me.

CHAPTER TEN

Jack

I HOLD onto her hand longer than I should, my eyes lingering on hers, and in this shared moment between us, there's only us. No one else.

She's vulnerable and scared. This is the real Maria Fraser, the one I caught a glimpse of during our interview. The moment she removed her sunglasses and looked me straight in the eye, I could see her. The real woman. She's not grieving for her husband. From what I've seen, she's already done that. A long time ago. No, she's grieving for herself, for the world she's played a part in.

A slow smile spreads across her face, but then she remembers where she is. Maria pulls her hand away first, her mask falling firmly back into place, and she takes a step back. Instantly, I miss her touch. The feel of her soft hand in mine.

What the fuck is wrong with me?

I shake my lingering thoughts away and try to remain professional. "The house has been made safe. If you could arrange your own security," I say, looking at Maria, but my words are meant for Pete.

It's Pete that answers. "I'll get on that straight away. Maria?" She finally turns away. Pete puts his hand on her shoulder and she flinches under his touch.

Surely he hasn't hurt her?

He had fucking better not. I'd kill him with my bare hands.

I stand and watch as all three of them leave the station. The door bangs loudly behind them, bringing my attention back to the fact that I'm standing in the station with people watching me.

I turn away from the door and start walking through the station. I don't get very far before bumping into Craig. "I can totally understand the attraction," he says, smirking.

"What the hell are you on about?" I bark at him.

"Hey, cool it. Maria Fraser. She's one fine-looking woman. It's no wonder you were standing there watching her. She has a mighty fine ass too. I would, and from the way you were watching her, you would too." I shake my head and continue to walk in silence until we reach my office. Craig follows me. "Well, you haven't denied it."

I sit down at my desk. "There's nothing to deny. As you said, she's a fine-looking woman."

"Yes, but she's danced with the devil himself."

"Now that I'm not too sure about. She's finally given her statement, and I'll be honest, it might've looked on the outside like she had everything, but deep down, all she had was a controlling husband who abused that position. Yes, she had a nice house, fancy jewellery, and money, but she's paid the price for it. Tony raped her that night and it wasn't the first time."

"I wasn't expecting you to say that," he says, sitting down.

"You can have a listen to her statement and see if you pick up anything else from what she says."

"I will do. Now, I was looking for you."

"Why's that?"

"Because there was a bit of a disturbance at the Fraser house shortly after you left there."

"What's gone on?"

"The neighbours reported a few men sifting through the debris."

"Men?" What would they be looking for? And who?

"Yes, men, but by the time our officers got there, they were gone. The neighbour couldn't give us a description, or rather, wouldn't."

There's a surprise.

"I don't want to put another officer back on duty. It's a waste of our resources and time."

"I agree. If we put officers at the house it means we'll be short when we need them."

"Craig, you're right. I know you said something about waiting for the storm, but I know there's one brewing, and when it lands upon us on, I think we'll have our hands full."

He nods, standing up and leaving the office, leaving me alone with the trail of destruction that's running through my mind. I want to know why I can't stop thinking about Maria Fraser. She's consuming my fucking thoughts, and right now, that's not a good thing. I need to be focused. One hundred percent focused.

I have a fucking murderer to find and bring to justice. I can't compromise this case because I've let a bit of skirt into my head. Fuck, it's not as though I've even had her in my bed.

But, if I'm truthful with myself, it's where I'd like her.

I need to shake these thoughts from my head, because with them lingering around, I won't achieve anything.

Papers and reports on my desk need to be dealt with. I call out to Jenny, asking politely for a coffee. She pops her head into my office and I know she wants to work out how my mood is because that depends on the coffee I drink. She truly is a diamond, one of a kind. A woman in her late forties who knows how to put everyone in this department in their place, including me.

"Milk and sugar," I say, and she nods with a smile.

Turning my attention back to the paperwork on my desk, I start reading through some of the reports. A gun found at the scene had two sets of prints, one of which was Tony's, so I can presume the other set is Maria's now. She stated that she held his gun against him. There were shots fired from it, but from the initial report, this wasn't the gun used to murder him. Not that I think Maria was lying to me, but she didn't kill her husband unless there's another gun somewhere with her prints on it.

Now, we just need to find the gun used in the shooting and we have ourselves a murderer. But even I know it's not going to be that simple. If it were, we would already have someone in custody.

I scan over a few of the other reports, but they don't tell me anything I don't already know. I lean back in my chair, folding my hands behind my head, and stare out at my office. An investigation like this goes one of two ways; really slow, information coming to us in dribs and drabs, or fast-paced, in that we get so much information we struggle to keep up.

Already, I can sense how this investigation is going to go, and I don't like it.

CHAPTER ELEVEN

Maria

TODAY, life is dragging me down, pulling me underwater, and if I gasp for air, I know I'll drown. Right now, in this moment of time, that might not be such a bad thing. I feel broken beyond repair.

Unfixable.

The pressure mounts. My heart is beating so fast, so out of control, that it's painful. My tears trickle slowly down my face. I will them to stop but they don't. To me, my tears are a sign of weakness. To others, my tears will be a sign of pain, of grief.

This isn't me.

This isn't supposed to be my life.

I'm better than this.

I'm stronger than this.

I deserve so much more than this.

Putting on a brave face for the last two weeks hasn't helped me. I wasn't prepared for the emotion that has overtaken me today, and not just because of Tony's death.

I'm suddenly scared for my future. A future that is no longer clear for me to see. Uncertainty surrounds my life.

The priest speaks to me and I stare, glaring at the hole in the ground as the coffin is lowered by six of my husband's closest friends, associates, whatever they want to call themselves. As my eyes cast over the men, I'm wondering which one of them a poor wife or mother will be burying next. Because no matter how invincible they think they are, the proof that they're not is now in the coffin that rests in the ground.

Tony thought he was untouchable.

Lou is beside me. Mark holds his wife in his arms. Her body has been trembling from the minute we left their house. Her tears for her brother are real. She worshipped the ground he walked on. Hopefully, through time, her pain will lessen and her family can have a happy life without violence and fears hanging over them. Lou and the girls deserve that.

Everyone here today will be waiting for some sort of reaction to his death, and I know they won't have to wait long. Pete and Mark might think they've been keeping things quiet, but I know they're planning something. They think they have an idea of who killed Tony, a rival gang, but I know they're wrong.

My attention turns to the handsome man who looks more like my father every time I see him. My brother, Giovanni De Luca, stands at the side with two of my cousins, Alesio and Leo. I was surprised to see the three of them here. I've wanted to reach out to him since the shooting, but I knew it wasn't wise. There's always someone hanging around me.

It still might not be wise, but I need to talk to him. Although, what I have to say, he's not going to be happy about. But he's my brother, and I know he'll help me.

It hasn't escaped my notice that there is a heavy police presence here at the cemetery. Some might not be in uniform, but I can tell them from a mile away. I understand why they would attend. After all, they have an investigation going on.

McKenzie stands closer than the others. I expect he's hoping to hear something that will help with his investigation. I've tried to avoid looking at him, but it's hard not to, especially when I've felt the warmth of his hand in mine. I've seen the way he looks at me. I know the way I look at him, and I'm hoping no-one else has noticed.

So, for today, I'm trying to avoid my growing attraction to a man I shouldn't be interested in.

Pete has warned all the men not to say anything. He doesn't want the police involved in his own private investigation.

I wish he would drop it.

"Maria." It's Lou that takes my arm. "Do you want a minute or are you ready to leave?"

"Can I have a minute? I'd like to speak with Giovanni."

"Under the circumstances, he is welcome to come back to the house," she says, her voice soft and her eyes filled with tears.

"He won't come back."

She nods, accepting my words. I know she only said that because of me. She doesn't want him there because of the history between my brother and hers. There was never any love between them, and Giovanni always believed that Tony was no good for me. But I was blinded by love. Or what I thought was love.

"I'll give you a minute." She kisses my cheek and walks away with Mark. She smiles, passing my brother. I can't see his expression as he has his back to me and is watching Lou. Everyone else is leaving the graveside. Pete stops when he sees my brother stepping toward me, but it's Lou that pulls him away with her and Mark.

"Maria DeLuca, anche nel dolore stai bene," Gio says, pulling me into his embrace. "Sei forte. Lo supererai."

"English, please," I tell him, not wanting to hide anything from anyone who happens to be eavesdropping on our conversation. "I don't feel strong today. I feel weak." Today, I'm mentally drained with the enormity of everything going on around me.

"Enough. My sister is one of the strongest people I know. You are a DeLuca."

"Are you forgetting I'm Mrs Fraser?"

"In name only, and that can be changed. It's Italian DeLuca blood that runs through your veins."

"I need help," I say, scanning the area. No one is in earshot, but McKenzie is waiting up ahead.

"The last time you asked for help…"

"Don't say it. Not here. I need to get away for a week or two."

"Of course. You can have my villa anytime at all, just say when. But I don't want you running away. You haven't done anything wrong. You need to be brave and show everyone that you're not weak."

He might be on to something. If I choose to go away on a break, that's how it will look to some. "I have to go to the lawyer's office this afternoon with Pete and Lou for a reading of Tony's will."

"You seem anxious."

"I am."

"Don't be. Everything will be okay. And if it's not, your brother will sort it all out. I promise. Have I ever let you down before?" His eyes roam the graveside and I know he's watching to see who is hanging around.

"No, but I've let you down."

"It's in the past. You're my sister and I love you. Don't ever forget that."

He takes my hand and I have one last look at the hole in the ground before walking away. I'll organise a fitting headstone and it will have lovely words from a dutiful wife, but I can say, honestly, that I'll never be back here.

I need the past to stay where it belongs.

"Mrs Fraser." McKenzie steps forward. It's hard not to see him. My eyes found him as soon as he arrived.

"Detective, what can I do for you?" His eyes dart between Giovanni and me. "This is my brother."

"Mr DeLuca." McKenzie greets my brother as though they know each other. I suppose he knows of him. Giovanni is a man everyone knows of, much like Tony. The only difference being, my brother doesn't intentionally get involved with murderers and prostitutes.

"Was there something you wanted?" I ask, hoping he'll get on with it. I don't get enough time with Giovanni and every second counts.

"I wanted you to know that I have officers coming back to the wake."

"Excuse me?" My voice is raised. Police officers at a gangland wake. It was bad enough having so many officers here at the cemetery. "Do you really think that's necessary?"

"Yes, I do. We don't have any leads on your husband's killers, and as you were a witness, that puts you in danger. They'll be posted outside."

"Officer," Giovanni starts speaking.

"It's DCI, but Detective will do." McKenzie corrects Giovanni in an attempt to put him in his place.

"Sorry, Detective. Do you really think those men are going to let anything happen to my sister? I might not like any of them, but even I know they look after their own. If I had any concerns, she'd be coming home with me."

"So, you and Mr Fraser didn't get on?" I can see through McKenzie; his mind has just gone into overdrive at my brother's admission.

"No, but if you had a sister who was marrying him, I don't think you'd be happy either."

"No, I don't suppose I would. Point taken. Mr DeLuca, I'd like to talk to you at a later date."

"Of course, Detective. Anything I can do to help."

My heart starts hammering against the walls of my chest and I swear it's going to burst through. I'm not sure I can do this.

"Mrs Fraser." McKenzie says my name before walking away.

"Breathe. Dai, mia cara sorella, puoi farlo. Non hai nulla di cui aver paura."

"I hope you're right."

"I'm always right. Now, you have family waiting."

"Talking of family, Lou said you, Alesio, and Leo are welcome back at the house."

He smiles and looks in Lou's direction. "For you, I'm going to stay away because there's been enough blood shed, and if Pete keeps looking at you the way he is, I'll kill him with my bare hands. But say thank you to Lou. The offer is appreciated."

I lift my head, and only a few feet away, Pete is waiting for me. "Maria, we should go," he says. "There are a lot of people who want to pay their respects and we have to go to James's office first."

Giovanni wraps his arms around me and my eyes fill with tears. "Go, you'll be okay, but keep an eye on him. Ti vuole nel suo letto. Stai attento e chiamami presto. Ti amo."

"I love you too," I say, my tears falling as I step back from my brother. Pete offers me his hand, which I take, because today isn't the time or place to inform Pete that whatever it is he wants from me, there's no hope in hell of me giving it. Not now. Not ever.

I reluctantly walk away from my loving brother with a man who is as, if not more, violent than my husband was.

And that's what frightens me.

CHAPTER TWELVE

Jack

"IF YOU KEEP LOOKING at her like that, I won't be the only one to notice," Craig says, stepping beside me. I glance at him and then turn my attention back to the woman who has just walked away from her brother.

I pretend to ignore his statement, but I know he won't settle for my silence, "I wasn't aware I was looking at her in any way." Of course, I'm well aware of watching her; I can't help it. The compulsion I feel to walk over there and remove Pete's hand from hers is so fucking strong. It scares the living daylights out of me.

"Yeah, well, you look at her as though you want to devour her for breakfast, lunch, and dinner. I would usually tell you to act on whatever you're feeling but, this time, you can't. You need to keep it firmly in your pants. And I remember what happened the last time I saw that look in your eyes."

I want to laugh at his words, but given where we are, it might not be the most appropriate thing to do. I try to ignore his last sentence because I don't want to think about that. Instead, I focus on the words, 'keep it firmly in your pants.'

"That's where my problem is," I say, smirking.

"Of all the conversations we had to have today. Totally inappropriate."

"Don't blame me. You brought up the subject. Now, I want a car to go back to Lou's house and I don't care who sees it. Have it parked right across the street in full-view. I want them all to know we're watching them. We're going to follow Mrs Fraser's car."

"Why?" he asks, watching as mourners get into cars.

"Because, today of all days, she, along with Lou and Pete, are going to Stevenson's office." I knew there would have to be a will reading, but why today? What can't wait another day or so? What is so important?

I speak to a couple of officers before getting into Craig's car. We wait. Looking out, I see Giovanni with his two cousins and they're watching Maria as she gets into the car with Lou. He looks concerned for his sister, and I suppose he has every right to, especially if he sees the way Pete looks at and touches her.

I need to look more into the history between the families because I can't understand what's going on. Maria and Giovanni look so close, yet they've not been pictured or seen together in a number of years. I need to find out the reason why.

I keep watching the three men, and from here, it looks as though one of the younger men has said something and Giovanni isn't happy with. He takes a step forward, his face inches from the other's, and it looks as though he's giving him a ticking off about something. I wish I knew what they are talking about.

"Are you ready, boss?"

"Yes, but what do you think is being said between them?" I ask, indicating to the three Italian men.

"I'm not sure," he replies, starting the car.

The car Maria is in has just left, and Craig pulls in behind it. I've no intention of hiding the fact that we're tailing them. I want Pete to be aware that, for the foreseeable future, wherever he goes, we won't be far behind him.

I've heard through the grapevine that he has his own investigation going on and I'm well aware that he will dish out his own punishment. If he does, I'm hoping that will be enough to put him behind bars.

As we enter the city centre, I know there's every chance we won't be directly behind them for long with the building traffic, but we know their destination, so if it does happen they won't get there too far in front of us.

I call into the station and speak to one of the men on my team and ask him to gather all information we have on the Frasers and the DeLucas. Hopefully, it will help my investigation. At this stage, I'll take any bit of information, no matter how small it may seem. Two weeks on and we're no further forward.

After a few minutes, their car indicates and slows down. We do the same until we've stopped behind them. I get out of the car, leaving Craig inside. The occupants of the other car haven't yet gotten out.

I open my suit jacket and lean against our car, pushing my hands into my trouser pockets, and wait. The driver gets out first, then Pete. They open the back doors for Lou and Maria. Pete stares straight at me whilst holding his hand out. It's Maria who takes it.

Hairs stand on the nape of my neck; I hate the thought of that man touching her. A look of smug contempt crosses Pete's face and I try not to let it bother me, but it bloody does. I don't know what his game is, but it's one he won't win. Not with me.

Pete has always come across as a man with all brawn and no brains. I smile at the thought. He thinks he's this mister-big-I-am, but he's not. Never has been, and if I get my way, he'll never be. Tony was smart. A highly intelligent man who played the game very well. Wasn't afraid to get his own hands dirty, but had an army of men that were prepared to carry out his dirty work.

Pete was one of those men.

Maria turns away from Pete to see what he's looking at. She smiles briefly before turning back to him. She walks toward the building, pulling him with her. Lou and the driver follow.

Lou still looks shaken. She cried all through the service and as the coffin was lowered into the ground. It's clear she loved her brother, but I'm wondering how much she knows about the family's criminal activities. She has two small children; surely she would want to keep them away from that side of things.

As they enter the building, Maria glances behind her toward me. I can only smile. She smiles again before turning back quickly, her hair flowing with the movement.

This case might be the death of me.

Or it might be the dark-haired Italian woman that has weakened all my fucking senses.

"You're fucked and don't even pretend you're not," Craig says as he rounds the car.

"Leave over."

"What? Only saying how I see it, and bloody hell. You, my friend, should not be playing games with Mrs Fraser."

"I'm not playing games."

"You might not be, but she is. There's something about

her. I know you don't want to hear it, but I think she should be on our suspect list."

"She didn't do it," I say quickly. Too quickly, as Craig's eyes scan my face.

"You don't know she didn't. And until we find out who did murder Tony, she should be a suspect."

I stare ahead at the building they have all entered. Of course Craig is right.

Did Maria Fraser kill her husband?

No. She didn't do it.

But does that mean I should stop watching her?

I think not.

CHAPTER THIRTEEN

Maria

"Have you been here before?" Lou asks me, her voice wavering as we sit in James's office with Pete. She's nervous and she has no reason to be. Everyone else has gone back to her house. James said this had to be done now. Not sure why it's so important today.

"Yes, I've been here more than a few times," I tell her, trying not to think about all the papers I've signed over the years in this office. All the dodgy dealings that I've played a part in. James's office is on the same level as the office Tony had.

I don't remember Lou ever being in this building. There was never any need for her to be here. She's never been involved in any of Tony's deals. He made sure everything with his sister was squeaky clean.

It's a pity he couldn't have done the same for me, *his wife*.

James, with his glasses low on his nose, sits fiddling with

all the papers on his desk, making sure he has everything before he starts.

He finally clears his throat. "Okay, I'm sorry I've had to bring the three of you into the office today, but given Tony's business and reputation, everything needs dealing with quickly. As much as this is a formal meeting, I'll keep things simple for you," James says, looking straight at me. Lou takes my hand. She's still shaking. Doing this today isn't fair on her. She's been through enough. She loved Tony with all her heart. I did too at one point, or at least I thought I did.

"Lou, Tony has always wanted to protect you and the girls. Make sure you had everything you could ever need. I have been instructed to clear down your mortgage and there is a bank account in trust for each of the girls. They get access to it on their eighteenth birthdays. There is also an account for you. I also have here…" He picks up a large brown envelope. "…The title deeds for the villa in France. The very one you and Tony went to with your parents." Lou's eyes fill with tears. "As you all know, almost everything has been lost in the fire that ripped through the house, but I have a key to a safety deposit box. The items within that are for you, Lou. It's mostly jewellery that belonged to your mother."

Lou sinks into the chair. Her tears fall and I know it's not the money that has her crying, it will be her mother's items and the villa in France. She's always spoken fondly of holidaying with her parents. They will all hold special memories for her. I rub her arm, offering her my comfort and support. "B…but…"

"Lou, I should stress that all money for you and the girls is, as Tony would say, clean. It hasn't come from the underworld. I have a letter for you that you should read in private. Your brother was very insistent about that." She nods, unable to speak.

"Pete, I have an envelope and a key for you. My only instructions were to give you both and that, when the time comes, you would know what needed to be done."

Pete smiles. I want to ask what it means but I stop myself. "What about the business?" Pete asks, edging forward on the seat.

"I'll get to that in a minute. Maria, I also have a personal letter for you, but I have many business papers that will require your signature."

"Why would I need to sign business papers?" I ask, suddenly nervous about what he's about to tell me.

"Because on everything business related, both yours and Tony's signatures are on all official papers. With Tony's death, everything he owned transferred to you. Money, businesses. You are an incredibly wealthy woman."

"Everything?" Pete asks, and I can hear concern and a hint of anger in his voice. He presumed everything business related would go to him.

"Yes," James says. "You are in sole charge of the Fraser empire, Maria. Pete will bring you up to speed on all aspects of the businesses."

"Surely that can't be right." Again, it's Pete that speaks. "She can't run an underworld empire."

I know they were like brothers, but his anger and frustration is starting to rub off on me.

"Pete! Why wouldn't everything go to Maria? She is his wife, after all. She's been loyal and faithful." Lou is standing up for me, and right now, I wish she wasn't.

"Let me get this right; my husband is expecting me to pick up where he left off?" I ask, more calmly than I'm feeling.

Pete is glaring at me, and I know he's cursing under his breath. I can see the ticking in his jaw. He's never been capable of hiding his emotions.

"Yes, Maria. Tony wanted the businesses to continue as they are now, but was always aware that, should anything happen to him, you'd most likely want everything to be above board. So with that, what you do with the businesses is up to you. I'll arrange for you to come into the office in a few days, when all this has sunk in, and we can sort out everything together." It was awfully nice of him to be so understanding. If only he'd been that understanding when he was bloody alive. Then things might've been so very different.

"What about you?" I ask James.

"I'll be your lawyer from now on. I've been taken care of and we can discuss that in private. There are also a few personal matters that we can discuss. I will act in your best interests and those of the businesses. Anything you need, you come to me."

"What about the clubs?" Pete interrupts.

Lou shifts in her seat. "Pete, have you not listened? It's all going to Maria and she can do what she wants with them."

"I've listened and, Maria, you know you're my friend, but I'm not sure you've got what it takes to take control of the Fraser empire."

"Is that because…" I allow the words in my head to trail off because I don't want to say them out loud. *A woman isn't capable of the crimes and murders he and Tony have committed.*

"It's been a long day for us all," James says. "We should all be back at the house with family and friends."

I agree. It's a lot to take in.

I wasn't angry or upset about losing everything in the fire. Expensive clothes, jewellery; all things bought for me by all Tony's illegal dealings. It's laughable. I thought all my ties would be cut to this world I've been living in, with the fire and Tony's death. And now I find myself being dragged into it. It's as though Tony knew I wanted to escape this criminal lifestyle and he's said, '*Fuck you. You're staying in it, and not only that, you're taking the reins.*'

Tony might think he's had the last laugh, but we'll see about that.

I STAND IN THE FRONT GARDEN WITH MY GLASS OF WINE IN my hand. Even outside, I can still hear the noise from inside, but everything here seems calmer. Inside, there are still plenty of tears and it's all starting to get to me. There are people here who shouldn't be acting as though they're grieving for a man that most of them hated and feared.

I tucked Rebecca and Daisy into bed, read them a story, and they are both fast asleep. I hope they sleep through the noise because I don't see it calming down in the house anytime soon.

I felt like a prisoner today. Pete's had his eyes on me at one side, and Detective McKenzie was watching me from the other. Both waiting for me to fuck up, or in Pete's case, waiting for the moment I break down so he can be the person I turn to. I'm not so lost in grief that I haven't noticed how friendly he's being, or the look in his eyes as he watches me. I may be a lot of things, but I'm not blind. Whatever thoughts about the two of us Pete is having, it's not going to happen. The devil himself would probably want to steer clear of Pete Jamieson.

He was being nice before today, but I'm sure now he'll be even nicer, hoping that I keep him around to help me with the businesses.

"What the hell do I know about his business?" I say out loud.

"You shouldn't talk to yourself, Mrs Fraser." Detective McKenzie is walking up the path toward me. I look past him and see a car sitting on the road; there's someone else in it. "They say that's the first sign of losing your marbles."

"I'm sure you're right," I say as he steps in front of me. "I thought you'd be long gone. You must have a death wish still being here."

"I'm a little surprised I'm still alive," he says with amusement, his voice husky.

"Me too," I reply before taking a sip of my wine. "Will you be following me from now on?" I ask, remembering he followed from the cemetery to James's office. I remember the look on Pete's face; it was priceless, and it makes me smile.

"No, not you, but if you feel threatened it could be arranged. Why is it, while everyone is inside, you're out here alone?"

"Just thinking, Detective."

"That must have been a surprise, your brother and cousins at the funeral. I thought you weren't on speaking terms."

"You thought wrong. Family is important, don't you think?" I ask. I don't want him prying into my family, although I'm sure a man such as himself won't have to dig far to get the history between them and Tony. I didn't get why the two families didn't get on. I still don't.

"I suppose so."

"That makes you sound lonely. Are you lonely, Jack McKenzie?"

"No." He might be saying no, but he's lying. I can see it in his eyes, the way they shift to the ground. He can keep his secrets. I have enough of my own without worrying about someone else's. "Now, getting back to business."

"Steer away from anything personal," I say with a hint of amusement in my voice.

"So, business. Who will be running this empire?" he asks.

"Me."

"You?"

"What's wrong? Don't you think I'm cut out for a life of crime?"

"To be honest, no. But you might surprise me. At least I know who I'll have to come looking for when there's trouble."

"What made you join the police force?" I ask him, curiosity getting the better of me.

"Truthfully?" I nod, because he doesn't seem the type. "My dad was a violent man who used to beat up my mum, and he was always involved in some dodgy dealing or another. From an early age, my mum told me that what my dad did wasn't right. But he was a lot like Tony and always avoided the law. The day I started my training, he beat my mum up so badly that their neighbours called the police. My mum died as a result of what happened that day, and my dad went to prison. I never wanted to be like him. I always wanted to protect. Keep others safe."

Wow. I never expected that. "I'm sorry about your mum."

"Thank you. Now, what about you. What are you going to do?"

"It looks like I have several businesses that need to be run. Although, I'm not sure if some will be happy with my plans. And I need to find somewhere to live."

"Does that mean I don't have to worry about arresting Mrs Fraser for bad behaviour?" I stare ahead and hold his amused gaze. The longer I stare, the more I see something I like. I swallow hard, hoping it will calm the fluttering in my stomach.

"Am I interrupting?" I swing my head around to see Pete standing at the door with a bottle of beer in his hand.

"No," McKenzie says. "I'm just leaving."

"Yes, I think that would be wise," I say, looking back at him. He smiles before walking down the path. He looks over his shoulder and smirks before entering the waiting car. I watch on as it drives away.

"What the hell are you doing talking to him? We don't talk to the likes of him voluntarily. It will cause us nothing but problems. Problems that I'll need to take care of."

"Talking. Nothing more," I state firmly. "I'm going to bed. You should maybe get home and do the same because we have an early start tomorrow."

"Do we?" he asks, surprised by my statement.

"Yes. Can you arrange for Joe to pick me up and take me into the office in the morning?"

I think he wants to ask why or at least tell me I'm not needed in the office, that he can take care of things for me, but doesn't. "Of course. What time?"

"Seven. That way, I can go through all the papers and accounts, and in the afternoon, you can take me to the clubs." Although, I'm not sure about going to all the clubs. Some I'd rather avoid for as long as I can get away with.

"Okay."

"And I don't want the staff at the clubs to know I'm going in."

"No problem. I'll see you in the morning," he says before walking back into the house, shaking his head.

Tomorrow is shaping up to be an interesting day. The only way it could be more interesting is if I get to see the handsome detective.

This thought shouldn't be in my head.

But it is and it has me smiling.

CHAPTER FOURTEEN

Jack

"I need a drink."

"No, you need to get fucking laid," Craig says, laughing. He might have a point, but I'm not sure. The last time I was with someone I ended up dreaming about Maria Fraser. That woman is everywhere, invading my life and thoughts.

"Pull over," I say as we approach a pub. "Are you joining me?"

"No, not tonight. Sorry. I'd rather spend time with my wife. It's been a long day and my boss is a bit of an arse. He wants me in the office nice and early in the morning," he says, laughing at me.

"Fine. In that case you had better not be late."

"I won't." I open the car door. "Don't do anything I wouldn't do," he calls after me.

I don't say anything, I just slam the car door closed and he drives off. I look around the street; no one lingering around. No one even standing having a smoke outside the pub which is unusual.

Pushing the door open, I go inside, and for a Thursday night, it's pretty quiet. I nod at a few old regulars as I walk toward the bar.

"Jack." The barman says my name, opening a bottle of whisky. He pours it neat and slides the glass to me.

"Thanks." I swallow it in one.

"Another?"

I nod and he pours. I know I can't stand here at the bar drinking all night, but I can already feel the warmth of the smooth liquid as it slides down my throat, and it's quietly comforting.

"You look as though you've had a tough day," the barman says, pouring another drink.

He's got no idea. "Yes, it's been long," I say and throw the third glass of whisky down my throat. He goes to pour another, but I put my hand over the glass, indicating no more, and hand him money. With a nod to the gents sitting, I leave the pub.

An early night is what I need. If I can stop thinking about this case and a certain Italian, I might get some sleep.

The walk to my house is only a few minutes and I'm hoping the cool night air will help clear my thoughts.

As I round the corner into the street I live on, the first thing I notice is that all the streetlights are out. The street is in complete darkness. Only a few lights on in some of the houses, so at least I know it isn't a power cut. A fault somewhere?

I climb the steps to my terraced house, and as I get close to the front door, I see it's open. It's been forced. Pulling my phone from my pocket, I switch on the torch and glance around, but there's no one about.

Why hasn't my alarm gone off?

I call Craig. "What the fuck is it?" he asks. "I wanted a quiet night with my wife. You're interrupting."

"Sorry. It looks like I've been broken into," I tell him.

"What the house? You're home already? You haven't gone in yet, have you?" The words rush from him but he knows me well and knows I won't be able to stand out here until he or officers from the station arrive.

"No, but I'm going in now."

"Can you wait until I get there? I'll call it into the station."

"You do that, but I'm going in," I tell him and then end our call.

Keeping my phone in my hand with the torch light still on, I push the door open and step inside. I pause and shine the light around the entrance. This morning's mail lies on the floor but broken glass is scattered on top of it. What the fuck? Lifting my head, I realise the glass on the floor is from the pictures that were on the wall.

I shine the light on the control panel for the house alarm to see it's been pulled apart. Wires hang loosely from it. That's why it hasn't gone off. Someone has taken the time to disable it, and completely destroy it.

Trying to avoid stepping on the glass, I take steps farther inside, the light from my camera leading the way. I turn left into my sitting room. It's been turned upside down. The cushions from the couch are scattered around the room. Picture frames and ornaments are on the floor, broken.

Who the fuck has been in here and what in the hell were they looking for?

A noise from the kitchen startles me. I leave the destruction of the sitting room and make my way quickly toward the back of the house. In the kitchen is the same mess, but no sign of anyone, although the back door is open. Rushing toward it, I open it wider, in time to see a dark figure jumping over the back garden wall.

Running up the garden, I jump, pulling myself up the wall, but whoever it is has gone and I'm not sure what direction they've taken.

I jump back down, walk back toward the house, and enter. The mess isn't too bad in the kitchen. I'd obviously disturbed whoever it was. A few drawers are open with bills scattered around.

Walking back through the house, I find myself taking the stairs, because I suspect the intruder has been in the bedrooms and the office I sometimes work in.

"Jack, where the hell are you?" Craig's voice calls out.

"I'm upstairs. Watch where you step," I call down to him as I enter my bedroom. Everything has been pulled apart. Clothes pulled from my closet and thrown over the floor. Drawers have all been opened and the contents is everywhere. The sheets have been pulled from the bed.

This has to be work related. But why?

There's no way this was just a random burglary. No, whoever was in my home was looking for something, because from the looks of it, nothing has been stolen.

I leave my bedroom and enter the office. Surprisingly enough, it looks as though it hasn't been touched.

"Fucking hell," Craig says as I leave the office. "Downstairs is a riot."

"I know. I disturbed the intruder. He got over the back wall and ran."

We walk downstairs as I hear the sirens. "You'll need to stay with me tonight."

"Thanks, but what about the missus?" Beth is lovely and I get on with her, I just don't want to be imposing on his time with her.

"She'll understand and wouldn't want you staying in a hotel."

"Okay." The boys in blue come in and start asking questions, shouting out that nothing should be touched until forensics get here. I tell them what I know. I give them a vague description of the intruder because, in truthfulness, I couldn't tell if they were a man or a woman. Craig tells them he wants to take me out of here and they agree it's okay for me to leave. I call the alarm company and they're sending someone out now. One of the officers has agreed to stay at the house until it's all made safe.

We leave behind the chaos and I make my way to Craig's car. My own car is still parked on the street.

"Well, what do you think?" I ask him.

"Not sure. It does look as though someone was looking for something. Do you think it's related to a case?"

"Yes. It must be, and I'm pretty sure it's connected to the Fraser case in some way. But if it was files they were looking for, they wouldn't find them. I don't bring anything like that home. Although, I can access the files from the computer."

He nods and I'm sure we both know that this is probably only the beginning of the storm that has been brewing.

CHAPTER FIFTEEN

Maria

"You look great," Lou says as I stand in her hallway checking out my appearance. Her black dress looks very smart and business-like on me, but I've paired it with some killer red heels. I really need to get out shopping for some things of my own, but I'm lucky Lou and I are the same size. I've left my dark hair down; it's flowing in soft curls down my back. I've inherited my mother's Mediterranean skin colouring so my make-up is minimal. After all, I'm meant to be a grieving wife. "Very much the important business woman."

"I'm not sure I have what it takes." It's true. I might look confident on the outside, but inside, my stomach is in knots.

"Of course you do. Even if you don't stay Maria Fraser forever. Maria DeLuca was the girl I first met all those years ago. She was strong, independent, and always put my brother in his place. She was my friend then and she's still my friend."

"Yes, but things changed." Our friendship is also bound to change in coming months. I know it will, even though I don't want it to. But I'm the one who will have to live with that.

"Yes, they did. I know Tony loved you, I just wish he'd shown you how much. It might've helped now. I don't know what went on between you in recent months and I'm sure you could tell me all about it, but you haven't. You haven't wanted to taint the memory I have of him any further. I'm all too aware of the person he was, but with me and my girls, he was different. I had thought he was different with you too, but seeing the bruising you have, I know he wasn't."

"Lou, I'm sorry. He was your brother and would've done anything for you and the girls. I don't know what was in your letter, but you have the opportunity to walk away from this lifestyle. To start over."

"The same could be said of you."

"My life was tainted before I met your brother, we all know that," I say, looking in the mirror whilst finishing fixing my hair. My own family were involved in all sorts. This is all I know. All I've ever known.

"Life is what you make it. You're still young. You can do anything you want. Even re-marry and have a family."

"Now you're talking silly. I don't feel very young."

"Nonsense. You're only thirty-two. You have time to do what you want. Rip out all the dead weeds and build a career for yourself. Make a name for yourself. Just go back to living your life your way. Don't let it be dictated by anyone else ever again." She leans over and kisses my cheek, and all I see is sorrow and hope in her eyes.

"I love you," I say to her.

"I know you do, and I love you. Always will. Now, go

on. Joe is outside. Go and do what you need to do for you. No-one else."

With a smile, I leave the house feeling a lot better than when I first woke up, although regrets are still lingering in the back of my head. Regrets that I'll never be able to share. But I can't let those regrets consume me or I'll end up like my mother and not living. Sadness sweeps through me as I think about her and the regrets she lived with. I try not to compare my life to my mother's, but my father was a highly respected man who held much the same power and control that Tony had. Although, I'm not sure if there was ever any blood on my father's hands, unlike Tony.

"Good morning, Mrs Fraser," Joe says, smiling as I approach the car.

"Joe. Good morning," I say as he opens the door.

"You do look well, Mrs Fraser."

"Thank you. I wish I felt it."

He closes the door and gets in the driver's side. "How you feel is understandable. But can I say something? And if I'm out of turn just tell me to shut up."

"Of course."

"Today, don't take any nonsense from anyone. You need to show them who's boss from day one because, if you don't, there will be some who will take advantage of the situation and your good nature."

"Thanks, Joe. I'll remember that." Smiling at my answer, he starts the car and we drive away. Joe is a good man. I'd say Joe is in his late forties/early fifties. He's kind but he looks aggressive if you don't know him. He's always been nice to me, and not in the way that he wants something from me. Unlike Pete, who has been giving me the creeps, even before Tony died. I know he's someone I need to watch. He would be one who would take advantage if he was given half the chance, but he won't get that from me. Tony might've trusted him, but I don't, and that's where all my issues will lie.

I don't know who can be trusted. I'm sure by the end of the day, I'll have a list in my head of who can't be trusted.

I sit back and enjoy the early morning journey into the city.

"Joe, can I ask a question?" I say as the car stops outside the stylish glass building.

"Of course," he replies, turning around to face me.

"How many of the businesses are legitimate?"

"Mrs Fraser, I really don't know. I'd say all the clubs and the security firm, but as for everything else…"

"That's all I need to know." Of course I know about the drug dealing and the girls on the street, but it's a side of Tony's life I pushed to the back of my head. It's also a part of the business I want no involvement in.

He gets out of the car and opens my door. "Mrs Fraser, will I be reporting to you or Pete?"

"Me. So, come on in with me. I may as well have someone in my corner today. I think I'll need it."

"I already know you won't need it, but I'm happy to help you in any way I can."

We enter the building, which is really quiet, unusual for this time of day and take the lift up to the top floor which has the office. My office. James Stevenson's firm is on the top floor too. It doesn't just seem like yesterday when he told me everything is mine.

We exit the lift, and behind the reception desk is Tony's receptionist/PA. I don't think she'll still be here by the end of the day; I've never liked her. She jumps when she sees me. "Oh, Mrs Fraser. I wasn't expecting you. If you're here to see Pete, he's not arrived yet," she says, looking flustered.

"I know, but when he does arrive, show him through to

my office. And when you have time can you bring me in anything Tony had you working on in the last month?" She looks at me, her mouth slack and eyes wide. Yes, I suppose she would be in shock. "Could you also please call Mr Stevenson and arrange a meeting for me? And get me a list of any meetings Tony had organised for this week, and next would be helpful too. Just when you have time."

"All the meetings?" she asks. I nod. "Of course, Mrs Fraser. I'll get on it straight away. Would you like tea or coffee?"

"Joe?"

"I'll have tea," he replies.

"Two teas, please, Colette."

Joe and I enter the office, leaving Colette flustered in the reception.

"That's how you need to be," Joe says as I stop and take in the office. I've been in here millions of times before, but it's only now that I truly take notice of everything. How bloody big it is. Who needs an office this size?

I walk over to the floor to ceiling window and stare out across the city. High flats stand tall in the distance, and church towers and roofs of all the local shopping areas are closer. "Let's hope I keep it up. Although, I'm not fond of her."

Joe smiles as I sit down. "I didn't expect you to keep her."

He's got a point. Every time I came here to see Tony, she was always hanging around like a bad fucking smell, flirting with him in front of me. That girl has no shame. Low-cut tops that her fake boobs burst out of. I can't be certain, but I'm pretty sure she and Tony had sex on more than one occasion.

"I suppose there will be a lot like her," I say as he takes a seat on the opposite side of the desk.

"Yes, there is, but don't let it put you off."

"I won't. Joe, what do you think I should do about all the other stuff?"

"You mean the drugs and the girls on the streets? That's up to you, but I'll say this, it brings in sixty percent of the weekly income."

"As much as that?" I had no idea. I knew that was where Tony started, I just never expected that it was bringing in that amount of income. I suppose that's how all the men get paid because I don't imagine their wages will go through the books of either of the clubs.

"The nightclubs do okay. But I imagine he only took them over so there was an avenue for cash to go through."

"Do you think Pete will be upfront with me about everything?" I ask the question but, deep down, I already know the answer to that.

"No. Pete will always look out for himself. He doesn't want to be someone's number two and we both know he's not happy with everything being left to you. As I've already said, you need to do what's right for you, not everyone else."

"Joe, you're a good man. How did you end up mixed up in all this?"

"Tony's dad helped me many years ago and I owed him. Yes, I know there's bad blood between your family, and rightly so. When he was dying, he asked me to look after Tony, so I've been here ever since." I wonder if he'll tell me about the bad blood. Or maybe I'm better off not knowing.

"You could have a life of your own," I say.

"Yes, but Tony was a bit like a son to me and, well, you need someone to make sure you're okay. I wish he had chosen a different path in his walk of life, but he didn't. If it's okay with you, I'll hang around just until you decide what path you'll take."

I smile fondly at the man across the table. "What if I choose the wrong path and fuck up?"

"Well, I'll be right by your side, Mrs Fraser. I think you'll do just fine."

I wish I shared his confidence, but maybe with a little help, I'll do okay.

CHAPTER SIXTEEN

Jack

I'M SITTING at my desk sifting through the piles of paper-work, wondering what the hell I should deal with first. There's so much here and I'm sure a lot of it is crap.

I decide to start with the break-in at my house. Nothing has been taken, there's no fingerprints, just a whole load of mess that needs to be cleared up. Officers did a door-to-door last night and what we've found out is that the alarm went off briefly at ten p.m., but my neighbours thought nothing about it because it was silenced so quickly.

This wasn't some random break-in. Whoever was in my house did it to get my attention. Maybe an attempt to frighten me. I find myself smirking as the last thought enters my head. I'm not a man easily frightened. If I was, I wouldn't be in the career I'm in.

Last night has to be about a current case. And the one that leaps out is the Fraser case.

But why?

We don't have any leads, and other than a break-in at my house and a few men sifting through the rubble of a fire-damaged house, there's been no sign of trouble. The streets have been quiet.

It's far too quiet, if I'm honest.

I look out of my office to the incident room beyond and my eyes settle on the board with all the pictures. Even from here I can see each one clearly. My eyes linger on Pete Jamieson. I think it was him last night, or he was behind it.

But what has he got to gain from breaking in to my house?

I can't pull him in without being sure. I need to be one hundred percent certain that he broke in. He didn't return to the house with Maria and Lou after the afternoon visit with Mr Stevenson. Why not? Where did he go? Who was he with?

And what time did he get back to the house? I saw him there at nine-thirty. Whoever was in my house was there at ten-forty-five when I got home and disturbed them. So, it could've been Pete. Maybe he left Lou's house shortly after me. Or maybe he was the one to orchestrate it.

He's behind it. I just need to prove it.

"Boss." Craig's raised voice brings my attention back to now.

"What's wrong?" I ask, noting the concerned look that's seldom on his face.

"We need to head on out."

"Why?"

"Because a body has been found by some bin men this morning."

I stand, pushing the paperwork back into a pile; this can all wait. "What happened?"

"The workmen were emptying bins at an Italian restaurant about fifteen minutes ago when they found the body."

Grabbing my suit jacket, I put it on and Craig and I leave my office. I call out for a couple of officers to follow us. "Dean and Smith, with me. Male or female?" There's a real buzz of activity as we walk through the station.

"Male. Two gunshot wounds, but his throat was slit. It also looks as though he might've put up a fight beforehand. His body is covered in bruises."

Fucking hell, and here I thought it was too quiet.

"Have we got an ID?"

"No, nothing yet. The restaurant isn't open yet but the owner is on his way so we can hopefully get a look at the CCTV. We might be in a better position after we see that and the body."

"What restaurant?" I ask.

"Casa De Luca." I sigh. Maria's brother's restaurant. I wonder if he'll play ball with us. "We not taking my car?" Craig asks as I open the doors to mine.

"No. Mine is faster," I reply with a smirk. The truth is, I don't want Craig's car seen out and about with me. It might've been my house last night, but I don't have anyone else to worry about. Craig has his wife and I don't want his house to be next on the list.

Officers Deans and Smith get into a squad car.

The squad car sets off first, siren blaring with blue lights flashing. Shifting my car into gear, we travel behind. The streets of the city are busy, and I swear other drivers are a pain in the arse. Don't they realise the blue lights and sirens mean we are in a fucking hurry?

We arrive at the destination within ten minutes. Officers already swarm the scene, blue and white tape in place keeping those who don't need to be at the scene of the crime back.

Craig and I seek out the officer that was first on the scene, so we can be brought up to speed. I instruct Deans and Smith to get statements from the bin men. Poor guys; they were only going about their daily job. I'm sure they never expected to stumble across a dead body.

"Where the hell is forensics?" I call out to anyone who is listening.

"They're on their way, Sir," a young police officer tells me. He looks physically shaken so I can presume this is the first time he's seen a dead body. He'll need to get used to it in our line of work.

I've been in his position and it wasn't pretty. It's funny how you always remember the first. It kinda sticks with you.

The forensics medical examiner, Natasha Miller, arrives on the scene. I watch on as she pulls on white overalls and gloves. "Jack, Craig, you both know what to do before I let you near that body," she says as her assistant hands us coveralls and gloves.

Craig and I walk over to where the body is and I cringe when I hear him gulp back as soon as we see it. There's blood everywhere we look. Natasha is urging officers to hurry and get the tent up to keep prying eyes away from the scene. She has her camera in hand and is snapping away at the body. I kneel down toward the body and shake my head.

"What is it?" Craig asks.

"We know this guy. Sam Christie. He was charged with possession a few months back. He's only a young lad, about twenty."

"He's obviously stepped on someone's toes and they're

not happy about it." I take a step back away from the body. What a waste of such a young life.

"McKenzie," Natasha calls.

"What?"

"Look here. He's been in a fight, and I'd say a few days ago," she says, pointing out bruising under his eye that has started to fade. "Looking at his injuries from the last few hours, someone wanted to inflict pain on him and watch him suffer before firing the two shots that took his life, although…"

A car stopping farther along the alley catches my attention. Giovanni DeLuca steps out, smartly dressed in a light grey suit, white shirt, and blue tie. "Natasha, can we talk later?" I say.

"Of course, McKenzie. Go do what you need to do."

Craig and I leave the cordoned off area and remove the white coveralls and gloves. "Mr DeLuca," I say, walking toward him.

"DCI."

"Detective or McKenzie is fine. I'm really hoping your CCTV is working," I say.

"It was when I left at one this morning," he tells me, opening the back door to his premises. The alarm starts beeping before he silences it. Craig and I follow him as he walks through the kitchen and a hallway until we're in his office.

"Take a seat, gentlemen."

Craig does. I can't. Giovanni sits down at his desk, keying in passwords to the computer. It comes to life and I stand behind Giovanni as he fast forwards the tape for the outside camera.

"Go back," I shout. Gio looks over his shoulder at me before turning back and rewinding the footage. "There."

Craig jumps from his seat and is now standing beside me.

Giovanni slows the footage down until we see a car on the screen. A car I don't recognise, and we can't see the plate. Two hooded men get out of the car, both walk to the boot, opening it, and they pull a man's body from it.

He's bound and gagged but still looks very much alive. They throw him down to the ground and his body slumps against the bin. The slightly taller of the two hooded men approaches him with something in his hands. He leans forward, his arm moving in front of his body before he steps away.

He stands back and I can see the blood. They watch him for a few minutes. It looks as though they're talking to each other, but at a second glance, they could be teasing the man who is bleeding to death in the alley. They wait about ten minutes before the second man pulls out a gun and fires two shots. They stand for a moment, looking at the man's slumped body before getting back in the car.

"I'll have one of my experts come in and take this recording."

"Of course," Giovanni says. "Do you need anything else from me?"

"I'm afraid the restaurant will be closed today."

"Losing a day's takings is the least of my concerns," he says. "Is my sister okay?"

His question seems strange. "Yes, as far as I'm aware she is. What makes you ask?"

"The dead body outside my restaurant is no coincidence. I was at the funeral yesterday. I think it's someone's way of telling me to stay out of my sister's life."

Now it makes sense and I think he could be right. "It might."

"If it is, there's only one person wanting me to stay away and that's *Pete Jamieson*." He spits the name at me. "If I have to take matters into my own hands to protect my sister, I will."

Of course he would. If I was in his position, I'd do the same. Pete Jamieson. But why does he want Giovanni to stay away from Maria? What's the connection?

What the hell am I missing?

CHAPTER SEVENTEEN

Maria

"Yes," I call out.

The door opens, and there stands Colette, still looking flustered. "Pete is here," she says in a soft, shaky voice.

About bloody time. I told him when I would be here. He's not making a good impression, but then again, he never does.

"Well, can you move from the door so he can come in?"

"Of course." She scurries away like a wee mouse. She must know her cards are marked.

Pete enters, looking somewhat amused. "What's got into Colette?" he asks, taking note that Joe is in the room as well. "Joe."

"I think she's a bit intimidated by Mrs Fraser," Joe says, smiling at me.

"What? Never. I've never known Maria to intimidate anyone." Pete doesn't sit down. Instead, he walks around the room until he's behind me, staring out the windows. "So, what is it you're going to be doing?" he asks.

"Well, if you'd take a seat, we can discuss that. I'm not going to talk to the back of someone's head."

Joe hides his smirk well when Pete walks back and sits down beside him. "I hope this isn't going to take all day. I have a lot to do."

"This will take as long as it needs to and I don't know what you think you have to do. I'm sure you'll find *I* have a lot to do." I put my hands down on the desk and stare at him. Who the hell does he think he is?

"Of course, Maria. We have a lot to do between us. We'll have fun working together," he says, smiling, and in this moment, I want nothing more than to wipe his smug smile from his face. Pete and I working together is out of the question. Joe maintains a straight expression on his face. "Let's get on," I say, looking at the list Colette has given me of all Tony's meetings. Both men nod in agreement and we start going through the list.

As we work through, Pete and Joe tell me what I need to know about each of the names. Who they are and what they do. Some names I know, people I've met at various events over the years. Councillors, wealthy businessmen, and a few lesser known gangsters.

"Now, McGovern. Who is he or she?"

Pete and Joe exchange glances and neither of them look happy.

"When is this meeting?" Pete asks.

"There's no date, just the name."

"McGovern is someone you don't want to be meeting. I can go meet him on your behalf," Pete tells me.

"Maybe not, but why would Tony have been arranging a meeting with him and why would you go instead of me?"

Pete hesitates. "Because he was planning on buying direct from him," he says, avoiding looking at me.

"Buying what?" I ask, my tone clipped. The hairs on the back of my neck stand and I'm suddenly unsure I want to hear what he has to say.

Joe starts to speak, but Pete stops him. "Arms."

It takes a minute for the single word to sink in. Arms. *Firearms.* Because that is just what is needed on the streets of the city. More bloody guns. My eyes dart between Pete and Joe. Joe doesn't look surprised, but he's waiting to see how I respond.

"I won't need you to go and meet McGovern. I'll do it myself, and I'll tell him we aren't interested in what he's selling."

Pete stands, running his hands through his hair. The chair scrapes across the floor. "Don't be so fucking stupid," he says, pacing around the office. "McGovern isn't the type of man we pull out of a business deal with."

"Pete, come on. I'm sure McGovern isn't expecting to be meeting with anyone, given the circumstances," Joe says.

"A gentleman's agreement is in place, and I was with Tony at the last meeting. McGovern will be expecting me to keep to the agreement."

"I don't care about an agreement Tony had with him. He's dead, and I will not play a part in bringing more guns to the city streets."

"The deal has been done, Maria. You don't get a say in it," Pete tells me, his voice raised. There's a tightness in his expression. I'm getting to know this look well. It's a look that tells me he's pissed off with me.

I sigh heavily. "We'll see about that."

"Oh, for fuck's sake, Maria. You can't start fucking

things up. There's certain things you won't be able to handle and that's what you have me for."

I open my mouth to speak but Joe shakes his head discreetly, so I stop. I glance at my new Gucci watch, a present from Lou, and note the time. "Pete, I have a lunch meeting today, so can I leave you to handle a few things and then I'll meet you at one of the clubs?"

"Of course. I need to make sure all our runners check in and account for all the cash." This side of the business I've never liked knowing about. I hate that my husband is responsible for most of the drugs on the city streets. Every time I heard about a drug-related death, I blamed Tony. Another death to add to his growing collection. I want to put a stop to this side of things, but I know I'll only be able to do one thing at a time.

"This money, where does it go?"

"Most of it goes through the clubs. Now, before you go… what about the security business? Then there's the drugs and the girls. I need to know what's happening. They've all voiced concerns. Tony always ensured they were well looked after."

"I'll leave you dealing with that for the time being. I think I have enough to be going on with." I don't want to deal with girls working the streets. In my opinion, they don't belong there. And as for drugs, I won't play any part in that. I'm also not happy with the money going through the clubs. I'll be putting a stop to that in coming weeks.

"Okay. Will Joe be driving you from now on?" Pete asks.

"Yes, although I want to revise what he's doing," I say, smiling at Joe. "Joe will be working for me directly. I'll be the only person he has to answer to."

"That's fine," Pete says. I wasn't running it past him, so I don't need his fucking approval. "Drop me a text when you want me to meet you," he says, approaching me. He smiles warmly, and for a split second, I think he's going to kiss the top of my head, but then remembers where he is. "See you both later."

Thank fuck for that. He's starting to freak me out.

Pete leaves the office and my body sighs in relief that he's gone. I rest my head in my hands.

"Mrs Fraser, I'll ensure you are never left alone with him, if that's what you want."

"Thanks, Joe. Let's go to our lunch meeting."

As I sit in the back of the car with Joe driving, I realise that Joe might've been just a driver for Tony and me, but he's a wise man. A man who really didn't want to become embroiled in this lifestyle. If I get a way out, one that means I can live a decent life, I'm going to ensure Joe gets out too.

It's ten p.m., and, boy, it's been a long day, but here I am on what I hope will be my last stop for the night. One of the clubs, Crave. The other club I'll get to tomorrow or the next day, even next week. I'm in no hurry to deal with Exquisite. The car stops and Joe gets out, opening my door. Climbing out, I wait on him as he locks the car.

The club has just opened and there's already a queue of people waiting outside. Joe and I walk toward the doors. The bouncer is about to tell us to wait in line until he realises who I am. "On you go, Mrs Fraser."

I nod. I'm sick of hearing the words *Mrs Fraser* today. The club is busy. The lights are low and the music is loud. Perfect atmosphere to sell drinks and dance the night away. Although, I know that's not the only thing that goes on behind closed doors.

Wandering over to the bar, a blonde whose name I can't remember stares at me. As recognition hits, she looks confused. "Mrs Fraser, we weren't expecting you," she says, her eyes darting to the doors that lead to the staff area and the main office.

"I bet you weren't," I say and walk toward the door. She attempts to stop me, but Joe interrupts, telling her to go back to pouring drinks behind the bar.

The staff area should be quiet, but it's not. There's lots of swearing and shouting. My eyes drift to the staircase that leads to the cellar, and I remember the last time I was down there.

I take a deep breath and slowly and steadily take the stairs with Joe right behind me. "Joe, do you have a gun?" I ask, pausing on the stairs.

"Of course. I always have one." He taps the back of his trousers.

"I won't ask you to use it…"

"I'll use it if I need to."

I nod and carry on.

Unlike the last time I was here, I don't hide behind boxes; I walk with confidence into the open space.

There's a chair in the middle of the room, a middle-aged man tied to it. Plastic sheeting covers the floor. Pete turns, I suppose hearing my footsteps crossing the floor. Mark is just about to strike the man in the face but stops when he sees me.

I recognise the man in the chair as one of Tony's men. Not a close friend or anything, but I've seen him and his wife at different events.

"What the hell are you doing here?" Pete's voice echoes around the room.

"I don't need an invitation. When I last looked, it was my name on the title deeds of the club, not yours. So, how about I ask you two what the hell you're doing?" I march right over until I'm standing toe-to-toe with Pete. I can't back down from him now because, if I do, he'll walk all over me.

My heart is beating furiously in my chest, and no matter how much I try to hold it together, I'm sure Pete can see through me.

"Teaching this arsehole a lesson on how to keep his mouth shut."

"Mark, get out of here. Get back to Lou and the girls."

"B… but."

"Do as you're fucking told." Mark's eyes dash between me and Pete, and when Pete nods, Mark leaves us alone. "Joe, make sure he leaves. I'll see you back in the office. As for you, Pete, get this out of my fucking club!" I roar at him. "Now. Take it some other place."

His eyes cast over me before he pulls a small pocket knife from his trousers and cuts the tape on the guy's hands. He pulls him to his feet and he can barely walk. I walk toward the door that leads out into a small alley and open it. "You don't deal with this shit in my club," I say, pushing his arm. He stops and pushes the guy out; he falls to the wet ground.

"I'll talk to you later," Pete says through gritted teeth, in the same clipped tone of voice Tony used to take when he was pissed off at me.

"Whatever," I say, pulling the door closed behind him and securing the bolts back into place. I look around the room. Pete was intending to kill a man in my club.

Pete Jamieson isn't getting the same control over my life that Tony had.

CHAPTER EIGHTEEN

Jack

I STAND on the pavement outside the club and stare along the street. Revellers are lined up, all waiting to get inside. As nightclubs go, from the public's point of view, it's always had a great reputation. Not so much from my point of view.

It's been the bane of my life the last few months. I know and everyone at the station knows there is money going through the tills that shouldn't be, but have we been able to prove it? No. Maybe now that Maria is running it, things will be different.

Stepping towards the bouncer on the door, I show him my badge. He talks into the mic before letting me inside, warning whoever is there that I'm on my way in. I could've waited in the queue to get in, but when my badge gets me instant access, why should I?

I feel the beat of the music beneath my skin as soon as I enter. It's hard not to let it consume me. On any other night, a club like this would be a good place to let my hair down and lose myself in a beautiful woman.

Tonight, for whatever reason, I've found myself here, wanting to see her. I know she's still here somewhere within this building, I've had an officer tailing her most of the day. I relieved him as soon as I arrived and he informed me that he saw Pete pushing one of his own men into the back of a car down the alley at one of the back doors.

Trouble in paradise, it would seem.

My eyes dart around the crowded room, taking everything in. That is until I see her. She's standing at the end of the bar, her eyes fixed on me, watching and waiting. She looks incredible. Joe, her driver, is standing close, but still giving her space. His eyes are on me too, as they should be. From what I've seen and been told, he's been very protective of her.

As I walk toward her, she takes a glass of wine from one of the waitresses behind the bar. She then asks the waitress for something, and as I get closer, a bottle of scotch is placed on the bar with a glass. "A drink, Detective?" she says slowly, her lips curving into the perfect smile that she always seems to be pictured with.

"Why not?" I take the bottle and pour it neat.

"What brings you here?" she asks, looking out across the dance floor.

"You."

Fuck.

The word is out of my mouth before I realise what I've just said. There's an awkward silence filling the air that surrounds us. I think fast. "I wanted to make sure you're okay. Giovanni was worried about you."

Her stance changes. Moments ago, she looked relaxed, but now, all I see is tension in her body. "Why is Giovanni worried about me? And when did you see him?"

"I saw him this morning when a dead body was found outside his restaurant."

If she already knows about this, she's hiding it well. I've seen the mask she wears, and there's no mask in place. She stands, frozen to the spot, staring ahead but looking as though she can't focus on anything. This is fresh news to her. "Are you here to tell me that the dead body is connected to my brother?" she asks, finally taking back control of the fear I'm certain I just saw.

"No. I don't believe it's anything to do with him. I think it's more to do with your husband's death." She doesn't flinch at my words, although I'm not sure if I expected her to. "Your brother was most helpful in our investigation and has advised that he'll continue to do what he can to help." She looks over my shoulder. Joe is still there. He's in earshot and I know he heard what I just said. "Joe, the detective and I are going to my office."

"Yes, Mrs Fraser," Joe replies. She takes her glass and the bottle of scotch and walks away. I follow with my glass in hand, enjoying the fine view I have of her sexy arse swaying from side-to-side.

She opens the office door, stepping aside, and I enter first. I squint against the bright light, allowing my eyes to refocus after being in the dimly lit bar. Silence is the next thing I notice. Nothing. No beat of the music can be heard or felt.

I stand as though on parade as she walks around me, placing her glass and the bottle of scotch on the desk. She moves the chair and sits down, dramatically crossing one leg over the top of the other. My eyes follow her slow movement; she's going to enjoy playing games with me. Her long, slender legs look amazing. But they'd look even better wrapped around my waist.

I grit my teeth and try to think of something else, anything, but nothing springs to mind. Blood pumps fast through my body and I have to tell myself that whatever attraction I feel for her, I can't act on it.

Even though, right now, it would be so fucking easy to part her legs and slide my hand up her thighs. The funny thing is, looking at her, here and now, I don't think she'd do a single thing to stop me. She wouldn't even put up a fight.

I need to change my direction of thought before I end up in a whole load of trouble. Picking up the scotch, I pour myself another drink. I feel her eyes on me as I do.

This is crazy.

I'm here in this office, alone with a woman I'm finding myself more attracted to every damn time I set eyes on her. This attraction I feel isn't one-sided. No, it's mutual from the glowing desire burning in her eyes.

Turning away, I take a deep breath and then a drink before looking at the woman who I know could bring me to my knees and leave me completely and utterly power-less. I laugh out loud. All my training has gone.

"What's so funny?" she asks.

"You," I say, stepping closer to her. Her face is flushed, her eyes wild with anticipation; a look I find so fucking hard to resist on a woman. I find myself having to bite back a groan before it leaves me.

I should move before I do something stupid.

But do I?

No. I can't.

I take another step closer to her. I take another drink and place my empty glass on her desk.

Yes, I'm heading into dangerous territory, and yes, I know all too well the consequences that I could face, but fuck it, it might well be worth the trip to hell. I reach out and take her glass from her hands and put it next to mine. I take her hands and she doesn't object when I pull her to her feet.

The mask is gone, and all I see is a woman who wants me. She doesn't want to, but she does. She's all mine for the taking.

My eyes skim her body and I smile, enjoying everything I see. I let her hands go and slide mine around her waist, pulling her against me. She smiles, pushing herself closer. She slides her hands slowly up my back before latching on tight to my shoulders.

She looks small against me, but her body fits me. *Perfectly*. I lean forward, my lips brushing against hers. With a soft moan her eyes close.

I take that as my invitation. Desperately needing to feel and taste what she has on offer, I crush my lips to hers. She groans, scraping her fingers into my shoulders, demanding more.

I want to control myself, but it's no use. All I want is her, right here, right now. The rule book is being thrown out the window. I gasp as her body presses harder against mine, feeling what she's doing to me.

Her touch and scent are everywhere.

I can't escape her.

I don't want to.

With my hands around her waist, I pick her up, her dress riding high. Maria's eyes lock with mine and she nods, giving me permission. Our lips are still locked, still attacking the other's. I carry her the short distance until her body is pushed against the wall.

Her moans get louder as she fumbles with my belt. I lower my hand, slipping it between her parted legs. Moving her knickers to the side, I slide my finger along her wetness. One quick move and it would be so easy to be deep inside her, pumping her hard against the wall of her office.

Her legs are clamped around my waist and my fingers dance across the warm, wet flesh. Soft lips leave mine and she buries her face in my neck, kissing and nipping at my throat. The urge to close my eyes and enjoy this moment is strong, but not as strong as my need to see her. To see that she wants me.

We both jump as the phone on her desk starts ringing.

"Fuck!"

"Don't answer it," I say breathlessly, capturing her lips once again.

She pulls her lips from mine. "If I don't answer it, Joe will be in here to find out what the hell is going on."

I smile, knowing I'm not the only one who's breathless. I release her and watch as she crosses the short distance to the phone, fixing her dress.

I use my time to re-do my belt and sort myself out. I don't listen to what she's saying. Instead, I pour myself another drink. She watches me as I down it in one.

"I wasn't finished with you, Detective," she says seductively after she ends her call.

I step toward her and watch on, smiling, as she struggles to control her breath.

"I'm not done with you yet either, but for now, I'll play my cards safe," I whisper in her ear as I lean toward her. "I'll see myself out."

I kiss her on the lips once more and do what I should've done earlier. I walk out of her office without looking back. I nod as I pass Joe in the corridor and make my way back toward the bar.

What the hell was I thinking?

Who is the one playing games now?

Me. Only this game could lead to me dancing with death.

CHAPTER NINETEEN

Maria

MY HEAD IS in a total spin. I've tossed and turned since I climbed wearily into bed at three a.m. If I'm going to stay at Crave until that time in the morning, I'll need to sleep during the day, or just longer in the morning. But I don't think that'll happen with me staying here. It's only gone on seven and I can hear the girls running around downstairs. They have too much energy for this time in the morning.

Today isn't going to be a good day. I'm lying in bed, in my dead husband's sister's house, and my thoughts are of the tall handsome man I nearly made a huge mistake with.

That's the story of my life.

Mistakes. Yeah, I've made plenty of them over the years. You'd think I'd learn my lesson. *Obviously not.*

What the fuck was I thinking? That's the problem, I wasn't, and I'm sure Joe has his suspicions of what went on in the office, although he never said anything. But he wouldn't; he's been used to keeping things a secret for my husband. I'll never know how many secrets Tony had kept from me, although I'm sure with each passing day I'll learn something new.

My encounter with Jack McKenzie has been playing over in my mind, on constant repeat. Down to every last detail. The look in his eyes as he stalked toward me, slowly tugging my hands, pulling me from the chair. The kiss… The more I think about him, the more my temperature starts to rise. I'm so turned on. *This is totally and utterly ridiculous.* He's only a man. A man I should stay well clear of.

But I don't think I can, and I'm not sure I want to. Although, I do know, if anyone found out about even our brief encounter, my life or his would be over. I'm sure Pete would ensure that.

Pete is someone I don't want to think too much about. I'd rather I didn't have to see him day in, day out. But I know after last night in the cellar, he's going to want to speak to me, and I know, without a shadow of a doubt, I have to stand up to him. If I don't, he will walk all over me and I don't want any man doing that to me again.

I have so much to think about. I need to set out my goals. What I want long term.

And that is to be completely away from the criminal lifestyle that Tony led. To live my life not having to worry about the next knock on the door. Not worrying about upsetting or treading on a rival's patch and living in fear of the consequences.

Instead of just lying here, I should give in and get up. It's not like I'm going to get any sleep now. When the girls are up, everyone should be up, or so they think. A good excuse to make a start on my to-do list, which includes going to see Giovanni to find out what's going on. Hopefully, we can get the chance to talk in private. I pick up my phone, scroll to the notes, and start typing.

Clothes shopping

Flat or house hunting
Call James
See Giovanni
Crave accounts.

I read over my list, and the club accounts are what I need to look over. Find out if the club is profitable on its own. If it is, I can start breaking everything else down. I know I'm meeting with James first thing on Monday morning, but I need to talk to him today.

I type out a text.

Me: Can we meet today? It's important.

I don't expect a reply straight away. Now to get myself up and ready for the day ahead. Hopefully, if I keep myself busy, I'll forget about Jack McKenzie.

"GOOD MORNING," I CALL OUT CHEERILY AS I ENTER THE kitchen and then pause. It's early, and Pete is already here. I take a deep breath and smile.

"Auntie Maria," the girls call at the same time, both excited to see me. They are sitting at the table, tucking into some toast and jam and a glass of milk each.

"Morning. I hope you're in a better mood," Pete says, his eyes raking over my body. Chills run down my spine as his eyes linger too long at the scooped neckline of the top I'm wearing. Mark coughs, noticing, and Pete turns back to him.

"God, you don't look so good," says Lou as she turns around, looking at me. "I'm making breakfast. Do you want anything?"

I sit down beside the girls. "Well, thanks, Lou. And, no. I'm not really hungry."

"What I meant was you look tired, and when was the

last time you had something to eat?" Everyone's eyes are on me. "Yesterday morning," I say.

"Well, that's not good enough."

"Bene, va bene."

"Never mind your Italian with me. Per favour, mangio."

"Si."

"Grazie."

"Will you two cut it out?" Pete says, and I can hear the simmering of his temper. Lou and I smile at each other, both of us remembering when we spoke Italian Tony would get mad because he could never understand us. Looks like Pete isn't happy because he doesn't know what we're saying.

Something I can use to my advantage.

My phone buzzes.

James: I can meet you at 1pm. Just tell me where.

I type out my reply.

Me: Not at the office or the club. Maybe go for a walk in the park?

He replies and I smile because he knows where without me telling him.

James: See you then.

I turn my attention to the girls, asking them about school and nursery. They both tell me about their friends and teachers. I love hearing the excitement in their voices. "What are your plans for today?" Pete asks.

"Oh, I have quite a list, starting with shopping and looking for somewhere to stay."

"Stop right there," Lou says, handing me some toast. "You can stay here as long as you want. I want you here."

"I know that, but what with the hours at the club, it's not fair on the girls. I don't want to wake them up when I come in."

"That's for me to worry about," she says. Mark sits quietly drinking his coffee, nodding in agreement with his wife.

"It's not up for discussion. Lou, I need to do this for me." My voice is almost pleading with her. I know she understands when she hands me a cup of tea and then rubs my shoulder.

"Well, okay, but you don't need to look. What about the flat above Crave? It would work for the time being until you find a home you want, and it does have all the latest security, so I wouldn't have to worry so much about you."

"Or you can just move into mine," Pete says, and I already want to throw up at the thought. Lou and I exchange glances and even she hates that thought as I see how horrified she looks. "We work the same sort of hours so you wouldn't need to worry about waking anyone up."

"Pete, thanks for the offer, but I have to learn to stand on my own feet again."

He looks disappointed, but I don't care. Mark offers me a smile and Lou turns back to cooking. I've always thought Mark didn't suit the life of crime he has been embroiled in since he and Lou first starting seeing each other.

Maybe once I get things at my own end sorted out, I'll be able to convince him to do the right thing by his family. They deserve so much better than this.

"Lou, fancy coming shopping with me? I'm sure the girls would love to spend the morning with their dad," I say, earning a scowl from Pete.

"Go on. You two have a girly morning," Mark says, standing and kissing Lou.

"Daddy, can we go to the park and then make cakes?" Rebecca asks, her big eyes staring lovingly at him.

"We can do anything you want, although I'm not sure I'll make cakes as good as Mummy," he says with a smile.

"Mummy doesn't make cakes, we do," Daisy shouts.

"Okay. We can make cakes for Mummy and Auntie Maria then."

"But we have things to do this morning," says Pete, looking at me. The scowl on his face speaks volumes; he's so pissed off right now.

"Well, I now have something more important to do," Mark tells him, standing up for himself.

"Fine," Pete huffs. "I'm going outside for a fag." He stands, walking away from the table just as Lou puts down a full plate of breakfast.

I stare for a moment at the food and my stomach starts churning. Bile rises in my throat, but internally, I fight not to be sick. I cover my mouth with my hand and take a few deep breaths. "Maria, are you okay?" Lou asks, her voice laced with concern.

"Just feeling a wee bit queasy. I blame my lack of sleep," I say, hoping my answer appeases her. She studies me for a long, drawn out moment before accepting my words. I'm just exhausted. Maybe the flat above the club is perfect for me. My own place, where maybe I'll get some peace and quiet to get some sleep.

"Right, Lou, you have ten minutes to be ready to go," I say.

"I'll be ready in five," she says, leaving the kitchen. I've noted that Pete hasn't come back inside and probably won't until I'm gone. In all honesty, I'm fine with that.

"So, what is going on with Pete?" Lou asks as we wander around another clothes shop.

"I'm not sure, but it's driving me mad. He had started paying me more attention before Tony died, but this, the way he looks at me, it's un-nerving. And I know he's not happy with me. I threw him out of the club last night."

"Mark said you sent him home, but wouldn't go into any details."

"I'm not surprised. Fuck, I don't know what to do. Pete was going to kill a man in the cellar last night. He even had the cheek to put plastic sheeting on the ground. If I hadn't walked in when I did, the guy would be dead. Like the dead body that was found at Giovanni's restaurant yesterday."

"What?"

"I need to see my brother today. He's worried about me, according to…" I stop myself. I carry on walking but Lou pulls me back and I turn around.

"Who told you Giovanni is worried about you?"

"McKenzie."

"Mmm, the dishy detective." We both laugh at her very true description of him. "When did you see him?"

"He came by the club last night."

"Was it business or pleasure?" I close my eyes briefly but Lou notices. "Maria DeLuca!"

"It was business. Purely business."

"For some reason, I'm not buying that."

"Well, you should. Tony's only been dead a little over two weeks." I don't know who I'm trying to convince, Lou or myself. But with thoughts of Jack McKenzie in my head, I'm fighting the urge to smile.

"Yes, that is true, but I want to know how long he's been dead to you." I'm not sure I'm capable of lying to her. "This is me. Yes, he was my brother and I loved him, but like you, I'm not blind. There's only so much a woman can take before she decides a man is dead to her. And let's face it, my brother over the last few months, or even years, didn't realise the good thing he had with you."

"Lou, I don't want to talk about it."

"Okay, but if you do, I'm here. Just for the record, if it was Mark, I'd probably have left him a long time ago."

"See, you have a good man. He loves you and he doesn't belong in this world Tony dragged him into."

"I know," she says with an air of sadness to her voice. Deep down, I believe it's taken Tony's death for her to realise that life could be so much better.

"I love you, but you have to make a safe life for those precious girls. Please don't let them end up living the way I have."

"I promise, I won't. Now, let's get you some clothes." She kisses me on the cheek and grabs my hand. Maybe Lou and I will be okay.

For both our sakes, I hope and pray that everything will work out just fine.

CHAPTER TWENTY

Jack

IT'S A DAMP, dark morning. *Too early for this shit,* I think as I climb out of my car. Half a dozen police cars are already here. Officers are taping off the crime scene. The tent is being erected around the body. I stare across the park. There's a young man with his dog—a beautiful black and tan German shepherd—talking to one of the officers. I'll speak to him in a minute.

Craig's car pulls up beside me. "Good morning," he says when he gets out, looking rather fresh.

"Nothing much good about it."

"True."

We get suited up to protect the crime scene from contamination and walk the short distance toward the area where all the activity is. "What do we have?"

"Morning sir. Male, two gunshot wounds, and his throat has been slit. It looks as though he was beaten up before he died."

"Has the body been dumped here after?"

"No. Take a look for yourself. From the splattering of blood, this is where he died." He's right; this is where he died.

"The young lad?" I ask.

"He was out walking his dog, just the same as every other morning. The dog was off the lead running backward and forward, barking, so he went to see what was wrong. That's when he found the body."

"Is he okay?"

"Yes. Shaken, obviously. Not what you expect to find on your morning walk. Especially when the body hasn't been hidden. We'll take a statement from him and let him get home."

"I'll speak to him," Craig says. I nod and he walks toward him, leaving me to assess the scene for myself. The officer hands me a torch and leads the way.

Stopping, I look around. There are no footprints in the mud, a few paw prints from the dog, but nothing much else to see. The man's body is before me, throat slit, the same as yesterday's body, and gunshot wounds in the same place. At least I know we're dealing with the same murderer.

The forensic medical examiner is already present, and for that, I'm grateful. Natasha can start working out the time of death. She's busy having a look at the body while her assistant writes down notes.

There's something familiar about the body, but I'm not sure. I don't think I know him, but then again, if this is gang related, which I think it is, then there's every chance I've seen him in person before, or even just his picture.

Turning around, I see how close the kids' play area is to where the body is. Fuck. I suppose it's been bad enough for the young man to see, but right now, I'm glad it wasn't a mum out with kids.

SATURDAYS IN THE OFFICE SHOULD BE FUCKING BANNED. On days like today, I can understand why some people quit the force. Today, I hate the conflict of the feuding gangs with a passion. Why can't they all get normal jobs and have the normal family life?

I wouldn't be in the job I am now if they did.

Events during the night and early hours of the morning have ensured Craig and I have been working since six a.m. Craig spoke to the young lad. He was a bit shaken up, which is totally understandable, but is otherwise okay.

Two dead men in two days, both killed the same way.

This is no coincidence. And I'm hoping and praying that there is the tiniest bit of evidence, so that I can bring in my number one suspect, Pete Jamieson. I can't bring him in for questioning without being able to link him to at least one of the murders. I'm hoping I get a lead soon, or even just identification of the body that was found.

The room outside my office is a buzz of activity, and has been since we arrived back in the station after being at the scene of the crime. I'm grabbing two minutes in an attempt to clear my head and concentrate. But it's not working.

All I see is Maria Fraser.

Craig would give me shit if he found out about last night. Never mind him, I'm giving myself a hard time over it. What was I thinking? I certainly wasn't thinking with my head. She is off limits and I should know better. Fuck, according to Craig, she could even be a suspect.

Don't get involved. Don't make it personal. That's what has been drilled into me over the years about cases like this.

But it's hard not to. I've crossed the line and I'm not sure I can go back. The truth is, I want Maria Fraser to the point I'm acting fucking recklessly. Where she is concerned, my vision is blurred. If it starts interfering with the case, I'll need to leave Craig in charge and step away.

That would be the right thing to do.

I close my eyes and rub my hands on my face. Nothing is making any sense to me. Maria, Tony, and now the two dead bodies. I know there's a link between them, but for the life of me, the only link I can think of is Pete.

Did Pete Jamieson kill Tony Fraser? Why? They were like brothers. Is there something going on between Maria and Pete? No. I've seen first-hand how she reacts around him. I think she hates him, passionately. Does Pete think he stands a chance with Maria?

I already know the answer to that. He does.

"Jack, come on." Craig bursts into my office.

"What the hell?"

"It's Jamieson. The body is Thomas Maxwell, an associate of Fraser and Jamieson."

"I know of him. What about it?"

"Pete was seen last night pushing one of his own men out the back door of Crave and into the back of a waiting car." Now I know why I recognised the man's body. "Should I even ask if it was Jamieson or Maria Fraser you had the officer tailing? No, don't say a word. I already know with the look on your face. We have enough to bring him in for questioning."

I stand and grab my jacket. "What are we waiting for? Do we know where he is?"

"Yes."

"Let's go."

CHAPTER TWENTY-ONE

Maria

IT's TURNED out to be not a bad day so far. I loved spending the morning just me and Lou. We used to do that often, but then everything seemed to change. Or maybe it was just me that changed. I now have more clothes than I know what to do with.

This area of the park is busy with lots of families spending time together. I've always loved coming here, even when I was a child. It's funny the memories that stay with you. For me, being here, it was always Giovanni, Mum, and me. She would bring us here on a Saturday afternoon for us both to run about and blow off some steam.

As I walk toward the bandstand, I can see James waiting there. "James, thanks for meeting me, especially on a Saturday."

"You don't have to thank me. You got me away from an afternoon of food shopping, so I should be thanking you. What can I do for you?"

"Let's walk. First, the office in your building. That's just leased, yes?"

"Yes."

"Can we terminate the contract? I don't need a separate office space when there's a perfectly good office that I can use in Crave. And Colette?"

"Yes. The lease won't be too much of a problem, but Colette might be," he says, his eyes narrowing.

"Why?" I ask.

"Because she could cause you problems, Maria. She knows too much." He doesn't need to spell it out for me. She knows every last detail of Tony's business. From the drugs, to the girls on the streets, to the money laundering.

"What do I do then? Because I don't want her around. I won't have anyone with dodgy dealings around Crave."

"What about Pete and Exquisite?"

"I'll get to him in a minute, and I've not been to Exquisite yet."

"If she wasn't around then she wouldn't be a problem."

I hear what he's saying, but I'm not Tony. That might've been his way to deal with things but it's not mine. "If I just terminate her contract, what harm can she do, really? Tony is gone. His dealings are nothing to do with me."

"The only problem with that is, your signature is on every bit of paperwork and she knows this. If you want everything you deal with to be one-hundred-percent legitimate then I'm going to need some time to sort everything out. Lose the paper trail."

"So, what? I should keep her around? Even though I know she's slept with Tony."

"Maria." He takes a deep breath and I can see he's having some sort of internal war of words with himself. He has something to say but is unsure. "She hasn't just slept with Tony; they were having some sort of affair, according to her."

I stop, turning to him, and pause. "What?"

"Yes, they had slept together, but the past four months she thought it was more than that because of the time they were spending together."

I stare across the pond, thinking about his words. Honestly, I don't know why I'm so surprised. I shouldn't be. Tony Fraser always did what he liked and took what he wanted. Me, I'm just the stupid woman that sat at home quietly.

Weak and stupid. That's exactly how I feel.

"What can I say?" he asks.

"Did you know?"

"I knew they had slept together, but Colette only came to me yesterday afternoon and told me her version of events and asked if she had been provided for."

"And has she?" I shout, forgetting we're in public. A few passers-by look in our direction. Why would he provide for her? She's just some bit of skirt he was having fun with.

"No. When I read the will, it was only you, Lou, and Pete. There's no second papers anywhere and she's not a family member so has no right to contest anything."

"I should fucking think not. Do you believe her?"

"Yes."

"There was no hesitation there. Why?" I ask casually, pretending I don't care, but already my heart is racing as I think about what he might say.

"Because she's twelve weeks pregnant."

Everything blurs around me. *Pregnant*. With Tony's baby.

"Maria, are you okay?" He reaches out and rubs my shoulder.

I'm not sure I am okay. "I'm surprised," I say. "Are you sure?"

"Yes. There was a scan picture in a drawer in the desk when I was looking to see if there were any other papers I should've known about. I presumed it was you who was pregnant until yesterday."

"I would never bring a baby into the messed up world Tony played a part of," I say, with sadness filling my heart. Tony knew it and this was what I know tore us apart. Tony wanted a family and I wanted a life that was crime free. If I'd got what I wanted, he'd have got his family. Turns out, he didn't need me for that. He got what he wanted. It's just a pity he won't be around to see his child grow up.

"James, you need to tidy up whatever paperwork trail leads to me so I can get her out of my life. I'm a reasonable woman, but I can't wait for this. She can't dictate to me. No way. If, when this baby is born, a test proves it's Tony's, you can arrange a trust fund, but as for Colette, she won't get a penny, not from me. Whatever company she is employed by will cease trading. There will be no big cash hand-out made to her." I sound like a bitch; maybe that's because I am. But what does she expect? That I'll smile politely and wish her all the best for the future, knowing she's carrying my dead husband's child?

"I understand and I'm sorry. Is there anything else you need me to do?"

He doesn't need to be sorry. This isn't his fault. I blame myself for a lot of things, and staying with Tony is high on my list. "Yes, the security firm; is it worth selling or will I just pull the plug on it? I have no interest in security and the problems it causes. I only want to run a business that I can be involved hands on with."

"I would think just pull the plug but let me speak to the accountant and see what he thinks. Again, there might be some paperwork that needs dealing with. Will you be okay?"

"Yes, I'll be fine. I'm thinking about moving into the flat above the club."

"That's not a bad idea. It's furnished. It was recently decorated for the club manager but he moved in with his girlfriend instead. I'm not sure where the key is."

"I can arrange to get the locks changed. That won't be a problem. Tony hasn't used it, has he?"

"No. From what Colette said, they spent time at her house on the south-side." Relief sweeps through me because I don't want to stay somewhere he had his bit on the side.

James's phone rings and he stares at it momentarily, as though unsure about the number flashing on the screen. "Hello, James Stevenson… Detective McKenzie…" There are butterflies in my stomach just hearing his name. "No, Mr Jamieson isn't my client… No, I understand. I can arrange for representation… Thank you."

He ends the call. "What's wrong?" I ask, noting the look of concern on his face.

"Pete has been pulled in for question, in connection with a murder."

"The body that was found at Giovanni's restaurant?"

"No. The body of one of Tony's men was found in a play park this morning. Although, I was aware of the incident yesterday."

I sit down on a bench and my eyes dart around the mass of greenery, and farther to one of the play areas. The man Pete had at the club last night.

"What's wrong?" James asks.

"I threw Pete out of the club last night. He was in the cellar, plastic sheets coating the floor, and he had a man…"

"Maria, this isn't anything to do with you. This isn't your fault."

"It is. If I just threw Pete out and kept the man there, he would still be alive today."

"You are not responsible for this. What Pete does is up to him and he knows the risks that come with being a criminal. There's always a chance that one day he'll get caught. Tony was lucky, or rather, had a good solicitor. You want out and don't want to play a part in any criminal activities and that's fine with me. More than fine. As soon as I sort out the paperwork trail we can both do what's best for us. That is, if you don't want me to help out Pete?"

"No, I don't."

"I'm your solicitor and I will always look out for your best interests. I will arrange representation for Pete with another firm."

"James, thank you for everything."

"I'm only doing my job."

"You and I both know you're doing more than that. Now, I'll try not to bother you until Monday. I'll go and see Giovanni now."

"MIA BELLA SORELLA, SONO STATO PREOCCUPATO PER TE."

I melt against his warm embrace, and I'd forgotten how comforting he could be. "No need to worry about me. Look at me?"

He stands back, keeping me at arm's length, but still holding me. "You, Maria DeLuca, look as beautiful as ever. Come and have a coffee with me."

He asks a waitress to bring us two coffees and we wander through the restaurant, finally sitting in a quiet corner. "Pete has been arrested," I blurt out.

"That's not such a bad thing." Giovanni's accent is much heavier than mine and I could honestly sit and listen to him all day.

"It's not."

"Is this because of the body found out the back yesterday?"

"Maybe, but another man's body was found this morning. So, I'm presuming they're linked."

"Most likely. So, tell me, sister, what are your plans for the future now that you're free?" he asks, changing the subject.

"Run Crave, move into the flat there for the time being, and at the moment, that's it. Take one day at a time. Deal with the other stuff and businesses when I've got my head around the current situation."

"Bella, bella. You do know my home is your home."

"I know. Lou has said the same, but I need to do this for me. No one else, just me."

"I understand. But remember I'm here for anything, any advice you need, any problems you face. You come to your brother and we can work them out together. Comprendere?"

"Si."

The waitress brings over our coffees and I look around. He's made lots of changes to the restaurant. It looks really fresh and modern. Our parents would've approved.

"What about the villa. When do you want to go?" he asks me.

"I'm not sure. When I asked I thought I'd take off straight away to clear my head, but now I'm unsure. There's so much for me to do."

"I can always help you with the business side of things. But you, bella, have a better business head on your shoulders than you give yourself credit for."

"Giovanni, I hope you're right."

"Of course I am. Now, tell me what else I should know."

"Colette, Tony's assistant is twelve weeks pregnant," I blurt out, tears filling my eyes.

Gio takes my hand. "Maria! Can I presume the child is Tony's?"

"According to her, yes. James found a scan picture in his desk and thought I was pregnant until Colette spoke to him."

My tears fall and I don't know why. Giovanni gets up quickly, his arms wrapping around me. "Maria, you shouldn't be crying."

"I know, but it's just hit me that there will be a baby that belongs to Tony. A baby that will grow up without knowing his or her father."

"Yes. They will never have to know him and everything he stood for. I will not have you getting upset about some cheap tart and her unborn child. You, my dear sister, are worth so much more."

I hear what he's saying, but this is going to be hard. And I still have to break the news to Lou that she is going to be an aunt.

I had so much I wanted to talk about with him, but with waiting staff and now my tears about Colette and her baby, our talk will wait.

CHAPTER TWENTY-TWO

Jack

I HAD EXPECTED James Stevenson to walk through the doors today, telling me he's now representing Pete. So, I'm a bit surprised by the old man in the dark suit that is sitting with Pete in the interview room. Although, it doesn't make any difference to me who represents him.

"Are you ready?" I ask Craig.

"Yes. Let's see what this fucker has to say for himself."

We enter the interview room. Pete and his solicitor both stop talking and stare ahead.

"Sorry we had to keep you waiting," I say, taking a seat.

"Detective, you and I both know you're not sorry, but now that you're here, can we get started? I'd like to get my client home."

Craig laughs and then presses record to tape our interview, introducing everyone in the room for the benefit of the tape. "Mr Jamieson, what can you tell me about Thomas Marshall?" I ask.

"Thomas Marshall. Family man, good husband, father of two, and a good employee. Not one for slacking, calling in sick. Why do you ask?"

I'm not playing his games. I'm here to question him, not the other way around.

"When did you last see him?"

"Yesterday."

"When?" Craig asks.

"The afternoon when he was leaving the building site down by the Clyde. We have the security there. It was payday. I went there to pay the lads. You still haven't said what this is about."

"Thomas Marshall was found dead in the early hours of the morning. He was shot twice and his throat slit, identical to the body we found yesterday morning outside Mr DeLuca's restaurant."

Pete's eyes glance toward his solicitor before looking at me. There's no expression on his face, no surprise. That's because he already knew about both murders. "I'm very sorry to hear that. His family will be devastated."

"So, the last time you saw him was in the afternoon?" Craig asks.

"Yes, when I paid him. I know some of the lads go for a drink after work. Maybe you should ask them if he went with them."

I glance at Craig. We both know he's lying to us. "Where were you last night?"

Pete shifts slightly in his seat and doesn't answer straight away, unlike the previous questions. "I was with Mark, helping him run a few errands for his wife. She's not coping well since the death of her brother."

And he expects me to believe this bullshit? His solicitor taps a pen against the table. "Is that everything my client can help with?"

"No." I focus on Pete, staring at him, and for the first time since we brought him in, he looks uncomfortable. "Now, how about you tell us the truth?"

"That is the truth," Pete says, his eyes darting around the room.

"I have a witness that puts you in the club last night. The same witness saw you throw a badly beaten up Thomas Marshall into the back of your car and drive off. That was the last time he was seen alive."

"Your witness is wrong."

"I'd like to speak to my client."

"Of course. Interview suspended at twenty-zero-four," says Craig.

I can't help but smirk as Craig and I leave the room.

"He'll make up a new story, you know that, don't you?"

"Of course he will. Men like him are evil to the core. We don't have enough to press charges, but we have rattled him, and for now, that's enough. He might start making mistakes, and when he does, we'll be there."

Craig nods in agreement.

I SLAM THE DOOR CLOSED BEHIND ME AND LEAN AGAINST the wall. "We're getting nowhere with him."

"We can try again later," Craig says, trying to sound hopeful.

We can try until we're blue in the face, but I've met the likes of him before and there's no way he'll confess to anything. Even if I had stood beside him and watched him pull the trigger, he'd still claim his innocence.

All I have to go on is one of the officers saw him pushing the guy into the back of a car. Yes, it was enough to bring him in for questioning, but not enough to charge him with anything.

The interview room door opens behind us, and Pete and his solicitor walk past. He doesn't say anything but has a smug look across his face. I don't get why he looks so fucking happy because he must know I'll have someone following him.

"Are the boys ready?" I ask Craig.

"Yes. Their car is farther down the road. Hopefully, he won't see them. Now, what are your plans? It's late and we've both been working for fourteen hours," says Craig, looking at his watch.

"I'm going home and you should do the same. And take your day off tomorrow."

"I'll have my day off if you do the same."

I laugh at him. "I might. We'll see what happens. Hopefully there will be no more dead bodies. Now, go and get home to that lovely wife of yours and do something nice tomorrow with her."

He smiles "I will. Goodnight."

THIS ISN'T WHERE I'M MEANT TO BE. I STARE AT THE building straight ahead. The queue to get in travels along the street. Bouncers stand at the door being very selective of who they let in. The streetlights highlight the skimpy dresses young girls wear. If I had a daughter, she wouldn't be allowed to leave the house looking like any of them. Sadness floods my body with my last thought. I don't know where it came from but I don't want it to stay.

I close my eyes and shake my head, mentally trying to push it away. It doesn't belong in the present.

The vision is there and I don't want it to be. Pain and

suffering. I've suffered enough already with a past that is full of darkness.

Opening my eyes, I shake my thought away and re-focus on now.

Maria is inside. She arrived early evening and hasn't left.

As I open my car door, I know I shouldn't be here. I shouldn't want to see her, but I do, and I find myself walking straight up to the bouncers and showing them my badge. "I'd like to see Mrs Fraser." I expect to go straight inside. "Hold on," says one of the men standing guard at the main entrance before he makes a phone call. "Come with me," he says as he ends the call. I follow him around the side of the building. Keeping my wits about me, my eyes dart around the dark street. "Through this door and at the top of the stairs." With that, he leaves me.

The sound of buzzing comes from the intercom on the wall and I open the door. It closes with a thud behind me and I also hear the clicking of a lock.

Lights come on and there's a spiral staircase in front of me. Where am I? I climb the staircase to the top and the door in front of me opens.

"What can I do for you, Detective?" Maria asks softly, standing before me in the doorway wearing jeans and a t-shirt, barefoot.

My eyes roam her body, and I know exactly what she can do for me. And more importantly, what I can do for her.

That is, finish off what we started last night.

CHAPTER TWENTY-THREE

Maria

I STARE STRAIGHT AT HIM, my eyes appreciating the man before me. He stands, holding his suit jacket over his shoulder. The white sleeves of his shirt are rolled up, showing off his arms, his biceps bulging. His dark grey tie hangs loosely, and the top button of his shirt is undone.

I snap my eyes away, bringing them back to his. Looks like my night just became a whole load of interesting.

"Can we talk?" His voice is smooth and trying to remain confident, but his body language doesn't scream confident to me. He's a man on the edge. Of what though, I'm not sure.

Something is troubling him and I can only guess it has something do with Pete and the murders. Or maybe it's just me and what happened between us last night. It's played over in my head all day.

"Come on in." He enters and waits. "It's a bit of a mess," I say, closing the door and leading the way through to the open plan living room and kitchen. My bags from this morning's shopping trip are still on the floor. I came straight here after my visit to Giovanni, and Lou, bless her, came over about five with bags of food and new bedding. I don't know what I would've done without her. She helped me clean up the flat; it was really dusty with not being used.

"Is this where you'll be staying?" he asks, his eyes darting around the enormous and well-decorated space.

I think it still needs a woman's touch, but for the time being, it will be home.

"Yes, for now. I had forgotten about this. It makes more sense. I don't need to worry about waking up my nieces in the early hours of the morning after working in the club. Can I get you a drink?"

"Just some water."

"I'm drinking wine. Can I not tempt you into joining me with a glass?"

"I have my car outside."

"You can always pick it up tomorrow. You look as though you need a drink. Stressful day?"

I don't know why I ask. I can see it has been and I know he had Pete in the station most of the afternoon and night.

"You don't make it easy," he says, taking a seat on the sofa.

"Don't make what easy?" I grab another wine glass and join him, sitting close but still leaving space between us, even though the last thing I want is space.

"For a man to say no to you."

I gasp and my already fast-beating heart picks up pace. I can't pretend and I don't intend to, although every part of my body says I should. We crossed the thin line last night and there's no going back. I've never wanted a man as badly as I want Jack McKenzie.

I pour him a glass of wine and I'm sure he notices the shaking of my hand. "Well, then don't say no to me," I whisper, handing him the glass.

He puts his hand on top of mine, mine still holding onto the glass. "This is wrong."

"Maybe, but maybe not. Something has brought you to me, McKenzie. Two nights in a row."

"It has, but my excuse, if anyone asks, is I had to ask you a few more questions. Although, I do have questions to ask, but that isn't what's brought me to you. You make me weak because I can't get you out of my head."

"So, you think after tonight you'll be able to forget about me?"

I've just said what's going through my head, telling him without the words that I want him.

A soft laugh escapes him and the corners of his mouth turn until he's smiling. "I'm not naïve enough to think a night together is going to be anything more than what it is, but I don't think I will forget about you."

It's funny, because I'm beginning to think the same.

Jack McKenzie hasn't been far from my thoughts since the day I met him in the hospital. I know this is all kinds of wrong because of who he is and who I am, but it feels so right.

He finally takes a drink of the red wine and sets the glass down on the coffee table, and then does the same with mine. Adjusting his body on the couch, he faces me. My breath catches in the back of my throat. His warm hand reaches out and trails softly over my cheek. I close my eyes, taking a moment to savour the warmth spreading through my body.

"Maria, if you tell me to leave, I'll go. But remain silent and we're going to end up in bed. You need to be sure this is what you want."

Opening my eyes, all I see is a man who is desperate to get what he wants. And in this moment of time, he wants me. "Stay." Maybe I've had too many glasses of wine, because when I open my eyes, the first words to come from my mouth are, "I want this. I want you."

My words are all it takes. He moves closer, wrapping his arms around me, crushing his body against me. His mouth meets mine, commanding and demanding.

My hands glide up the front of his shirt as I succumb to the forcefulness of the kiss. I reach for his tie, pulling it off and undoing the next few buttons on his shirt.

His hand stops me and there's nothing I can do about it. He forces me back until I'm leaning down, his body pressing hard against me. I wrap my arms around his neck and thread my fingers through his hair, pulling him closer, wanting and needing there to be no space between us.

He's tasting and taking, and I return the kiss with equal ferocity.

I have to remind myself to breathe as we continue to kiss. His fingertips dance across the bare skin on my neck, teasing.

For the first time in my life, I willingly surrender myself to a man. I'm allowing him dominance over me and my body.

This time, I'm not a victim.

I'm not weak.

I'm full of passion and burning desire for a man who I know could ruin me. The intensity of the feelings flooding through my body shock me.

And, yes, I know I should put a stop to this but I can't and I won't because I want this, and badly.

This kiss is everything I never thought I wanted, yet, at the same time, everything my body and mind wants. Jack

McKenzie's demanding kiss is so much more than I'd thought or dreamed about.

His lips are soft but very, *very* commanding. Almost punishing. His hand trails down my body, not lingering anywhere too long, but pausing briefly on my breasts, igniting a fire deep within. The warmth between my legs needs to dampen down just a little or this will all be over way too soon.

"Stop," I whisper against his lips.

He stops and stares, his glazed eyes full of desire. "Why?"

"Because I want to take this somewhere more comfortable."

He stands, taking my hands, pulling me to my feet. "Lead the way."

With my hand still in his, I walk toward the bedroom. The room I spent the most time cleaning this afternoon, and now I'm so glad I did. This room is certainly more me, especially with clean, crisp, fresh white bed linen.

In the bedroom, I let go of his hand, turn to face him, and pull my t-shirt up over my head, taking it off and discarding it on the floor. His eyes follow my every movement as my fingers loosen the belt on my jeans before I remove them completely.

I now stand before him in my bra and knickers, and I'm thankful they're a matching set.

"You are a very beautiful woman," he says softly, his thumb rubbing over my cheekbone.

He takes two steps forward, and I reach out, grabbing his face, closing the short distance between us. I press my lips to his. "You're not so bad yourself, McKenzie," I whisper and then kiss him.

Wrapping his hands around me, he pulls my body flush to his. Warm hands glide up and down my back as he deepens the kiss. I'm under no illusions of who is in control, and it's certainly not me. I smile against his lips, feeling his fingers fiddle with my bra fastener.

With my bra straps falling from my shoulders, I release him and allow it to fall to the floor. Breaking our kiss, I take a step back. "You're wearing far too much clothing for my liking."

"I can rectify that," he says. "Go and climb into bed."

I do as I'm told, not because I have to, but because I want to. And tonight, I've just realised there is a difference.

Lying on my side, I take great pleasure in watching him undress. The vision before me is quite breath-taking. It's very clear Jack McKenzie works out and looks after himself. I suppose, in his job, he would have to. Every muscle on his body is well-defined, from his broad shoulders, all the way down his chest to that hint of a V. I smile, raising my eyebrows when he's just about to climb into bed beside me with his boxers still on.

He shakes his head in amusement before removing the boxers, and I now get to see him in all his glory. My eyes fall down his body and I don't even try to hide that. The vision I had about him, about wanting to know what he looked like beneath the suit, is no longer in my head. It's been replaced by the real thing.

Climbing into bed bedside me, he lies on his side, his eyes staring into mine. I hold my breath, and for a split second, I panic, wondering, if he can read me. See through the beauty on the outside and see the ugliness within.

My cheeks flush beneath his heated look as he leans in, capturing my mouth once more with his. He knows how to kiss, I'll give him that. He's reduced me to jelly, and I'm thankful I'm not standing.

"What are we doing?" I whisper the question against him, not really wanting him to answer, because to do that, he has to stop kissing me. And, right now, I don't want him to stop kissing me, ever.

"We're finishing what we started last night. Now shush and let me enjoy our time together." He kisses me again, this time more deeply, and yet still soft. His tongue sweeps against mine and I gasp from the force of the kiss.

Leaning me back on the bed, he kisses me roughly, leaving my body humming with desire. His hand slides down, stopping at the waistband of my knickers. He pushes them down and I wriggle my legs until they're off.

Our bodies come together, his hard cock pressing against me.

I close my eyes.

This is wrong. So bloody wrong. Yet it feels so right. He pushes lightly against me. It feels like heaven and hell at the same time.

He's a detective and I'm a gangster's wife. *A dead gangster,* I remind myself.

His warm lips kissing my neck send shivers across my skin. Hands glide back up my body and he rolls my nipple between his fingers, teasing me. His breath is hot against my skin. I push my hips toward him, seeking more than what he's offering.

I need him inside me.

Now.

My lungs are burning with each breath I take and I'm not sure if it's because of desire or fear. Fear that he might realise he shouldn't be here with me. I try to let go of my feelings and thoughts and hold on to the blood-pumping desire I feel for a man that makes me feel human.

Wrapping my legs around his waist, I open my eyes as he thrusts into me. I can't breathe. I can only see and feel. His face tells me how much he wants this, and his throbbing cock inside me tells me the same.

Yes, this might be wrong on so many levels. And yes, we'll both most probably have regrets, but it's everything I want it to be.

We live in different worlds, but with his skin against mine and his soft kisses trailing my neck, you'd never know we shouldn't be together.

This is a secret that can't be shared.

Not ever.

CHAPTER TWENTY-FOUR

Jack

I STILL. She feels like heaven. And even in my desire-filled state, I know I shouldn't be doing this. I also know, feeling her wrapped tightly around my cock, that this one time is never going to be enough for me.

And that is going to be a problem.

A big problem.

My other problem is that I wanted to take this slow. I didn't want to rush this because I know our time together will be limited, but now I'm deep inside her, I want to take her hard and quick, then again softly, over and over.

I move slowly, allowing her to adjust. Her eyes glaze as I pull almost fully out and plunge deep inside, once, twice. Her eyes close. It would be so easy to close my own eyes, but I force myself to keep them open, wanting to watch the effect I have on her. Take her so close to the edge then watch on as she helplessly falls over, calling my name. Because she will be calling my name, if only so I can hear how it sounds from her perfect lips.

I can't help but smile in appreciation of the beauty beneath me as my eyes travel down her sexy body. She's everything a man could want and a whole lot more. I pause again for a brief moment, enjoying the feeling of her muscles contracting around me.

She moans softly and wriggles beneath me. For a gorgeous, sexy woman, right now she looks quite cute. And cute isn't a word I would've used to describe Maria Fraser.

Her back arches and she pushes her hips closer to me. The sexy legs that were wrapped around my waist are now falling to the bed. I lower my face to hers and her lips meet mine, softly and slowly. She slips her tongue inside my mouth, demanding more from me, and I realise that as much as I want to be in control, she's controlling this. I'm the one under her spell.

The pace changes. Warm, soft hands grab hold of my shoulders, desperately pulling my body closer to hers. There's no space between us. Sex fills the air. The scent of us together has me smiling and I pull back from our kiss.

Her soft moans turn to heavy pants. Those beautiful eyes are completely glazed and I can see she's struggling to keep them open as her need builds. She's so close to falling apart and I want to fall over the edge with her.

I thrust against her, over and over, and watch as she gives in to the orgasm that is rushing through her body. My own is building at a lightning quick pace and we both surrender and fall at the same time.

Fucking perfection.

I want more.

I press a chaste kiss to her lips before I lift my body from hers and roll to the side, taking her with me so we can be face-to-face. Our deep breathing is all that can be heard around us.

My gaze lingers on her and I know I should leave but I

don't want to, and that is a first for me in such a long time. I use women, have done for more than a few years, never letting anyone get too close because all a woman does is cause pain and disruption. They take everything they want and leave you with nothing.

"What's wrong?" she asks, her face so close to mine I can feel her breath against my skin.

"Nothing, although I should go."

"What if I say I don't want you to go?"

"I'd say we're playing a dangerous game that could lead to disastrous consequences if we get caught together."

She lifts her hand and holds it against my cheek; the warmth of her touch has me questioning my own sanity. "I'm sorry," she says softly, and all I can hear is sadness in her tone.

"Don't be sorry. We both wanted this." Her eyes drift closed and I hate the fact that she's hurt and that it's my fault. "Maria…"

She opens her eyes. "What sort of person am I?"

"Don't you dare. You are someone with strengths and weaknesses like everyone else. Someone who, for months, maybe even longer, tried to put on a brave face as she suffered at the hands of a man she once trusted completely. You are someone who is trying to pick up the pieces of a life you don't belong in and move on."

"How do you know?" She sits up in the bed, staring across the room, pulling the covers up and over her body. I sit up, wrap my arm around her, and smile as she snuggles into my body.

"Because I can see you. The real you. Not the woman you pretend to be."

"I don't want to pretend anymore. I don't want to live my life filled with secrets and lies."

"Only you can change that."

"I'm too busy trying to change Lou's life."

"What do you mean?" I ask, curiosity getting the better of me.

"She and the girls shouldn't be mixed up in this life of crime. Mark doesn't belong in it either. He never has. He was just pulled in by Tony as soon as it was clear he and Lou were serious about each other."

"I can help," I say automatically.

"No. She won't turn anyone in, if that's what you're getting at. I want her to walk away to keep my nieces safe. They deserve a normal life. The normal life Lou and I never had."

"I understand that, and what about you? What does Maria Fraser want?"

"Not to be Maria Fraser. I hate that name and every-thing it stands for."

"A name is easily changed."

"It is, but everything else… I'm just so confused."

My phone starts buzzing. I ignore it, but it buzzes again. "I'd better get that," I say before climbing out of the bed and taking it from my trouser pocket. "Craig."

"Well, boss, so much for a night off," he says.

"What's happened?" I ask, pulling on my boxers and trousers.

"There's been an incident at Saint Cuthbert's school."

"Saint Cuthbert's?" I ask, but my eyes are already on Maria.

"Yes. It's been broken into."

"Okay, but why is it our problem?"

Maria is out of bed and getting dressed, concern etched on her face.

"Because there's another dead body."

"What the fuck? Seriously, you'd think people would have better things to do on a Saturday night."

"I'll come by the house and pick you up," he says.

"No, it's fine. I'll meet you there."

"Okay." I end the call before he starts questioning me.

"Saint Cuthbert's?" Maria says.

"Yes, why?" I ask, pulling my shirt back on.

"MFJ is the security contractors. Anything I should know about?"

I pause for a moment and take in what she's just said. Tony and Pete's security firm. Well, it's hers now. "Shit. I didn't realise."

"So, is there anything I should know?"

"Yes and no. If I tell you now, I'm putting my own arse on the line."

"It's fine, McKenzie. No doubt I'll be seeing you again soon."

We walk back through the flat until I'm standing at the front door, not wanting to leave her alone, but knowing I have to.

She opens the door and presses a kiss to my lips. "Go." With the taste of her on my lips as I walk down the stairs, I'm glad I only had a mouthful of wine, because there's no way I could explain myself if I had to ask Craig to come here and pick me up.

I CLIMB OUT OF MY CAR AND ADJUST MY TIE.

"Well, look at you. No wonder you didn't want me to pick you up. You haven't been home yet." I'm not sure I have the energy to listen to his crap now. It's the middle of the night and I should be somewhere else, like back in Maria's bed with her wrapped snuggly against my body.

"What do we have?" I ask, not wanting to listen to him anymore. God, the next few hours are going to be long enough without him asking questions about where I've been.

"Okay, I understand. Jack McKenzie is all about business. Fine," he huffs. "So, the school has been broken into, new carpets and flooring have been taken. All security cameras are down and a body has been dumped in the middle of the sports field."

"Do we know who?" I ask, already dreading his answer.

"Yes. Leo DeLuca."

Holy crap. Not the name I had expected. "Fuck. Same as the others?" My thoughts drift to Maria. I need to see her. But for now, I have to follow protocol.

"Yes."

"Three dead bodies, all killed the same way. What the hell is the connection?"

"Someone is unhappy with others stepping out on their turf?"

I rub my head and we walk towards the crime scene. I can see a pattern forming and I'm already dreading to find out who we might find dead tomorrow.

CHAPTER TWENTY-FIVE

Maria

I PACE THE FLOOR. All I want to do is call Pete and ask him what he knows about Saint Cuthbert's, but if I do that, he'll wonder where I got my information from. And that's something I'm not prepared to tell him. This is all such a fucking mess.

I suppose I'll just have to wait until Jack McKenzie knocks on my door again. Only, next time, I'm sure he will be all business. Nothing like last night or Friday night. God, I can't stop thinking about him, about us together. I'm certain if he hadn't taken that phone call, I would've woken up in his arms this morning. That's what I wanted.

I look at the time; ten a.m. I hadn't realised it was so late. I didn't go to bed until after two, but I couldn't sleep, all manner of thoughts going through my head.

I've given myself a sore head with everything that is spinning around in it.

Jack McKenzie is the type of man I should stay well clear of, and not just because he's a detective, but because

he's the type of man I could fall for so easily. I'm so
confused by my feelings for him. I want to not want him,
yet I long to have him again.

Why am I so damn attracted to him? Maybe it's the
forbidden I'm attracted to because, let's face it, he and I
are from the wrong sides of the fence. He fights for justice
and, well, I've sat back and allowed crimes to take place.
But there's more than just a sexual attraction between us. I
know it and I'm sure he does too. He's hot; off the
charts hot.

I called Lou earlier to see what her plans are today and
what she got up to last night when she went home. I was
trying to find out what Mark was doing without coming
out and asking her. Turns out she and Mark had a movie
night in the house with the girls, and today they're taking
them down to the seaside. The girls will love that,
spending the day on the beach, running around and playing. All that fresh air. It sounds like a perfect family
day out.

I couldn't help but smile as she told me because at least
I know that whatever happened last night, Mark played no
part in it.

After speaking to Lou, pangs of jealousy filtered
through my mind and that isn't fair to Lou. She has Mark
and her girls and I know without a shadow of a doubt that
they will all move forward with their lives, away from all
this crime that has plagued us for years. They have each
other, while I have no-one. No family of my own. Yes, I
have Giovanni and my cousins, but I don't think it's the
same.

It's hard at times, especially when I see the closeness
between Lou and her girls, but it was my choice not to
have children with Tony. And, for me, it was the right
choice. Kids should be allowed to be kids and not have a

lifestyle inflicted on them, especially the one I've become accustomed to.

The intercom buzzes and I look at the screen to see who it is; Pete. He's standing downstairs, eyes darting everywhere as his body moves from side-to-side. What the hell is wrong with him? "Come on up," I say, giving him access.

I walk to the front door, unlocking it, and leave it open while I go and stick the kettle on. From the look of him, he needs a strong black coffee. "Morning," I call over my shoulder when I hear the door closing and his footsteps on the floor.

He doesn't speak, only stalks toward me. An icy chill runs down my spine as I feel the closeness of his body next to mine. I try and hide the fact that my heart is beating fast. I'm nervous. My eyes fill with tears as he kisses my shoulder.

Gathering my composure, not wanting him to see me weak, I make him a coffee. "Here you go," I say with a fake smile on my face.

"Thanks. I need this, although, maybe something stronger would be better. But, I'll settle for a coffee and the company of the most beautiful woman I know."

"Pete Jamieson, you should know flattery will get you nowhere with me. So, what brings you here?" I step away from him and sit down at the dining table because, if I sit on the couch, I know he'll sit down right beside me and I don't want that.

Fuck. I don't even want him here.

"Just thought I'd pop in and see how your first night was." He sits opposite me, and straight away I notice the slight shake of the cup in his hand.

"I'm fine. Tired, but I'm sure in a few days I'll have settled in."

"Don't you think it's a bit small for you? Not what you're used to."

"No. It's perfect for me."

"I'm not so sure. I'd prefer you living with me."

"This isn't about what you'd prefer, or even Lou for that matter. This is about me and my independence."

"Of course it is," he says, mocking me. "So, what did you do last night?"

"Would you believe me if I said Lou and I cleaned this place?"

"Really? I know she spent the night with Mark and the girls." He's questioning me and I don't like it. Who the fuck does he think he is?

"I know she did. She was here earlier. She brought me over food."

"Did you go into the club after she left?"

"No. I just sat with a bottle of wine and enjoyed some TV."

"On your own?"

"What the hell, Pete? What the fuck is with the twenty questions? Yes, on my own. Who else would I be with?" I stare at him, willing him to say something else, because I'm ready to throw his sorry arse out of the flat.

"I don't know. Part of me thinks you might be seeing someone else with how quick you moved out of Lou's."

"I'm not like my fucking dead husband. Just because he fucked his whores, doesn't mean I've been doing that. Is that what you think of me?"

"No, of course not." He shakes his head and at the same time rubs his temples.

"Just get out. I don't have to listen to your crap."

"I'm sorry, Maria." The buzzing of the intercom distracts us both. I get up, walk to the monitor, and sigh seeing Jack McKenzie and another officer. I let them up. "Who is it?"

"Detective McKenzie and another officer." I go and open the front door and try to control my rapid heartbeat because I know this isn't good.

"Detective," I say, holding open the door and inviting them both in.

"Mrs Fraser, we need to speak to you," the other man says. I know I've seen him before. He tells me his name is Craig but I've already tuned out and don't hear his surname. The atmosphere within my flat is icy, and I'm not sure if I'm ready for what McKenzie is about to tell me.

"Detectives," Pete says, approaching us, putting his hand on my shoulder. I shrug away from him and I'm sure both men before me have noticed, but I don't care.

"Jamieson."

"I think you should sit down," McKenzie says, his eyes darting between Pete and me.

I don't like this.

I sit down, and Pete sits beside me closer than I'd like. From the look on McKenzie's face, he doesn't like it much either. Fear grips me. Jack sits down while Craig stands behind him.

"Mrs Fraser."

"Please, just Maria," I say, trying to remain calm even though I'm anything but. My insides are churning because I sense I'm not about to be given good news considering the sombre look on both their faces.

"Maria, I'm afraid we discovered a body last night."

"W…who?"

"Leo DeLuca."

"No!" I scream. "No, it can't be. Please tell me you've made a mistake."

"I'm sorry," he says.

Pete's arms engulf me, pulling my body to his. Tears run freely down my face. I can't lift my head to look at any of the men in the room. "Maria, just let it out. I'm here. I'm with you. I won't leave you," says Pete, trying to comfort me, his hands rubbing gently against my back.

After I'm not sure how long, I lift my head and my eyes meet Jack's. I can see he's wondering what the hell I'm doing in Pete's arms.

I try to pull away from Pete, but he's gripping me tightly. "Pete, I need space!" I shout, and he finally frees me.

"Maria, what you need is your family." Pete tries to hold my hand but I pull it away from him. I hate that he's here. I don't need or want his foolish attempts at comforting me. No, the man I want to wrap me in his arms and tell me everything will be okay is standing before me looking as confused as I feel.

I can see the frustration on Jack's face. He wants to be the one comforting me and he hates the fact that he can't.

With Pete's mention of family in my head, my thoughts turn to Giovanni. "Detective, does my brother know?"

"Yes, I'm sure he'll know. Officers have gone to inform Leo's next of kin," Jack tells me.

I stand, wiping away my tears. "I need to see him."

"Maria, you can't go anywhere in the state you're in. I'll take you to Giovanni soon," Pete tells me.

"I don't want you to take me anywhere!" I turn, screaming at him. "Especially not to my brother's. He'd kill you. You'd be a fool to even consider it."

Pete chuckles and I don't even want to look at the detectives. I'm sure my outburst has given them something to think about. "Maria, you're being irrational."

"Irrational. Really? I've just found out my cousin is dead, what the hell do you expect? For someone that is meant to care, Pete, you've not said the one thing you should in these circumstances."

"What's that?" he asks.

"That you're sorry to hear the news…" I stop myself from adding the rest of the sentence. Because it isn't news to him.

Turning away from Pete, because I now feel sick at the thoughts running through my head, I'm faced with Jack and Craig. My flat isn't big enough for the commanding presence that fills the air around me.

Jack's eyes are still on me, and Craig is looking between his partner and me. I'm sure he's put two and two together and come up with the right answer. Craig is a smart man, after all. Or with the job he has, that's what I would expect.

"Can you all leave?" I say and move toward the door.

"Maria, I'd like to stay," says Pete in a soft voice.

"No. I want you to go. I want to go and see *my* family on my own."

His eyes cast down toward the floor and his shoulders slump in defeat. "Fine. I'll call Joe."

"I can do that myself."

He steps toward me and kisses my cheek before leaving.

"Are you sure you'll be okay?" It's Craig who asks the question. "We could take you to your brother's."

"Thank you, but I'll be okay."

"We're very sorry for your loss." I nod at Craig and he turns away and walks toward the door.

"Maria." My name is almost a whisper from Jack's lips.

"Please just leave," I say, trying to avoid making contact with his eyes.

"My card should you need anything."

I take it from him and don't look up as he walks out the

door. I push it shut and sink to the floor, allowing my tears to fall.

Why Leo? He's always been a good person. This is all my fault. I'm the one who married a mad man. I'm the one who brought shame on our family.

Now, as my tears stream down my face, all I see is my beautiful cousin. No words are going to fix this mess I find myself and my loved ones in.

CHAPTER TWENTY-SIX

Jack

"WHAT THE FUCK HAVE YOU DONE?" Craig asks me as we walk down the spiral staircase. *He knows*. I can hear it in the tone of his voice. Long gone is the caring voice he used to speak to Maria, and in its place is anger. "You've fucked her, haven't you?"

I don't know how to answer him without my own anger spilling out. "Craig, this isn't anything to do with you."

"Maybe not, but come on to fuck we are in the middle of not one, but now four murder investigations. She might only be a witness in your eyes for the murder of Tony, but for me, she could also be a suspect."

I hear him. I don't want to, but I do. But I know he's wrong about her being a suspect. Maria Fraser is a victim where her husband is concerned.

"What do you want me to say?" I ask as we open the door and find ourselves out in the warm sunshine, not that the weather will lift my mood.

"You could tell me I'm wrong."

I spot Pete sitting in his car across the street, staring at us. "We're not leaving until he does," I say. Craig looks across the street to where my gaze is and then nods, agreeing with me.

I can't stand that man. Right now, I'd take any excuse to lock him up. Maria is anxious around him. Her body stiffens and her eyes are always watching and waiting, as though unsure of what he might do next. Where Pete Jamieson is concerned, I don't have a good feeling and my instincts rarely let me down.

"I can't tell you that you're wrong. I won't deny it. But I also can't explain my feelings."

"Holy crap! *Feelings*. Jack McKenzie doesn't do feelings, not since…"

"Don't say it. Don't you fucking dare." I glare at him, frowning. I can't believe he's even brought it up. After all this time. I don't need him reminding me. I have a constant reminder in the picture that sits on the dresser beside my bed. There's not a single day that I don't think about her.

"I won't, but wouldn't your time be best spent on the case?"

"Yes. But she's part of the case, and you've seen how Pete looks at and touches her. She flinches every time. I'm worried about her."

"So you slept with her out of pity?"

"No! What do you take me for?"

Pete's car moves away, and as much as I think we should follow him to see where he's going, I know I should get back to the station. This was meant to be a day off. Whoever said, 'Sunday is meant to be a day of rest,' talks shite.

"Craig, you should go home."

"What about you?" he asks.

"I'm going back to the station. I have a few things I want to do and some loose ends of paperwork to sort out."

"I can come back with you."

"No. Go home to your wife. All this crap shouldn't be interfering in your life."

"Same could be said of you."

"What life?"

"You'd have a good life if you'd only let yourself and stop using the job as your excuse. I'll see you tomorrow." He opens his car door and gets in. I stand on the pavement and watch as he drives away.

He's trying to prove a point, one I'm not prepared to listen to. I throw myself into my job for a very good reason. It gives me a focus in life. It fills the gap.

A black car pulls up on the road side and I can see Joe, Maria's driver. I turn around, hearing the door we exited from open. Maria. She stands looking as distraught as she was when we left her. Her dark hair is tied back elegantly. She's wearing her trademark dark sunglasses. She's changed from the jeans she had on and is now wearing a black dress.

"I thought you'd be gone," she says, looking around.

"I was waiting until Pete left." Her eyes dart around the surroundings, looking for him.

"He's gone."

Joe gets out of the car and opens the back door. He nods his head in my direction.

"Maria, can you do me a favour?"

"What's that, Detective?"

I hate how harsh she sounds.

"Keep Joe with you, at all times."

Joe steps forward, hearing his name. "Detective, I'll look after Mrs Fraser," he tells me, and for some strange reason, I believe he will.

"Is there a reason you think I need looking after?" she questions me.

"Yes and no. Your husband was shot dead. A young man who was supposedly dealing on your husband's patch was murdered, his body dumped outside your brother's restaurant. One of Tony's own men was murdered, and now your cousin. Until I have someone in custody for all of that, I'd say the threat to anyone inside the criminal world that Tony lived in is high."

"I'll be careful, McKenzie. I have Joe and I have your number. If I feel threatened in any way, I'll call you. I'll also pass on your number to Joe, just in case. Now, if you don't mind, I should leave. I have family I'd like to see."

"Of course. I'll be in touch."

She gets in the car and Joe closes the door. "Detective, is Mrs Fraser in danger?" he asks.

"I honestly don't know. I'm wary of Pete Jamieson."

"You and me both." His statement takes me by surprise. "Detective, don't be so surprised. My loyalty isn't to Pete Jamieson. Mr Fraser was my employer because I owed him a debt, but Mrs Fraser… she's very hard not to like. Over the years, I've grown fond of her and before you jump to conclusions, I look at her as family. She might think of me as only her driver, but I'll do whatever it takes to protect her."

"That's good to know. I think I've had the wrong impression of you."

"That wouldn't be hard, considering the circles I mix in. I should go, but I will be keeping a closer eye on Mrs Fraser, and if I think she's in any danger, I will call you. Although, I may act first."

"I understand."

He rounds the car and gets in the driver's seat. I can't see Maria through the blacked-out windows. Maybe that's not such a bad thing, but I know she can see me. The car drives away and my phone beeps. Taking it from my pocket, I stare at the unknown number before opening the text

Thank you for letting me know about Leo. I know you shouldn't have done that, but I do appreciate it. Can I call you later? M x

I stare along the street, see the black car turning a corner, and smile.

Me: Call me any time, day or night. I type out before putting my phone away.

Jack McKenzie, time to get your head screwed on and figure out who the hell is committing all these murders.

CHAPTER TWENTY-SEVEN

Maria

IT'S BEEN a long day and it's not anywhere near finished with yet. I'm sitting in the back of the car, heading back into the city, and I'm going to the club. Thoughts of how the day started off are firmly embedded in my head. Pete, McKenzie, and Leo. I can see each of their faces so clearly.

Leo's poor family is devastated at what's happened. Life isn't fair. Why are the good taken when the likes of Pete Jamieson get away with murder?

Tony got away with murder more than once, and if he was still alive, he would still be getting away with it because he was lining the pockets of some very influential people within the city. I wonder if Pete is smart enough to do the same, or if he will eventually trip himself up and be put behind bars.

I believe his timing was spot on today to be at the flat when McKenzie came to tell me the news. But how did he know McKenzie would come to me? I'm not Leo's next of kin, so technically, he shouldn't have told me. I should've heard that from family.

Has Pete been watching McKenzie? If he has then he knows what I've done and that would make sense with his questions. This isn't good.

It was strange being around family today, especially given the sad circumstances. Some welcomed me with open arms, but others made it clear I shouldn't have been there. My aunt and uncle, Leo's parents, and my mother's sister, were pleased to see me. They told me more than once that I shouldn't be a stranger with them. My aunt also told me that the past is in the past and that I need to move on and be happy.

'Trovati un bel uomo italiano e hai un sacco di bambini. Ti meriti di essere felice e avere una famiglia da amare,' she said, more than once.

Maybe one day I'll have a proper family of my own, but I'm not so sure of an Italian man. They come with their own problems, and I think I've had my fair share of those.

Giovanni and I didn't really get a chance to talk today, but with the brief conversation we did have, I know he's doing his own investigation into Leo's murder, and he'll make someone pay. He and Joe held their own private conversation, much like when Joe spoke to McKenzie when I was sat in the car wondering what the hell they were talking about.

When I first entered my aunt's house with Joe, I thought my brother might kill him, but the icy air changed after their conversation. All Giovanni said to me was to keep Joe close. I also saw them exchange phone numbers.

Between Joe, my brother, and McKenzie, I'm a bit on edge tonight as we drive across town. I'm nervous, and even after everything I've been through, I've never felt as anxious as I do now.

Shit.

I haven't spoken to Lou. She doesn't know about Leo. I grab my phone and call her, hoping I don't disturb the girls.

"Hey, I was just thinking about you. Where are you?" she says, answering in her usual cheery voice.

"I'm heading back through town to the club."

"Where were you?"

"I was with Giovanni and the rest of my family." I try to keep the tone of my voice even, but even I can hear the waiver in it.

"Maria what's happened?" The words leave her in a rush.

"Leo has been murdered."

"No!" she cries out, and I have to hold the phone back from my ear. I catch Joe glancing in the rear-view mirror, making sure I'm okay. Lou knows my cousin well; we all hung out together in our teens. Back then, everything in our lives seemed so simple. None of us had a care in the world. Little did we know that our worlds would be turned upside down. "When?"

"Last night. He was found in the early hours of the morning at Saint Cuthbert's."

"Why don't you go straight to the flat and I'll come over and be with you. Mark will be fine with the kids. You shouldn't be alone."

"No, I'm okay now. I'm going into the club. I may as well get the hang of running it and keep the staff on their toes. It will help me keep my mind off everything."

"Only if you're sure? What about the other x-club? Have you been over to it yet?"

I laugh at her nickname. She hates it as much as I do.

"Not yet. What the hell do I want with a club like that?" We both laugh.

"You'll need to go sooner or later and then decide what to do with it."

"I know. If I'm honest, I've been putting it off. Now, enough talk of x-clubs. Tell me about your day with the girls."

I listen on as she excitedly tells me all about her day at the seaside with Mark and the girls. They loved it, playing with the sand and splashing in the water. It sounds as though they all had a great day, finished off with fish and chips. Nothing better after a day at the seaside. We end our call after I reassure her for about the fifth time that I'm okay.

The car comes to a stop outside the club. "That's us here," Joe says.

"You can get off home then," I tell him.

"I will do no such thing. I'll be with you tonight. I've made promises today and I'm a man of my word."

"Joe, I'll be fine in the club."

"Humour an old man?"

"There's nothing old about you, Joe. But okay, I'll humour you. We'll both go inside." He gets out of the car and opens my door. I can't help but smile at him. Around Joe, I don't have to pretend to be anything I'm not. He accepts that I want to change things, unlike Pete.

I've been dreading having a full conversation about anything business related, because he expects things to carry on the way they did when Tony was alive. I get the impression he wants to be the big shot in the city now, and for me to fall into line with him.

There's no way that's going to happen.

I stand on the pavement, looking at my club, Crave, and if I'm truthful, I'm happy with just this place to run and look after. I have money in the bank and I'm sure I could make a decent living from the club. The rest of Tony's empire, I couldn't really care less about. Although, Lou has a point; I'll need to go to the other club sooner rather than later and deal with it.

An X-rated club, catering to every gentleman's needs and kinky fantasies. I have no idea who has been keeping an eye on Exquisite since Tony's death. I suppose Pete has taken it upon himself to look after the books, and I'm sure he's had various women from the club looking after his needs.

I should speak to James about these. I'd happily close the doors and pay the staff off, but I imagine it won't be as easy as that. Nothing in my life is never easy, as I'm finding out.

"Joe, how often would you go to the other club?" I ask, even though I'm unsure if I want to hear the answer.

"Mrs Fraser, do you really want to know?"

"Yes, and please stop with the Mrs Fraser. Maria is fine."

"Okay. Mr Fraser was in the other clubs most nights. I would always wait. If he was any longer than thirty minutes, it usually meant he was with a lady."

I sigh. "I'm not sure I would call any of the women who work there ladies."

"A valid point," he says with a smile as we approach the bouncers at the door. "Why do you ask?"

"Because Lou mentioned it and I know I should deal with it. Decide what to do with Exquisite. Close the doors or try and offload it."

"It's the only club of its kind in the city. Clients are usually very wealthy businessmen. As far as I'm aware, it's profitable, but you would have to speak with the manager. She would be able to tell you more than me."

"I think that should be on my to-do list for tomorrow. I'm not sure I'll be comfortable running a sex club."

"No. For some reason, I don't think it would suit you."

"Let's go and get some work done," I say as we enter the club.

"Yes, boss."

IN THE DAYLIGHT, YOU WOULD NEVER ANTICIPATE WHAT goes on behind the doors of the building in front of me. It just looks like the rest of the buildings in this street. Not even the name above the door, Exquisite, gives anything away.

It's one p.m. and I'm not sure what to expect when I go inside. It's been a few years since I was here with Tony on opening night. From what I remember, it's very classy inside. It should be; I designed it.

"Maria, are you sure about this?" Joe asks.

"Yes, but if this makes you uncomfortable, you can wait here."

"No. Where you go, I go, unless you're with someone I can trust."

"Okay."

Opening the door, we enter, and the plush reception area is how I remember. All soft greys and light wood.

"Mrs Fraser, lovely to see you," Sandra says, rounding the reception desk and shaking my hand.

"Please, Maria is fine. You already know Joe?"

"Yes. Hi, Joe," she says, shaking his hand too. "I was wondering when I would see you. We can sit in the lounge, have a coffee, and talk."

She leads the way into the relaxing yet sensual surroundings of the lounge. I can imagine if you're here at night, with the right music setting the atmosphere, it wouldn't be long until you were sucked into what this club offers.

At the moment, the club is brightly lit, and I'm guessing there are currently no clients making use of the facilities, although I could be wrong. Joe and I sit down while Sandra makes coffee, asking us both what we'd like.

"I'm glad I came here during the day," I say to Joe, looking around me. I note there is one member of staff behind the bar. I'm not sure I'd be comfortable here when the club is busy. I can only imagine what the staff here think of me considering my husband used the services provided on a somewhat regular basis, or maybe he didn't use any of the ladies and he brought Colette with him.

Sandra joins us with the coffees and takes a seat. "I was pleased to get your call last night," she tells me. "Although, after Pete talking and reassuring me, you didn't have to come here under what I'm sure must be a very difficult and demanding time."

Joe and I exchange glances. "What do you mean, Pete reassuring you?" I ask, feeling mighty pissed off, and I'm sure Sandra knows it.

"He told me that everything would continue as normal and put all the staff's minds at rest because some thought they would lose their jobs after your husband's death."

What the hell is it with Pete Jamieson?

"Well, Sandra, Pete had no right telling you that. He doesn't own this club. So, how about I make myself clear on this, just in case you are unaware; I own this club. Pete has nothing to do with it. I'm now your boss."

"I'm sorry, Mrs Fraser, really I am. Does that mean I have to stop, how shall we say, putting money through the bank?"

"Yes, it does. I'll be upfront with you. I'm not interested in running a sex club."

"Mrs Fraser, I can understand that, but I do think you should take a look at my set of accounts. Not the ones Pete has me doing. This is a members' only establishment. I run a tight ship with both staff and clients and I've never had any problems. Mr Fraser was happy with the work I've done here."

"I'm sure he was. I'll have a look at the accounts but I'm not making any promises. One of the options for here is selling it as an ongoing concern."

"I understand," she says softly. We continue talking about the club and staffing. I ask for all the important paperwork. "Mrs Fraser, I have another meeting with a potential new client soon. If you'd like to come back later today or another time that is convenient to you, I could show you the accounts and go through the software I use to keep everything from staff details to client accounts."

I don't want to come back here if I can help it, but I suppose I should. Get it over and done with.

CHAPTER TWENTY-EIGHT

Jack

No OVERNIGHT BODIES FOUND, which meant I gave some of my staff the morning off. They deserve it; they've all been working extra shifts since the death of Tony Fraser. And with our workload increasing by the day, I'm not sure when I'll be able to give them another day off.

My phone buzzes; I smile seeing her name on the screen.

Maria: Sorry I didn't call. I've had a few things to do. M x
Me: It's fine.

I had hoped she would call last night, but with everything going on and the death of Leo, I knew she wouldn't. But it didn't stop me thinking about her. Thinking about our time together.

She's everything; amazingly intelligent, shy yet confident, beautiful… my list could go on, but I don't think there are enough words in the English dictionary to do her justice.

Maria: Have you been thinking about me, Detective?

Me: I'd be lying if I said no. Where are you?

Maria: I've just left Exquisite and I'm heading back to Crave.

Me: Well, damn woman, I didn't realise you were a member. Maybe I should risk my salary and take out a membership.

Maria:I'm not a member, Detective. I own it.

She what? I pick up and press call. I hope she's on her own.

"This is a surprise, Detective," she says, her voice full of mischief.

"How long have you owned Exquisite?" I ask.

"Since Tony's death. This is the first visit I've made to it since then."

"Why the hell did I not know he owned that place?"

"I'm not sure."

"Sorry, Maria. I didn't realise I said that out loud."

"What's wrong?" she asks, sounding concerned.

"Nothing, I just thought I had all bases covered in this case. Yet, every day, something new crops up. I hope you're with Joe."

"What is it with you and my brother? Yes, Joe is in the front of the car, driving. The only time he's left my side is after checking my flat last night and ensuring I locked up after he left."

"At least Giovanni and I care enough to look out for you. I don't think we can say the same for Pete. And Joe cares too. I'm glad he's on your side."

"You can't possibly care about me, Detective."

I'm not sure how to respond to that. What the hell do I say? Because, the thing is, I do care. More than I should. And that small fact worries me. "I wouldn't be any good at my job if I didn't care," I say, and straight away I regret the words because it sounds like I only care about my job. "That's not what I mean."

"I know it's not. Because I'd hate to think Jack McKenzie was abusing his position."

"Maria…"

She laughs. "So, you don't appear to have a sense of humour."

"Not where you're concerned." A knock on my office door has me lifting my head. Craig stands there waiting to enter and he doesn't look happy considering he's had the whole morning off. "Maria, I'll have to go. Something has come up."

"Okay, call me later. I like hearing your voice." She ends the call and I wave Craig in.

"Someone looks happy. I'm not even going to ask any questions today," he says, taking a seat.

"You'd better tell me what's wrong."

"We have nothing to go on. No evidence in any of the four deaths to bring anyone in for questioning. Anything we do get leads us to a dead end," he tells me, and I can see the frustration seeping from him.

He's not the only one frustrated with this. "I know. So, time to go back to basics. Who was Tony's biggest rival? Charlie Knox. He wanted control over the drugs on the streets, everyone knows that. We need to look at him. Down to every last detail. Have someone on him. I want his movements documented. And see if there's anyone on the streets prepared to talk. Next, Pete Jamieson. I want someone on him twenty-four hours a day. My gut tells me he's involved in the other three murders. Could he have killed Tony for his own financial gain? That's something we should look into as well. Why was he at the reading of the will? Was he jealous of everything Tony had?"

"I never considered that Pete might've killed him," Craig says. "What about Maria?"

"As a suspect?"

He nods. "I've listened to her statement. He was a man abusing his position as her husband. She sounded hurt. I had never envisioned her as a weak woman, but in that recording with you, that's how she comes across. As a victim."

"I'd say yes, she was a victim to him, but I don't think she's capable of murder. And remember, we have eye witness statements saying two cars pulled up at her house shortly after Tony arrived home."

"I know all that, but something in my gut is telling me we should be looking closer to home for Tony's death. And, yes, Pete could fit that too."

"Do what you have to do today. I'll be here in the office catching up with paperwork and going back through reports from the fire. I'm going to chase up a few other things as well."

"I'll go and get on it," he says before leaving my office.

He's wrong about Maria. I know it. I just need to find out who killed Tony to prove it.

I BANG MY FISTS ON MY DESK. TODAY IS FUCKING tiresome. All I seem to be doing is going around in circles, and all I'm doing is making myself dizzy going over all the information I have before me.

I keep coming back to the same name. Pete Jamieson.

He had lots to gain from Tony being dead, but is that motive enough for him to murder his boss and lifelong friend? They were like brothers.

Pete has stepped in and taken charge, and from what I've seen, he's making moves on Maria. Moves that she doesn't seem flattered about. And, although she hasn't said in as many words to me, I get the impression she wants out. Away from all the criminal activity that she has been surrounded in. Is that motive enough for Maria to murder her husband?

I shake my head. It's not. She was there, but why was she left unhurt? There has to be a reason she was left.

This is stupid. I need a break.

For fuck's sake. It's after nine p.m. I should just leave all this until tomorrow. Gathering all the paperwork up, I put it in a neat pile. I switch off the light and notice the main office is now empty. Nothing new there, me being the last one leaving.

As I walk through the station, it's pretty quiet. I don't like it when it's this quiet, because you just know there's something around the corner.

I'm just about to say goodnight to the officer at the front desk when I hear two officers talking about a call that has just been received. The hairs on the back of my neck stand to attention hearing where they're heading to.

"Guys, do you mind if I come along?" I ask them.

"It's only a disturbance," one says.

"That's okay. It's just that venue has popped up today during my investigation. Gives me an excuse to have a look around with my own investigation."

"Okay," he says. "Just go in with an open mind. It's not your average club."

"I've heard what goes on behind the closed doors."

Yes, I've heard all about Exquisite, but I've never stepped foot inside. But now I get to see it for myself. I've always been curious of the type of men who would pay the ridiculously high membership fees.

This should be interesting. I text Maria: *Where are you?*

Maria: In Crave. Why?

Me: I'm on my way to Exquisite. There's some sort of disturbance.

Maria: I'm just leaving.
Me: Joe will be with you?
Maria: Yes.

I sigh with relief getting into my own car, knowing she's with Joe.

I know I shouldn't have told her. I'm putting my job on the line giving out even a simple piece of information. But it gives me an excuse to see her again and that brings a smile to my tired face.

I wonder what Maria plans on doing with a gentlemen's club? I still can't believe it was Tony's. Although, nothing should really surprise me where he is concerned.

Time to see if Exquisite lives up to the name it has.

CHAPTER TWENTY-NINE

Maria

OUR CAR PULLS UP outside the building. I can see McKenzie's car parked and there's a police car in front of his.

I'm nervous and unsure about what to expect when I go through the doors. My heart is already racing at a ridiculously fast pace and I've not even got out of the car.

"Maria." Joe has opened my door and is waiting for me to get out.

"Sorry," I say, leaving the comfort of the car.

"It's fine. I'm not thrilled about being here. I know McKenzie told you about the disturbance, but you can't let on that's what brought you here."

I hear what he's saying. "I know. I'll just say things were quiet at the club and I thought Sandra could give me access to the office."

"Sounds good."

He presses the buzzer and we wait. "I'm sorry. We're not admitting anyone at the moment," a woman's voice tells us.

"Mrs Fraser is with me, so I suggest you open the door," Joe says with confidence and authority. The door opens and we step inside.

"Sorry," a young girl says. "I didn't know you would be here tonight." This girl can't be a day over twenty-one. "I'll let Sandra know you're here."

"If you could," I say, before walking in the direction of the main lounge area. Joe quickly falls into pace beside me.

Everything hits me all at once as soon as we're in the lounge. The smell, the music, the lighting; it all sets the mood for a sensual atmosphere, completely different from when I was here yesterday afternoon. And here I stand, looking around, with poor Joe by my side. One glance at him and I can tell he's uncomfortable. "Joe, if you would rather not be here, I honestly don't mind."

"I'm fine. It's not like I haven't been here before, and anyway, I'm meant to be keeping an eye on you."

I wander over to the bar and a member of staff approaches me. "Can I help you?"

"Yes. Can you take me to the manager?"

"Erm, not at the moment. She's busy."

"Yes, I'm aware she is and I, being the owner, would like to know why the police are here."

"Sorry, Mrs Fraser. We've never met."

"No, we've not. Now, can I be shown to where Sandra is or do I have to start going from room to room and unsettling clients when I barge into their rooms looking for her?"

"I'll take you. She and the officers are upstairs in one of the rooms. The other rooms have all been cleared. All clients on the premises are here in the lounge."

I glance around. I hadn't taken any notice of the people. Men sitting with beautiful women, enjoying a drink.

My eyes dart to a darkened corner, where one man sits kissing a woman, but there's a woman kneeling on the floor unbuttoning his trousers. I find myself getting hot as I watch the three of them in the corner. There's nothing discreet as the woman on the floor takes his cock in her hands, drawing them up and down his length.

I turn away. I was always under the impression the lounge was only for having a drink. Anything else had to be taken to one of the many rooms within the building.

"Lead the way," I say.

In the hallway, I pause and admire the impressive grand solid oak staircase that splits off in both directions at the top. It reminds me of the one I had at our family home, before it was all destroyed. The hallway is brighter and still looks very luxurious. Beautiful shades of grey line the walls. Deep dark grey velvet curtains hang at the windows.

I smile, remembering designing the main areas of this building. I left the rooms to someone who knew what they were doing with those. I had no interest in seeing what was going into them. Looking around, it makes me think Crave needs a bit of a re-vamp, and I'm just the woman to do it, after all.

As we reach the top of the staircase, I can hear lots of shouting. I follow the noise, turn right, and push open the first door.

"Sandra," says the girl who was leading us upstairs. And then I see him. Jack McKenzie. He's leaning against the wall, his arms folded across his chest, letting the other officers in the room do all the talking. He looks amused.

"Thank you." Sandra dismisses the young girl and she scurries away. "Mrs Fraser. Joe."

"Everything okay?" I ask, looking at Sandra and trying to avoid McKenzie's lingering gaze.

"Everything is not okay," shouts a woman. Well, I'd say she's more a girl, standing in the middle of the room with a bed sheet wrapped around her body. Her face is red and her shoulders and arms are the same, as though someone's been gripping her tightly.

It's only now I notice the naked man lying grumbling and moaning on the floor. I step farther into the room, noting that Joe remains in the doorway. "It's not my place to say, but wouldn't it be better if Miss…"

"Chloe. My name is Chloe."

"Wouldn't it make more sense for Chloe to get dressed?" I say, offering the young woman a smile.

"Thank you," Chloe mouths at me. She grabs her clothes and rushes into the bathroom.

"Yes," McKenzie says. "That makes sense to me."

"Sandra, I'm not sure what's gone on, but I would've thought it made sense to ensure staff feel safe and comfortable. And Chloe did not look comfortable standing there with everyone else in the room with only a sheet wrapped around her," I say quietly to her.

"You're right, Mrs Fraser."

"Please. Maria is fine." I'm going to have to take out an advertisement on the front page of the paper telling everyone that I'm changing my name. Mrs Fraser is a constant reminder, but then again, so is all this.

"Sorry, Maria."

"Tell me what happened."

Sandra and I step away from the officers and turn our backs to them. "Chloe pressed the panic alarm. We have an alarm in each room to ensure the safety of our girls. When I got here with Phil, he was forcing himself on her. She was shouting no. You've seen the red marks on her shoulders, and I'm sure in the morning she'll have bruising on her face. He slapped her several times. He's also been a bit too rough with her in his games. Phil pulled him off and Chloe kicked him, but he was swinging his arms about and Phil punched him."

"Okay."

"I called the police."

"That's fine. Where is Phil?"

"Downstairs. With everything kicking off up here, we cleared the other rooms that were occupied." That might explain the three sitting in the darkened corner of the lounge.

"You've done the right thing."

"I hope so. We haven't had any sort of trouble here before."

"I know that, but I'd maybe go downstairs and sort things out in the lounge. I wasn't aware that clients could do what they wanted in the public space."

"Oh! Will you be okay here with Chloe and the police?" Sandra asks.

"Of course I will."

Joe steps aside, allowing Sandra to leave the room. The man on the floor is still grumbling. "Are any of you going to move his sorry arse?" I say to no one in particular but with my eyes on McKenzie.

"Once he can get up and put some clothes on, it won't be a problem," one of the police officers says.

Shaking my head, I walk toward the bathroom door. "Chloe, are you okay?" I ask.

"Yes, you can come in," she says softly.

Entering, I gasp and cringe seeing her back. It looks like he's taken a whip to her. Bright red lash marks mar her well-toned back. There's a small trickle of blood on one of the marks. This isn't right. "Chloe, are you sure you're okay? Can I get a doctor for you?"

"I can't see it all, but I take it my back is in a right old mess?"

"Yes," I say as she pulls a t-shirt over it.

She stands before me, now clothed. "This will have to do. The dress I had on earlier would no doubt stick to my skin and irritate it even more. And if I could see a doctor at home. I don't want to go into hospital and have to explain."

"Of course, I'll sort it for you. My driver can take you home, make sure you're safe."

"That's very kind, Mrs Fraser. Thank you. Do I still have a job?"

I smile at her. "Yes, if you still want it." Why would the women who work here put themselves in danger? The money might be good, but it's a huge risk.

"Yes," is all she says and we both leave the bathroom. In the bedroom, the man is now standing, or being held up; whichever way you choose to look at it. At least he has his trousers and shoes on now. One of the officers is attempting to put his shirt on him.

"Officers, do you need Chloe for anything else?" I ask. "If not, I'd like my driver to take her home."

"That's fine," McKenzie says. "I'm sure the officers have everything they need."

"Maria, I'm not sure about leaving you, all things considered." Joe's eyes dart to McKenzie and I already know what's going to be said.

"Mrs Fraser will be fine. I'll stay here until you get back," McKenzie says, and the two officers raise their eyebrows, wondering what the hell is going on. "My investigation," he says, and the officers nod, accepting his answer. Although, I'm not sure about him being here. Joe nods and says he'll be back shortly.

"Thank you," Chloe says before leaving with Joe.

The officers now have the man in handcuffs and are walking him toward the door.

My heart starts racing as I look toward McKenzie and the surroundings we're in. I take a deep breath, trying to stop my racing heartbeat. If I ignore the scene that was before me when I entered, I could easily find myself distracted. The deep, sensual tones on the walls. The dark wooden four poster bed that is not for sleeping in. The array of what I can only describe as torture instruments on the table. If I ignore those, I can imagine myself being chained to the bed with Jack…

We can't be left alone. Especially not here in this club. Was this his plan when he called me tonight? To get me here with him so we could be alone?

I hope not, because too many people have seen us both entering the club.

CHAPTER THIRTY

Jack

"AND THEN THERE WERE TWO," I say, stepping toward her. "I think the owner of this establishment should give me a tour."

"I don't think that would be a good idea," she whispers when I'm standing right before her, toe-to-toe, nose-to-nose. Her body shakes involuntary and I sense her weakness. Her delicious body gives her away. Her cheeks are flushed and I can almost feel the heat spread through her veins.

"Oh, I don't know. I think it sounds like the best idea I've had in weeks," I say softly, wrapping my arms around her shoulders. She struggles for a moment with my touch. Wanting, yet not wanting me at the same time. It takes a moment but she finally gives in. Her body melts against mine and everything feels so damn right. I close my eyes and I know I could easily drown in the scent of her.

When I feel her body relax, I know without a shadow of a doubt that, in this moment of time, with the warmth and comfort I'm providing, she feels safe. "Maria, what's wrong?"

"Nothing and everything. This. Us. We shouldn't be doing whatever it is we're doing. There's too much risk."

"Says who?"

"Me. This is your career. If we get caught, it won't only be you paying the price…" I hear the pangs of regret as her voice trails off. And it hits me that she could very well pay a high price for a secret liaison with me. *Her life.*

Tilting her head, her eyes meet mine. "I won't let anything happen to you. No one will hurt you ever again."

"Don't make promises you can't keep, Jack."

I smile. "That's the first time you've called me Jack. It's always Detective or McKenzie," I say, pressing a kiss to her forehead.

"They both come easier to me."

"Keep talking like that…"

She playfully slaps my arm and grins. Not a full on happy smile; it's filled with sadness and seeing that, it hurts. Like no pain I've ever known before. "Stop it. Behave yourself. I need to get out of this room," she says, her eyes going to the door.

"Call Joe. Tell him I'm taking you home."

"I'm not sure."

"Maria, don't you think you'll be safer with me?"

"No. That's the problem. I'm not safe around you. We both seem to lose our senses around the other."

"And that's such a bad thing?"

"You and I both know it is. But, I'll let you take me home. I need to have a word with Sandra."

I nod and we exit the room and walk down the stair-case, back into the main lounge. I wait at the bar, leaning against it, my eyes following Maria as she walks toward Sandra. I'm too far away to hear what's being said, but it looks as though Maria isn't happy with something. Sandra's body sags and she finally nods. Maria walks back toward me.

"What was that all about?" I ask.

"That was me telling her to close for the rest of tonight because she can't control what's going on in the lounge. She might be running the place, but it's me for the time being that owns it, and I don't want there being any problems coming back to me. I have enough to deal with. Now, if you're taking me home, can we leave?"

"Come on then." She steps in front of me and I reach out and place my hand in the small of her back, then quickly pull it away, remembering we're in a room full of people. This is all too fucked up.

"Goodnight, Mrs Fraser." Phil, the man who was in the room upstairs when I arrived, nods his head in her direction, before casting his suspicious eyes on me.

"Night, Phil. See you tomorrow when I check in."

She walks to my car with a certain air of confidence. Her guard is back in place in public. It's like she's two different people, but then again, with the way she's lived her life over the years, that's how she's had to be. Tough exterior, always putting on a brave face, hiding the pain. But alone, her defensive wall crumbles and the cracks are there to be seen if you go looking for them.

I open the passenger door and wait as she climbs in gracefully. When it comes to getting into a car, there are two types of women; one that doesn't give a fuck how they look or what body parts they show. The other gets in elegantly, never revealing too much and always looks picture perfect as she does.

I know which one I prefer. The lady that leaves it all to my imagination.

Climbing into the driver's seat, I glance at her, and

not only does she look tired, but she's also lost in thought. "Penny for them?" I ask as she quickly types out a text.

Her smile is weak. "You can have my thoughts for free if it leaves my mind clear." She turns her head and stares blankly out the window, and with a sigh, I start the car, driving in the direction of the club. Her phone buzzes. "Joe says I've to be careful."

"He seems a good man," I say.

"He is. It's funny, he's been driving Tony for years, but it's only now that I feel I've got to know the real man he is."

"Which is?"

"He's loyal, warm, and caring. Not qualities you expect from someone who has worked for Tony Fraser all these years." She sniggers. "Let's face it, Pete doesn't possess even one of those qualities."

"No. We can safely say that. Maria, do you think Pete killed Leo?"

She sighs heavily at the mention of her cousin's name. "I want to say no, but I can't. I know him well. I know what he's capable of."

"I'm sorry." I wish I could offer her some words of comfort. I don't have a scrap of evidence that I can charge him with. "Are you going into the club or straight to the flat?" I ask as we drive along the street. There's still a queue of people outside it waiting to get in.

"The flat. I don't want to have to start explaining myself as to why you're back in the club. I don't see the point in arousing more suspicion."

"Good point." I turn my car into the side street and park. "Come on. I'll just check over the flat, then I'll leave."

"What if I don't want you to leave?" she asks, her voice

low and soft. I shift in my seat, taking her hand in mine. "If you want me to stay, I'll stay."

Her eyes fill with sorrow, and I'm not sure why. We both get out of the car at the same time and I stand back, allowing her to enter the security codes that will open the door. "MD1303," she says to me as the door clicks open. "No one else knows this code, not even Joe. I've had it changed recently."

"Why are you telling me?"

"Because I think there will come a day when you need it…" She stops and takes my hand, pulling me inside. The door clicks shut behind us. "Up until Leo, I didn't think my life was in danger, but now I'm not so sure. I'll give Joe the code in the morning because I trust him completely. But no one else will get it, and especially not Pete."

I wrap my arms around her, pressing her against the wall. "You shouldn't have to live like this. I can keep you safe."

"I can't go into hiding because I'm scared. I want whoever killed Leo caught and put behind bars and, somehow, if I disappear, I don't think he will get caught."

I press a soft kiss to her lips, not taking anything else from her. Just trying to reassure her. "Thank you."

"For what?" I ask.

"For being here with me tonight."

"Where else would I be?"

"Safely tucked up in bed with someone whose life isn't as fucked up as mine."

"Where would the fun be in that?" I stare into her eyes, and for the first time, I realise this is where I want to be. Here with her. Not with some stranger that I'd hopefully never see again. Maria's life might be fucked up, but it's not the only one.

I let her go, taking her hand and leading her up the staircase to the front door.

"Take me to bed," she says, taking me by surprise as soon as the door is closed and locked behind us.

"Only if that's what you want," I whisper against her skin, and as I inhale her scent, I'm praying that she doesn't change her mind.

"I do want you and *now*." She tugs my hand, pulling me toward her bedroom. We don't put the lights on, but already my eyes have re-focused to the darkness, scanning the area as we walk, making sure everything is okay.

I hate the fact that she now feels scared. After all the years she was married to one of the most notorious men in Glasgow, it's now that he's dead she fears for her life.

Tonight, I have to show her she has nothing to fear. I'll be forceful and soft. I'll give her exactly what she needs. And tonight, she needs me to be me.

The lines are blurring.

As we enter her bedroom, I pull her back roughly. Her body collides with mine, my hands cupping the side of her face and my lips finally melting against hers, as I've wanted to do since she walked through the door in the club.

I walk her toward the wall, our lips still connected. Her hands pull against my back, wanting more, needing more. Her mouth explores mine with a hard-hitting passion that sends shockwaves of electricity through my veins.

"I need you." She breathes hard against me. "I shouldn't want you, but I do, and I can't control my feelings when you're around."

I brush my thumb over her cheek. "It's just as well I want you. But I'm fighting with my demons to have you."

"Don't fight them. I'm all yours."

As she says it, my mouth crushes against hers. She's fucking addictive. One taste, that's all it took, and I'm now an addict. And if I'm not careful, I'll be so far out of it that I'll fuck up. I'll miss something so important to the case and it will end up costing me dearly.

Tonight, I can't think about that. Tonight, it's just us. Whatever the hell the definition of us is. I pull back and our eyes collide. I know she sees me. The real, damaged, and fucked up me.

"Detective, I want you naked and in my bed, now."

Holly hell. I'm not used to being bossed around, but coming from Maria, it's kinda hot. I step back, and with her glazed eyes on me, I start to undress; jacket, tie, and shirt. I unfasten the belt on my trousers, but that's it. That's all she gets for the moment.

She walks to the bed with her back to me and pulls off her dress then kicks off her shoes. She unclips her bra, allowing it to fall to the floor. I stand almost drooling as she slips her fingers under the waistband of her lace knickers and pushes them over her hips. When they fall to the floor, she steps out of them.

My eyes chase over her body, not knowing where to stop first. They're still glued to her as she lays herself on the bed.

I've never been a man to leave a woman waiting. It's not my style.

I stalk toward her, still keeping my trousers on. For what I want and need right now, they don't need to be removed. With her eyes still on mine, I push her legs apart and crawl onto the bed, settling myself where I want to be. The first moan is like music to my ears. She closes her eyes, her body wriggling, desperately waiting for my first touch. Lowering my face between her legs, I'm done for as I taste her. Fucking heaven. Tantalising. And all mine.

I'm like a teenage boy, high on life, as I continue to taste and tease.

CHAPTER THIRTY-ONE

Maria

HOLY SHIT. What the hell is he doing to me?

Oh, I know what he's doing to me. He's driving me fucking crazy. Each teasing movement of his tongue has me clawing at the bed sheets beneath me.

I can't breathe. My world is revolving and all I see is two. Two people who shouldn't be together, but when they are thrown together, they're the perfect fit for each other.

I arch my back and push my hips closer to him, yet at the same time, I want to leave some space between us, all because it feels too damn good. And I want it to last forever.

I bite my lip and moan as his tongue flicks across me. Heat rushes through my body as he continues his lavish assault, pushing me close to the edge.

Then he stops without any notice, leaving my body hanging and wanting more. My breaths come in deep, uneasy gasps. I groan in annoyance at his deliberate failure of pushing me all the way over the edge. Opening my eyes, he's standing now, removing his trousers and boxers. I glare at him, because I was more than happy where he was mere moments ago.

He laughs before turning me quickly and roughly over until I'm lying face down. The bed moves and he grips my hips, pulling them into the air. This isn't what I expected, but as I feel the end of his cock brushing against me, my head tilts back, I know this is what I need.

I need to have him buried deep inside me.

With one hand still on my hip, the other slides over my back. I gasp when fingers thread through my hair, pulling it tightly, yet not quite tight enough. I slide my hand between us and guide him to where he needs to be.

He grips my hair, pulling my head back farther. I risk a glance over my shoulder. He's watching me as I watch him as two become one and he slides easily inside me.

He stills while I savour this moment. Nothing is rushed, although my body aches for him to take me.

The deep intensity of his gaze completely and utterly steals my breath. In the depths of his eyes, I see desire and determination, but there's something else. Dare I say it, a protective warmth.

A look that I've never been on the receiving end of. It's a look that terrifies me, yet excites me.

He leans forward, softly kissing my lips, our eyes still lingering on the other. This moment now—everything has changed. I feel it deep inside.

"You are mine now." Something about the slow and steady way he says it has me believing it.

"Make me yours," I whisper against his lips.

With a smile, he tugs on my hair, pulling out and thrusting deeper into me. I close my eyes, savouring this moment.

Everything that should be wrong with us, isn't. It's so

right that it makes no sense, but at the same time… it makes sense. This is insanity yet perfection all at the same time.

His grasp on my hip is hard and desperate as he thrusts against me. Each grind faster and deeper than the one before. I'm clenched so tight around him. I push myself closer to him, needing to feel everything. Feel our bodies together. His skin on mine. My fingers wrap tightly around the bed sheets, pulling and clawing with each thrust.

This is fast and furious, and so fucking head-spinningly intense. This is crazy. This is us. This is probably the most fucked up relationship I've ever had, but it's one I want. If that is what the offer on the table is.

He releases my hair, both hands now on my hips, pulling me closer and pushing me to the brink of an earth-shattering orgasm.

My heart stops.

My skin tingles.

My stomach is in knots.

His name leaves my lips in a long cry as he calls out mine.

All the rushing, and now, in this moment, sweet kisses trail my neck, leaving me useless. My body relaxes, falling into the softness of the bed. Slowly, Jack pulls out of me, moves from on top of me, and lies down on the bed before turning me so I'm facing him. "You are mine." As I hear the deep rough growl as he says the words, I get it. I understand what he's saying.

"Yes, but…"

"No buts. We can worry about details tomorrow. I'll work this out. I won't put you at risk. Now, for the rest of the night, I'm staying here with your heavenly body tucked up right beside me."

God, I have no words.

He wraps his arm around me and I snuggle up, resting my head on his chest. Slowly, I trace my fingers up and down and around his stomach, still coming down from my high. "You keep that up and there won't be much sleeping getting done around here tonight."

I stop and smile, taking note that my fingers have trailed a little farther down and are now lingering on that delicious V that I have a perfect view of.

"Sorry," I say softly.

"Don't be sorry. I just don't want to leave you so exhausted that you can't function tomorrow. Or maybe that's what I do want."

I CAN HEAR HIS VOICE AND I CAN FEEL HIS BODY BECAUSE I'm still draped around him. My legs tangled with his. His fingers run through my hair. My eyes flutter open. I lift my head. He smiles but there's something wrong, I can sense it.

"Craig, just deal with it. No, don't bother with coffee because I'm not sure when I'll be in." He stops talking to hear whatever Craig is saying. "Look, unless there's another dead body you have to tell me about then I'll be in the office when I'm ready. I have a few things to take care of." He ends the call and I wriggle a little farther up the bed. "Good morning," he says, kissing me. "Sorry I woke you."

"You need to work. You are a very busy man, Jack McKenzie."

"Yes, I am, but right now, I'm making some time for you."

"That sounds interesting," I say, allowing my hands to dance down his skin.

"As much as what's in your head right now appeals to me, we should talk."

"Spoil sport. If we need to talk, things change."

"Nothing is going to change. You're still mine. But…"

"But you have a job to do," I say heavily.

"I do, and right now, I have to find out who killed Tony and prove that Pete is responsible for the other three murders."

My body freezes and I know he feels it. I can see it in the way his eyes search mine, looking for an explanation.

In this moment, with the mention of Tony, it hits me that if he finds out everything he needs to know about Tony, there will be no us.

Secrets and lies.

Nothing good ever comes of them.

I should know.

"What's wrong?" he asks, still fiddling with my hair.

"Nothing, except I need to use the bathroom."

He smiles, but it doesn't reach his eyes. His instincts have kicked in and he knows there's something more troubling me. Of course he does. He's a fucking detective, after all. A DCI at the top of his game. He didn't get there by standing back and looking on. He got there by working hard and proving he has what it takes.

I'm such a fool.

"Go on then."

"I'll grab a quick shower," I say. "Then you can shower and I'll make us some coffee if you still want to talk."

"Of course I want to talk. Nothing has changed. I want you, and if you didn't look so unsure, of what I don't know, I'd be following you into that bathroom and we'd be taking a shower together." He looks puzzled as I climb from the bed.

"Well, what are you waiting for?"

I know later I'll regret this, but now I want him, and I want to make him happy.

He smiles, casting his eyes over my naked body. "You have two minutes, then I'll join you."

"COFFEE AND TOAST? WHAT WILL I NEED TO DO TO GET A full breakfast?" he teases, pulling my hand and taking a bite of my toast.

"Here, you have your own," I say, shoving him playfully away. "And if you want full breakfast, you'll be doing the cooking."

"That can be arranged. Now, are you going to tell me why you freaked out at the mention of Tony's name?" He sits down at the table and I honestly don't know what to tell him. I don't want to lie.

"What do you want me to say? I'm trying hard to move on. Everywhere I turn, there's something or someone reminding me about my husband. I'd love to put Tony to the back of my head, the part I can keep closed and never need to open again."

He reaches across the table, taking my hand. "Maria, I get that. I understand. But I do have a job to do and I need to bring in someone for his death. Fuck, my life would be easier if he was alive because I'd be bringing him in and he'd be getting locked up for a long time for all the crimes he's committed."

"We'll have to differ on this, because I'm glad he's dead. I don't have to sit back and suffer in silence anymore. I don't have to pretend to be the dutiful wife who sits at home while he is out fucking every damn slut that works for him."

He nods; his eyes are soft and caring. He understands

what I'm saying. I don't need to tell him about Colette, although I'm sure with his investigation, he'll find out soon enough.

What I've said isn't a lie. It's the truth.

It's what I haven't said I know he'd be more interested in.

CHAPTER THIRTY-TWO

Jack

I WISH MORE than anything I could be anywhere but here. This damn office feels so claustrophobic. People in and out, not giving me so much as two minutes fucking peace and quiet to think for myself. The only person who has stayed out of my way is Craig since we had words.

He pushed question after question at me about where I was, and who I was with this morning. Deep down, he knew, so fuck knows what he was hoping to achieve in hearing me say I was with Maria.

And that's where I wish I was now.

Craig left my office, telling me I'm compromising the case. Regardless of my feelings and relationship with Maria, I will not under any circumstances compromise the case. I need to put Tony's killer behind bars, along with Pete Jamieson, before he kills again.

I stare blankly at the notes I've made on the papers before me, hoping that something will tell me what I need to know. And right now, I don't know if I want to find

Tony's killer more than I want to have Pete Jamieson behind bars. I want to believe that Pete is responsible for all four deaths, but there's something in my gut telling me he's only killed three times, *recently*.

And unless someone comes forward and can identify him as the murderer then I have absolutely nothing but my hunch to go on.

Mark!

His name has entered my head more than once. Maria would love nothing more than to have him, Lou, and the girls away from this life of crime and destruction. Maybe he is who I should be concentrating on. Maybe I should look into what I can do for him. For his family. For Maria's sake, if I take down Pete, I don't want to have to take down Mark too. Which, ultimately, I know will happen. I believe Mark isn't a bad man, he's just been thrown in with the wrong crowd.

My office door opens again. "What the hell is it now?" I bark before looking up.

A young rookie stands looking at me as though he's just shit his pants. In fairness, he probably has.

"Sir, I'm afraid you're needed downstairs."

"Fine." I gather everything on my desk, piling it up, and slip on my suit jacket. This had better be important. Walking through the station, I can already tell whatever is going on *is* important.

Craig stands at the front reception, barking orders to a couple of plain clothes officers. "What's going on?" I ask.

"A man was found in Saint Cuthbert's."

"The school again. What the hell is wrong with that place?"

"Yes, the school, but here's the thing. He's not dead. We don't have another dead body on our hands. We have someone who is in a critical condition in hospital."

"So, what are we waiting for?"

"Nothing. We'll go in my car," Craig says as we walk out of the station.

"Tell me, do we know who he is and what happened?"

"Nothing like the murders. This is one of Pete's men and he's been badly beaten up. From early indications, something heavy was used to hit him."

"A baseball bat?"

"Something much heavier. He's in a bad way and I'm not sure if he'll pull through."

"Pete?" I ask.

"No. I think this is more to do with Leo's death."

"Revenge. So, now on top of everything else we have to deal with, there's going to be a tit-for-tat war."

"Looks like it, and your bit on the side is going to be stuck in the fucking middle of this." He glares at me, and in this moment, I'm glad we have the car between us because my anger is brewing quicker than a cup of tea.

"I'll go in my own fucking car." I turn away from him before I say something I'm going to regret, because no matter what happens, I need to work with him. He's the best man, other than myself, I have on this case.

But that doesn't mean I have to put up with his crap.

I start my car, put my foot down, and speed off.

With Maria now in my thoughts, I want to call her, see what she's doing. I want to be back in her flat with her tucked into my side, and not thinking about the big bad world on the outside. If only it were that simple.

But life is rarely simple. I of all people should know that. Life is fucked up. Or at least mine always seems to be.

I try to focus on where I'm going, but it's hard. This could be what we need, a break in the case.

With our conversation playing over in my mind as I

pull into the hospital ground, Craig parks his car and we both get out of our cars at the same time.

"I'm sorry," Craig says, approaching me with caution. "But you have to see it from my point of view."

"I see it from every point of view and that's what you need to remember," I say firmly, letting him know that this is a conversation that we're not having.

"No, you have to remember it was me who had to watch you fall apart and nearly lose everything you'd worked so damn hard for all because of the woman you had let into your life."

"That was different, and we're not discussing my past."

"Fine."

I flash my badge and tell the woman sitting at the desk why we're here. She tells us where we need to go. Craig and I walk in silence until we come to the ICU. "I'll go and find a doctor see if anyone can give us information."

"Okay," I say as he walks away.

A doctor comes and gives us all the information he has. It will be a while before our victim can tell us anything, if he pulls through. We're told the next twenty-four hours are critical.

"What now?" Craig asks as we leave the hospital.

"I'm not sure," I reply, throwing my hands in my face and rubbing my eyes. "We can go back to the office and sift through the files for each of the cases, or we can go and visit Giovanni DeLuca."

"Do you think that's wise?"

"I have no idea, but this has to be linked to Leo's death. I can't sit back and do nothing. At least if we pay him a visit, that might be enough to stop anything else happening."

"Do you really think so?"

"No, but we can live in hope. I'm getting a bit tired of all this."

We drive separately over to Giovanni's restaurant, and more than once I've wanted to call Maria and tell her what's happened and who I'm certain my suspect is, but I haven't.

Why do I get the feeling this whole case is going to explode in my face?

It's almost seven p.m. and I'm sure the restaurant is going to be busy when we enter. I park out the front and wait for Craig before we enter together.

"I need to see Mr DeLuca," I say, flashing my badge at a waiter who comes over to greet us.

"I'll tell him." He rushes off, frowning in the direction of the kitchen.

After a few minutes, Giovanni finally appears. "Gentlemen, can I get you anything?"

"Just a few minutes of your time."

He walks into the restaurant, taking a seat at a table, surprising me that he hasn't opted for the privacy of his office. "What can I help you with?"

"I want to know what you know about the man that was found injured today at Saint Cuthbert's."

"I have no idea what you're talking about, Detective."

"I don't think it's a coincidence that a badly beaten man was found where Leo was found murdered," Craig says.

"At least it's not another dead man," Giovanni says, avoiding looking at either of us. I wonder why. "How is the investigation into my cousin's death going?"

"It's an ongoing investigation. So, you can't tell me anything about Saint Cuthbert's, Mr DeLuca?"

"No. If I had any information, I'd be passing it on to you."

Craig and I exchange glances and neither of us believe a word he's saying. I stand, knowing we're not going to get anything from him. "I'm sorry we've disturbed you tonight, but if you do think of anything, please get in touch. You already have my number."

"Of course, and sorry I couldn't be of any help." He stands, offering us his hand. Craig shakes it first and steps away. "Detective, my sister... she's very important to me. I don't want her stuck in the middle of any crossfire."

"What are you saying, Giovanni?" I ask.

"I'm saying that while Tony was alive, I was always worried about her. Now that he's dead, doesn't mean I'm any less worried. Especially where Pete Jamieson is concerned."

"I understand your concerns." I do. I have the same concerns myself, although I'm not for telling Maria's brother why. Why I feel so protective toward her. Shit, I can't even explain it to myself.

"Detective, whatever happens with everything in this, I need to know that someone will get my sister to safety."

"I can offer Maria safety, but you and I both know she won't take it."

"My sister can be stubborn, but if anything should happen to me, I need to know Pete Jamieson can't hurt her."

"Off the record, I want Jamieson behind bars and I'll do whatever it takes to make that happen," I tell him, and as I stand before him, I realise that I will do what it takes.

Even if it's not legal.

CHAPTER THIRTY-THREE

Maria

ME: Can I see you? M x

I hit send before I change my mind for the millionth time. I've typed the same words over and over, only to delete every single time. This is crazy. I shouldn't want to see him, but I do.

My feelings are so overwhelming that it would make more sense for me to stay clear of him. He's the perfect mix of good and bad. Combined together making a perfect man. In my eyes, anyway. I sit back with my wine glass in my hand and stare ahead, enjoying the first few moments of today that I've had alone.

It's hard to believe that the club is right underneath me. You really would never know because it's so peaceful. Taking a drink, I almost spit it out when my phone beeps.

Jack: You should let me in then.

He's here.

Standing, I walk over to the security screen and see his

face before me. I smile. I buzz him into the building and walk to the front door, open it, and wait.

His footsteps get louder the closer he gets to the top. "We must be on the same wavelength." He's holding a bottle of white wine in his hands. "I come bearing gifts. Happy new house," he says, leaning in and pressing the softest, quickest kiss to my now tingling lips.

"Gifts are always appreciated. Thank you," I say, moving from the doorway and allowing him access to the flat.

Closing the door, I follow him back into the main area. He puts the bottle of wine on the work surface and turns to face me. "Come here."

He beckons me over to him, holding out his hand, and I can't help myself. I walk straight into his arms. He leans forward, and sliding his hand over my arse, pulls my body closer to his.

His mouth finds mine as I wrap my arms around his neck, and our lips and tongues are mixing together as he kisses me.

Warmth spreads through me as his tongue flicks over my lips. His hands glide up my back, grabbing hold of my hair, tugging tightly. Our kiss has changed from playful to desperate in a flash. I slide my hands down the front of his shirt, pulling it free from his trousers. My fingers trace the dips of curves of his muscles as they dance back up the front of his body.

This is what I need tonight. The idea of losing myself in Jack McKenzie is more than appealing. To feel and breathe only him. This what I need, and from the look on his face when I first saw him, he probably needs this more than me.

With his hands exploring my body, I know we're both overdressed.

"Jack," his name is but a whisper from my tongue.

He stops, and I hate that our kiss has been brought to an end. "Maria, I need you."

Hearing the desperation in his voice, I take a step back from his hold. I undo the buttons on his shirt and tug it, allowing it to fall from his shoulders to the floor. I pull off the top I'm wearing. My bra is next, and both fall to the floor. His eyes widen as he watches me remove my jeans and underwear.

I stand before him, completely naked, all his for the taking. He loosens his trousers and frees his erection, his eyes darting between me and the work surface. I smile when he moves the wine farther along the counter.

I laugh as he picks me up and not-so-delicately places me on the counter. I wrap my arms around his neck, pulling his face closer to mine. My lips find his, his crushing against mine, reclaiming what he believes is his. All I can feel is the depths of hunger in his kiss. There's nothing calm or slow about this.

His warm hands explore my back, my waist, before settling on my hips, pulling them, moving me closer to the edge. I moan softly as his erection presses against me. He pushes inside me with an ease that makes me think we belong together. A thought I shouldn't be thinking, but yet again, I do.

He grips my hips, pulling me so tight to him that all I feel and see is him. There's no space between us. No layers to rip through. Tonight, like previous times, I've given myself to him freely, and it doesn't matter whether it's soft and gentle or hard and fast, because this is what I want.

We move together, each thrust going deeper and harder than the last. My arms feel weak as pleasure flows through my veins.

His mouth leaves mine, and all I can do is sigh heavily,

missing our contact. His hot breath sweeps across my skin. Goosebumps spread over my body when he kisses me. Small, sweet kisses. Not what I had expected. I moan.

I use my hands to keep me balanced on the edge of the work surface. I wrap my legs around his waist, sensing that he's almost as close as me. He pulls on my hips again, harder than before, and quietly groans my name as he drives into me harder. Every muscle on his delicious body tightens as my back arches.

My orgasm hits me, exploding like fireworks lighting up in the dark night sky. Jack's body falls on top of mine and he holds on to me. In this moment, I don't want him to ever let me go.

"Thank you," he says softly, kissing me right below my ear. The softness and intimacy of this single act doesn't go un-noticed by me.

"Hey, you have nothing to thank me for. We both wanted... no. We both needed that," I whisper, breathing heavily.

"How about we both get cleaned up then we can open the wine I brought?"

"How about we share a bath then we'll open the wine. And then, when you've relaxed, you can tell me what's troubling you."

"A bath with you sounds perfect, and the wine sounds good, but for tonight, I'd rather forget about everything except you."

"I can help you forget," I say, pressing a kiss to his lips.

"I'm counting on that."

———

"Now, get your fine ass into my bed, Detective. I'll get the wine and some glasses."

"Has anyone told you you're kinda bossy?"

"Nope. Not yet anyway. I'm sure all the staff that work for me will find that out soon enough."

He laughs. With the towel wrapped around my still naked body, I leave the bedroom. In the main area, I pick up his clothes, folding them neatly. I grab the wine, glasses, and his clothes, and walk back to the comfort of my bedroom.

"A woman of many talents," he says, sitting up in the bed, watching me. I put the wine and glasses on the drawers at my side of the bed, and his clothes at his side of the bed.

I stop and stare. I've just given him a side of my bed. Fuck, that happened really quickly. "What's wrong?" he asks.

"Nothing. Nothing at all," I say, dropping the towel and climbing in beside him. I hand him the bottle of wine and I hold the glasses.

I smile as he pours the wine. "A toast," he says as I hand him a glass.

"I'm not sure either of us has much to toast."

"Oh, I don't know. Here I am in the company of a very beautiful woman, and I'm happy that she hasn't turned me away. So, a toast to a very beautiful woman." Our glasses clink against the other's and we sit in bed, sipping on the wine.

"Are you going to stay here tonight?" I ask, trying not to get my hopes up.

"Do you want me to stay?"

"Of course. I believe it's your turn to make breakfast in the morning," I say, sounding playful.

"So it's like that, is it?"

"Yes."

"Okay, then I'll stay because it's my turn to make

breakfast. Wouldn't want you going without in the morning on my behalf."

"Sounds good. So, in the morning, I'd like you first, then breakfast," I tease, pressing my lips to his.

"Maria, you are definitely bossy."

"I'm just me."

"And that's the way you should always be. Don't change for anyone."

"Not even you, Detective."

"No. There'd be no fun if you did."

He wraps his arm around my shoulder and my body fits perfectly against his. This must be a sight; me snuggling into the detective's arms, both of us drinking wine in my bed. It must look strange, but the strange part is, it doesn't feel it. It feels right.

"What are you thinking about?"

"Truthfully, I'm not too sure. Although, it has gone through my head more than once how long will we be able to keep this quiet."

He sighs and moves, putting his glass down. He takes mine from my hand and puts the glass beside the now half empty bottle. I screech as he pulls my body over on top of his. "You shouldn't be worrying about that. Not now. I don't want to think of the consequences of our actions. But now… now, you are in a very interesting position." My eyes travel down his naked body and I smile in approval.

"I'm always happy to take advantage of the situation."

"Now, that's what I was hoping you'd say." He raises his eyebrows and smiles when I lower myself to exactly where he wants me.

I already know I'm going to be tired in the morning, but tonight will be worth the sleepless night.

CHAPTER THIRTY-FOUR

Jack

I'm sick of Saturdays in this fucking office. Today is no different from last week or the week before. This investigation has taken over my bloody life. I've been so consumed by everything that's going on within it that I feel like I'm missing something big.

And whatever it is I'm missing is bound to have been staring me in the face all along.

Four weeks since the death of Tony Fraser and we're still no farther forward. I still need more evidence to bring Pete Jamieson in for the other three murders.

The guy who was beaten up is still in a coma, and the longer he's in it, I know it will be unlikely he'll make a recovery. Even if he does recover, I doubt anything he would tell me would be able to link to Pete. No, his beating was one of revenge, of that I'm sure. Giovanni was making a point to Pete.

The point being, he can't get away with the murder of Leo DeLuca. I don't want that to happen, but as time goes on and at this stage in my investigation, it's looking likely that I have three, possibly four unsolved murders.

Like everything else, I don't have any evidence to prove that Giovanni was behind the attack, but I know it, and he knows I know.

This is all a fuck up.

The only good thing I have to look forward to is tonight when, hopefully, I'll get to see Maria after she finishes working in the club. Technically, it will be the early hours of the morning, but I don't care. I'll see her.

I've spent almost every night this week with her at the flat, and it's working out okay considering there's so much going on in both our lives. She's been busy with Crave; that's the one business she wants as her own. The one place she'll manage. And I know she'll make a huge success of it when she can put a stop to dodgy money going through the tills.

She doesn't need to tell me or spell it out; I'm all too aware of what has been going on within the walls of Crave. I'm not sure how she'll stop it because, from what I can see, Pete is trying to control things the same way Tony would've done.

We've skirted around the subject of Pete and all the dodgy dealings that she might be part of. She's hinted that she wants everything above board, but even I know that will take time. And time is the one thing I'm running out of. The powers above are putting pressure on me and my team to solve the cases. Too many criminals have got away with murder in the past.

Lifting my head, I look out to the room beyond my office; only a handful of officers are on duty today. My officers have been working some crazy shifts lately. They need some down time. They're not the only ones.

I've promised myself a holiday once these cases are closed. I'll need it.

I pick up my phone and stare at it before typing out a text: *What are you doing today?*

Maria: I'm at Exquisite M x

Me: I'm hoping you're just checking up on the staff and not actually working. A man could get a bit upset at that thought.

Maria: Green is not a good colour on you unless we're talking about your eyes, then it's perfect. M x

Me: I smile. *At least I know you like my eyes.*

Maria: I like a lot more than your eyes but your ego is already big enough it doesn't need stroking. M x

I'm highly bemused as another text comes through.

Maria: Shit, wrong choice of words. Can you stop distracting me, I'm trying to get some work done. The quicker I sort things here the sooner I get to leave. M x

Me: Sorry for distracting you. But I hope I'll be distracting you in the morning when I see you. And then you are more than welcome to stroke more than my ego.

Maria: Then you are allowed to distract. Now go and do some work. Surely you have plenty to do? M x

She's right, I do have plenty to do.

I shrug my shoulders and start looking through all the reports on my desk. There has to be something here in amongst all this. Although, it's like looking at a giant jigsaw and wondering which piece to start with.

I pick up the first report from the night of Tony's death and read it front to back then back to front. Might sound silly, but it's what works for me.

Items removed from the property;

Two electronic safes.

One pair of black ladies' shoes.

A key.

A diamond necklace.

Why the hell have I not looked at these items for myself? I stand, opening my office door. "Can someone please find out where all the items are that were removed from the Fraser property?" I call out. According to this report, the items were removed by the fire investigators, but I'd have thought forensics would've had them. As I look through the papers on my desk, there's no mention of them in any other report.

I need to know what the key is for and what's inside those safes and there's only one person that will be able to tell me the answers I need. I pick up my phone and press call.

"I thought I told you to get on with some work?" she says, her voice teasing.

"Yes, you did, and that's why I'm calling."

"This sounds ominous. What's wrong?" It's brief but it's there, a slight shake to her voice. Anyone else probably wouldn't pick up on it, but this is me. I can even hear the grass growing.

"There were a few items removed from your house the night of the fire. I'm waiting on them coming from the fire investigation team, but can you tell me what was in the safes?"

"Oh! You say safes as in more than one. I only know of one. It was in our bedroom. It contained money and a few pieces of jewellery." She sounds surprised.

"There's two listed on the report, along with a pair of your shoes, a key, and a diamond necklace."

"When you find out about the other safe, will you tell me about it?"

"Yes," I say, because she should know. Although she might not like what's inside it. "I'll let you get back to whatever you're doing over at Exquisite."

"Detective Jack McKenzie, I care as much for your

tone of voice as I do for spending time here. If you have a problem, that's yours to have. And if you're still in the same sort of mood, then maybe you should revise coming to the flat. Now, I'm just as busy as you so I'll speak to you when you're in a better mood and the green-eyed monster has been safely stored away."

She hangs up on me. I stare at the phone in my hand.

Fucking hell. She hung up on me.

I'm struggling here. I'm struggling with my growing feelings for a woman who, because of my job, I should stay away from. But I can't change what I want and feel. At the moment, I don't see my strength. All I see is my weakness.

And I know that's what Craig sees in me.

My weakness for a woman.

I need to re-group. Call on my strength to see and help me through this case and pray that Maria will still be there at the end of it.

Fuck, this is going to be hard.

"Boss." My office door opens and I find myself looking at Jenny. "Come in," I tell her.

"Thanks," she says, taking a seat. "Okay, so you wanted to know about the items removed from the Fraser house. The fire investigation team messed up. The items should've been handed over to us three weeks ago."

"What the hell?"

"It's okay. They are being hand delivered to forensics now. The safes haven't yet been opened if you want to be there when they open them."

I smile. "Thanks, Jenny."

"Can I get you anything or are you leaving the station?"

"I'm leaving," I say, standing and putting on my jacket.

"I thought you might."

STANDING IN THE ROOM, I STARE AT THE TWO SAFES. ONE I know from Maria contains money, so what does the other have inside it? The officer at my side is ready to open the first. We both have gloves on to avoid contamination of evidence. "Ready?" Rose asks. I nod.

She gets the first one open and takes out the items, placing them on the table. Money and jewellery; a lot of cash from the look of the bundles. This is the one Maria knew about. "That's all in this one. A lot of cash that's been kept at home."

"Yes, but not as much as I had expected considering it's Tony Fraser. Next," I say.

It takes her a few minutes to open this one. It's slightly damaged from the fire. She opens the door and steps to the side. "It's all yours, Detective." I step in front of it, and the first thing I see is a semi-auto hand gun. I remove the gun and check it over. It's fully loaded, so I unload it, putting all parts on the table. There's more money and two large padded envelopes, both with a name on the front. Miss C. Donnelly.

The first envelope contains what looks like business letters, private letters. I sift through them, wondering who the hell Miss Donnelly is, and then I see it. A scan picture. At the top it says Baby Donnelly. Why would there be a scan picture with that name in a private safe?

"Tony was having an affair."

Rose leans over and has a look at what I'm holding. "Looks like it, with a baby on the way." Shit. I wonder if Maria knows about this. Or am I going to deliver fresh news when I tell her?

I take a closer look at the papers inside. There's title deeds for a house, with Miss Donnelly's name on it. A bank account too. There are a few other items as well, but for the time being, this gives me something else to work on.

"Rose, thanks. If you find any prints that don't belong to Tony can you let me know straight away?"

"Of course."

Leaving her office, I know where I need to go. Back to my own office to find out who Miss C. Donnelly is.

CHAPTER THIRTY-FIVE

Maria

"SANDRA, this is getting tiresome. We are going over the same issues. Your staff should be your first concern; they take priority over any client. I don't care who that client is. The client that was with Chloe is no longer a member. Any client that treats staff in that way will have their membership terminated. There will be no second chances," I tell her.

So far, I've been here in Exquisite for nearly five hours, and I'm slowly losing my patience with Sandra. I'm not the only one. Poor Joe. He hates being here as much as I do, but it's been one problem after another today. I'm stressed just from listening to Sandra moan about everything, right down to the tiniest detail.

I'm surprised Tony put up with her. Or maybe he put up with her for his own selfish reasons. I wasn't enough for him, so maybe Colette wasn't enough for him either. I shake that thought away as quickly as it entered my head.

Although, I'm certain Tony has, at some point over the last few years, slept with Sandra.

"But these men spend a lot of money with us," she whines.

"Sandra, I'm sorry I'm not making myself clear. Our staff come first and I don't care if it's the president of the USA. If he mistreats our staff, even he isn't welcome."

"But…"

"I'm not listening to this anymore. Sandra, go home and take tomorrow off as well. While you're at home, have a think about what you want, because at the moment, you are making my decision on this place really easy."

She stands and stares at me before casting her eyes over Joe, who has stayed pretty quiet. She shakes her head before grabbing her bag and jacket and leaving the room.

"Thank Christ for that. She was starting to irritate me."

"Yeah, me too, but now it looks like I'm stuck here," I say.

"Well, then I suppose I should find something to do around here because there's no way I'm leaving you here alone. I can only imagine what the detective and your brother would do to me."

"Joe, about Jack…"

"Maria, what you do in your own time has nothing to do with me. But I'll say this, you look happy."

"Thanks, Joe, but there's many who wouldn't be happy with my current arrangement with the detective, including Lou."

"Yes, I understand that, but I'm sure even Lou would be happy for you if she knew everything about her brother. What I'm trying to say is, it's good seeing your smile."

"I always smile."

He laughs. "Yes, you do, but there is a big difference

when your smile is real as opposed to the fake one." I know what he means. "Now, if you have work to do, I'll go and find myself something to do."

"Like what?" I ask him.

"Some bar work or clear out the cellar. Just anything downstairs. Although, if there's any trouble, just let me know."

"I will."

Joe leaves the office and I know he'll keep busy even though he doesn't have to stay. He could've gone to Crave and checked that everything was okay. The club manager has told me it is, but I'm still a bit unsure about him. Tony employed him and he's used to things not being above board. And I've seen him a few times on his phone almost whispering. I'm certain it's Pete he's been talking to.

I'm still very suspicious of most people at the moment.

I look at the time; it's nearly seven-thirty p.m. I know I should be out of the office and in the main lounge area. I've been putting it off. I stand up and smooth down my black and cream dress. Grabbing my handbag, I take out my make-up and stand in front of the full length mirror that's on the wall.

Earlier today, I had wondered why there was a mirror here. Now I understand why as I freshen up my make-up. When I finish, I take a step back, staring at my reflection. The woman before me still carries the weight of the world on her shoulders. But something about me has changed over the last few weeks.

And I'm not talking about physical appearance, because no matter what shit was going on in my life, I always made an effort with myself. Although, before it was always for Tony's benefit, now it's for me. Because I don't want others to see my weakness.

My phone buzzes.

Jack: How are you?

I smile seeing his message.

Me: Still at Exquisite and going to be here until closing.

Jack: Ok, but on the plus side doesn't that close before Crave?

Me: Yes.

I smile again as I realise I might get to see him sooner than originally planned.

Jack: Perfect. How about I stop by and pick you up later?

Me: Sounds good to me. Joe is here now but if I know you'll be here later I can let him go home. He doesn't like this club.

Jack: I can understand that. See you in a few hours.

Me: See you then M x

Switching my phone to silent and with another glance in the mirror, I leave the office with a very real smile on my face.

The lounge area is already busy, and as I look around the room, I take in that there is a member of security standing by the bar keeping an eye on things. It's nice to know that Sandra has listened to some things I've said to her considering she's put up arguments for everything else today.

Joe is behind the bar. "You look at home behind there," I say.

"I've worked a bar a few times in my life," he says, finishing off pouring some drinks.

"That's good to know, but if you want to go home, you can."

"I won't leave you," he tells me.

"Jack will be here to pick me up later, and there is enough security here should there be any problems."

"I'm not sure."

"It's up to you, but honestly, everything is fine here."

"Okay, I'll go," he says with a sigh, and I know he's relieved he won't be spending the night here. I wish I didn't have to, but hey, it's my own fault for sending Sandra home. Joe spends a few minutes talking to a member of security before telling me he'll see me tomorrow night at Crave, although if I need him before that, I've just to call him.

In some ways, he reminds me of my brother with how protective he can be towards me.

――――

IF I DIDN'T KNOW ABOUT WHAT GOES ON UPSTAIRS IN THE private rooms, I wouldn't mind keeping this place on. Tonight, so far, everything looks as though it's going well. Nothing out of the ordinary happening in the lounge. The atmosphere is relaxed, and from where I'm standing it looks almost, dare I say it, normal.

I walk back toward the bar and almost trip over my own feet when I see him entering the room. He shouldn't be here. He pauses momentarily, his eyes scanning the room, and I'm not sure what or who he's looking for until his eyes meet mine.

With a smile on his face, Pete walks slowly and steadily toward me and I inwardly sigh because him being here is not good. Especially for me.

"I didn't realise you were *working* tonight?" he says, stepping forward and kissing me briefly on my lips. *What the fuck?* I hear the way he says *working* and it sends shivers through my body. Alarm bells ring loudly in my head. "Come and have a drink with me?" He's already had a drink or two tonight; I can smell it.

"I can't, sorry. Need to keep an eye on the girls."

"Nonsense. That's what security is paid for." He grabs my hand and tugs me toward the bar. What is he doing here?

"A bottle of the finest champagne," he tells the bartender. "With two glasses."

"Pete, I really shouldn't." I want to ask what he's cele-brating but I'm scared of his reply. I don't even want him near me, knowing that he played a part in Leo's death. He turns my stomach and all I want to do is run to the bath-room and be sick.

"You can't leave a man sitting on his own in an estab-lishment like this."

"Fine."

"Glad to hear it. Now." He turns back to the bartender. "Can you bring that over? We'll be sitting over there," he says, pointing to a corner of the room.

"Of course, Mr Jamieson."

With my hand still in his, we walk toward the seating and alarm bells are already ringing loudly in my head. He sits down and pulls me right beside him. Shit, any closer and I'd be sitting on top of him, although I'm sure that's what he had in mind. "You seem very tense." He has no idea how tense I am. He places his hand on my thigh. My eyes dart from my thigh to his face, urging him to move it now. My body stills. I want to move away from him, but fear is holding me back. My heartbeat is racing so furiously I'm scared it might explode.

I shouldn't be feeling this scared of him. I'm surrounded by all these people, yet I feel so alone, as though there's only the two of us in this room. Why am I scared? What is holding me back from pulling away and causing a scene?

Doubts.

Part of me thinks no one will take me seriously. Pete is well-known and seemingly liked here, whereas I'm just Tony's wife. The woman who would put up with anything.

"Pete, what are you doing here?" I ask as a member of

staff brings over the champagne and opens the bottle. He asks if we'd like to taste. I can only shake my head as I can't find the words. I'm totally speechless. Once the champagne has been poured, he leaves us alone.

"I think we should have a toast," he says, handing me a glass. "To the most beautiful and perfect woman in my life." I cringe at not only his words, but the lustful look that's in his eyes. "Well, say something?"

"What do you expect me to say?"

"Tell me that you're in my life."

"Pete, we have a working relationship, so of course I'm in your life."

"That's not what I mean and you know it. You've been teasing me for months, holding out on me because of your marriage. But, you don't have to now. Tony's not here to stand in our way of happiness."

Oh, dear Lord. I need to get away from him. "Pete, you and I are friends, we can't spoil that," I say, trying to sound sincere.

"Nothing could spoil what I know we'd have together." He inches his body closer to me and wraps his arm around my shoulder. I hold the champagne flute in my trembling hand, hoping that he's too drunk to notice.

"Pete, now isn't the time or place to be thinking about what we'd have together. Have you forgotten I've just lost my husband?"

"Maria, you and I both know your feelings for Tony changed in recent months. You forget how well I know you. I'm very good at reading between the lines." *That's what he thinks.* "There's nothing to stop us being together. We can have a happy ending. You and me and some kids. Just like I always wanted."

He kisses my neck over and over. I squirm as he holds me and I know if I don't get away from him now, something bad is going to happen. Something that not even I can bounce back from. I hate him. He's turning my stomach. My eyes search the room. I'm looking to grab a member of security's attention.

Why is it when you need someone, they conveniently disappear? Pete had this planned. I know it. Deep down in the pit of my churning stomach, I know it.

"Pete, I need to go to the bathroom," I say softly, hoping that he won't hear the panic that has already set in.

He stops kissing my neck. "You taste delicious. I can't wait to taste the rest of you. Go on and hurry back."

I stand and he swats my arse as I step away. I turn around and offer him my fake smile before walking quickly in the direction of the office. Once out the way of the bar, I type out a message.

Joe. I have a problem Pete is here drunk and is expecting me to…

I can't even bring myself to finish the text but I hit send.

My phone rings instantly. "Maria, what the hell is going on?"

"Joe, he's scaring me and I'm not sure how to handle it."

"I'll come back now."

"No, you can't. If you do, he'll know I've been in touch." There's a minute of silence and I can hear him thinking.

"Do you trust me?"

"Yes."

"Leave it with me."

I end the call just as I reach the office. I rush into the private bathroom just in time.

This is my idea of a nightmare.

I gasp when I see him as I leave the bathroom. He's standing in the middle of the room, his eyes roaming my body. The corners of his mouth twitch slowly into a smile and I know he's just mentally undressed me.

"Come here," he says softly, holding his hand out to me. I stare at him, frozen to the spot. "I said come here."

This time, there's more authority to his voice and I'm scared. I step toward him with a smile, hoping that I'm hiding how I really feel.

Right now, I feel weak and stupid. Again, a position I had hoped I would never be in again. *Dear God, please give me the strength because I don't want this.* Images of what might happen flood through my mind and it all starts feeling a bit too much. The room spins and my body shakes uncontrollably. I'm now seeing two of him. One was fucking bad enough. I hold my breath, gulping down hard in an attempt to stay quiet so that I can think. I need a moment to think straight.

"Maria, come and have a drink of water. You don't look so good. But I can help make you better."

CHAPTER THIRTY-SIX

Jack

SOMETHING IS WRONG. Not a name I expected to see brightly lit on my screen. I take a deep breath, unsure what he wants, and answer. "Joe what's wrong?"

"Pete's at Exquisite and Maria is scared."

"Where are you?" I ask, grabbing my car keys.

"She sent me home. I didn't want to leave her but when she told me you were picking her up, I reluctantly left. Can you do anything? If I go charging in there he'll know she called me."

"I'm leaving now," I tell him, hearing the anguish in his voice.

"If you go in there alone, Pete will put two and two together."

He's right, but I don't care what Pete thinks. The only thing I care about is ensuring Maria is safe. And if she's scared of Pete, she's not safe. I don't think anyone is safe when it comes to Pete Jamieson. Standing, I shrug my suit jacket on, wedging my phone between my ear and shoulder. "I know, and it's fine. I'm still at the station. I'll think of something. I'm leaving now so I'll be there in ten minutes."

"Do you want me to meet you there?"

"No. I think if we both show up it will raise more than a few eyebrows. I'll text or call you as soon as I know she's okay."

"Thanks, and please take care of her."

That goes without saying. I end the call as I walk through the station. He cares a great deal about Maria, and it's not hard to understand why.

Two uniformed officers are coming in through the front door and I ask them to come with me to Exquisite, telling them I've just had a report of a disturbance. It was all I could think of. They take off in a marked car and I follow in my own car.

Pete is still bound to wonder what the hell is going on, but I don't care. I'm sticking to my lie about a phone call about a disturbance. It does sound plausible given the fact we were called to an incident there only last week.

The speed at which everything is moving in all our murder cases and our investigations into the crime world that Tony Fraser and Pete Jamieson are a part of is giving me fucking whiplash. This back and forth, and not getting any real leads into who committed the four murders is doing my head in. For every damn step forward we take, we jump back three. I feel like I'm chasing my tail. We're no closer to catching any killers. And it doesn't matter what the hell is going on and where, Pete Jamieson's name is always in the mix. He's always in the thick of it, causing all sorts of trouble and problems, in not only this investigation, but now with my relationship with Maria.

Although, I'm not sure what my relationship with Maria is.

But, I do know one thing. I want no harm to come to her, especially from Pete's fucking hands.

The patrol car stops and I pull in behind it, in front of Exquisite. Nothing looks out of the ordinary, from the outside anyway. Getting out of my car, I'm trying to act calm. It will do no one any good if I go barging into the club, especially not Maria.

I show the security guy on the door my badge, even though the officers beside me stand in uniform. I recognise him from last week; I'm sure his name was Phil. "We've had a call regarding a disturbance," I say, entering alongside the security.

"Not to my knowledge, but Mrs Fraser is here and you're welcome to have a look around. Follow me," he says, leading the way through the lounge toward the office.

He knocks on the door but there's no answer.

"Open it," I say.

He uses his security pass to open the door and I enter. She's not in the office. I check the bathroom and she's not in there. There's a strong smell of smoke in the room. Maria doesn't smoke, so that means Pete has been in here, with her. "Where is Mrs Fraser?" I ask, my voice slightly raised. The two officers are now in the room, looking puzzled.

"She's not left the building."

"Is Pete Jamieson on the premises?"

"Yes. He arrived about forty minutes ago."

"I want Mrs Fraser found. Every room in this building has to be searched."

"But, there are clients…"

"I don't care who is doing what. I've been informed there is a disturbance and Mrs Fraser can't be found. So that makes me think she might be the one in trouble."

He frowns for a moment then realises what I've said. "Okay, follow me."

We walk back through the lounge, lots of eyes turn in my direction as clients whisper amongst themselves. My eyes roam the space, taking in every person here. None of them draw much suspicion from me before we take to the stairs. I'm not thrilled at having to go through each room, especially when who knows what people are getting up to behind those doors.

Phil has his phone in his hand and looks to be going through some sort of list. "What's wrong?" I ask as we pause outside the first door.

"This room is locked but it's not booked out to anyone. Strange." I look at the two officers and they nod in agreement to what I'm thinking. The big, bulky man takes a key card from his pocket and opens the door.

"Get off me," she cries, but he doesn't.

Her dark, tear-filled eyes find me and I can almost see the relief in her body. My eyes take in the scene before me as I storm into the room. Pete has Maria pinned down on the bed. He's gripping her arms and using the weight of his own body to hold her in place beneath him. The only positive I can take from the situation is that his clothes are still on.

"What the fuck? This room is taken!" Pete shouts before turning to see us.

"I'm sure you heard the lady, because I know we all did. She said get off her and I'd advise that it's in your best interest to do just that." I can hear the calmness in my voice, but I'm feeling anything but. Right now, all I want to do is grab this bastard and do what he's done to many others. Fucking kill him.

Slowly, Pete releases his hold and moves off the bed, allowing Maria's whole body to relax. Pete walks toward us looking so fucking smug with himself. What I would give to wipe that look from his face.

"Take him outside," I say to the officers. Pete walks past me and I swear he's lucky there are others here.

"What brings you here, Detective?" Pete asks as one of the officers grab his shoulder.

"Someone called in a disturbance, so here we are."

"How convenient," he says, his eyes darting back toward Maria before he leaves the room with the officers. Phil walks towards Maria. "Mrs Fraser, are you okay?"

"Yes, thank you, Phil. I'm fine now. Can I have a word with Detective McKenzie?"

"Of course, Mrs Fraser." Phil leaves the room with a nod of his head in my direction and I'm left alone with Maria. I take a step toward her. She stands, wiping away tears from her eyes. I know she sees her tears as a sign of weakness, but I don't.

"What are you doing here?"

"Joe phoned me. He sounded really worried about you. And now that I'm here, I can understand why. Come here." She steps toward me and I wrap my arms around her because I can now that we're alone. "Maria, tell me what happened and how the hell did you end up in this room with him?"

"Long story. But we ended up here because I was trying to buy myself some time," she whispers.

"I've got time to hear it."

"I'll tell you everything, but not in here."

"Okay." I kiss the top of her head and hold her tighter for a moment because I know when we open that door, and there are people around, I'll have to keep my hands to myself. That thought alone cripples me. I hate that I have to hide my feelings and my relationship with Maria from everyone.

"What's going to happen to Pete tonight?"

"What do you want to happen? My officers can take him into the station, but I'm not sure we will be able to press charges."

"Can you give him some sort of warning and then we can ask him to leave the club?"

"Yes. Come on."

We leave the room and walk down the stairs where the officers are standing with Pete. His eyes dart between Maria and me, and he smiles. Surely he can't know about us.

"Mr Jamieson, you're meant to be staying clear of trouble," I say. "Not causing it. No matter what I'm investigating, you're always somewhere near."

"Detective, you've interrupted my night, not the other way around."

"Okay, if that's what you claim, but I think we all know differently. Now, I'd hate to be your enemy if that's how you treat a woman who is meant to be your friend. You owe Mrs Fraser an apology for your behaviour before you leave the premises."

He glares at me. "Maria, I'm sorry. Please forgive me. I'm not sure what came over me."

Maria straightens her posture and looks him straight in the eyes. "Apology accepted, but do yourself a favour, Pete. Go home."

He leans over, kissing her on the cheek. "Sorry," he says then turns and walks away. I speak to the officers, telling them to ensure he leaves the club, and thank them both for coming with me. They can go back to the station and fill out their report.

"How long before you can finish?" I ask Maria.

"Now. I'll leave Phil in charge for the rest of the night."

"Good, because I'm taking you home."

CHAPTER THIRTY-SEVEN

Maria

WHAT A LONG NIGHT it's been. I kick off my shoes and sigh heavily as the door closes behind us. I've never been so pleased to be home in the flat. *Home*. It's funny because it has become home to me. Well, until I have time to look for something else. Jack wraps his arms around my waist and I lean back, accepting the warmth and comfort he's offering.

We were both really quiet on the drive from Exquisite. I didn't know what to say to him about Pete.

"Are you sure you're okay?" he asks again, moving my hair and pressing a kiss to my neck. I swear he's asked the same question over and over. It's strange hearing someone being so concerned about me.

"Yes. Honestly, I'm fine." I've been through a lot worse than Pete Jamieson forcing himself on me. "But I could do with a drink."

"Is there wine in the fridge?" he asks.

"Yes, and there's beer too, and whiskey in the cupboard."

"Sounds like you want me here."

I turn in his arms, standing face-to-face with him because I want him to see the conviction behind my words. "Of course I want you here. It's where I'd hoped you'd end up tonight, much like the other nights this week you've been here with me. Do you want to be here with me?"

His eyes are dark as he holds my gaze and a slow smile graces his perfect lips. "There's nowhere else I'd rather be. I want to be here with you. Only you."

I press a soft kiss to his lips. "Let's get that drink."

"I'll sort the drinks. You go and get changed then I just want to sit and hold you in my arms."

I leave his hold and go to the bedroom. I stare at the mirror, and all I see is a woman who is tired. She's had enough of Pete *fucking* Jamieson. But I don't know what the hell I'm going to do about him.

I wish he was dead like Tony.

I know I shouldn't be thinking that, but Pete is trying to mess with my head. He wants to pick up exactly where Tony left off. He wants control over me. And there's no way that's happening. I will never willingly have that man in my bed or sharing my life.

I need to cut all ties.

But how?

The popping of a cork has me looking toward the bedroom door. Jack. He might well be the man to help solve my problem with Pete. I *know* he's the man to solve my problem. Yes, I could give Jack all the information he needs to put Pete away for a very long time, but at what cost?

I'd be incriminating myself in a lot of dodgy dealings.

I run my fingers through my hair. Right now, I hate my past. Why couldn't I have met a nice man, who treated me right?

If I did, I wouldn't be here now with Jack.

"Maria, have you fallen asleep?" Jack's deep voice carries through the flat.

"No. I'll just be a minute," I reply.

I quickly change into a pair of silk pyjamas and make my way back to him.

Jack is sitting on the couch. The TV is on but the volume is low. He turns, hearing my footsteps crossing the floor. "Maria, what's wrong?" he asks, concern seeping through his voice.

"I want Pete out of my life. Once and for all."

"Come here." He holds out his hand, which I take without hesitation as I sit beside him. "I want him out of your life too. Maria, I wanted to kill him tonight when I saw the position he was in with you. Fuck, that goes against everything I've worked for over the years. If I can get enough evidence for a conviction, he'll be behind bars for a very long time."

"Pete Jamieson behind bars won't do me any good."

"Maria, look at me." I turn to face him. "I won't let him hurt you."

"Don't make promises you won't be able to keep. If he wants to get at me, being behind bars won't stop that. He has too many connections, like Tony."

"I only make promises I can keep and I won't allow him to hurt you."

I can hear the promise he's making, but he doesn't know Pete like I do. He doesn't know all the pain and heartbreak he's already caused to not only me, but countless families across the city.

My eyes drop downward and my body sags.

"Maria, what's wrong? What aren't you telling me?"

"Nothing. It's fine."

He tilts my chin, ensuring I'm looking him directly in the eyes. "Nothing good ever comes of secrets and lies."

"I know, but my life has been full of those."

"I know that, and if you want to talk, just know I'm here for you." A few weeks ago if he had said that, I would've thought he had an ulterior motive, but now I can see he means what he says.

"I know that."

I pick up the glass and settle myself into the warmth of his arms, neither of us saying anything else. This feels good. I don't ever remember feeling this comfortable in a man's arms. I suppose I must've felt comfortable with Tony at some point because I married him. I'm not sure where or when everything changed for me over the last fourteen years. I just know that fateful night in the club, I couldn't take any more.

"Maria, you're very quiet. Is everything okay?"

"Yes. Just thinking about the past and how I've ended up here."

He pulls my shoulders, turning my body to face him. He's smiling, "The past is the past. But it's brought you here to me. So regardless of how bad it's been, I don't care, because I have you in my life and I intend keeping you there, if you let me."

"What are you saying?"

"I'm saying I want to see where this takes us." He pulls me closer, leaving little space between us. He swipes his thumb over my lips and such a small movement has my skin tingling with desire.

I want him; there's no doubt in my mind about that. I want more with him. Although what, I'm not sure. "This, us, if anyone finds out it's putting us both in danger," I whisper.

"I've promised you I'll keep you safe. And Joe already knows. He wants to keep you safe too."

"I know he does," I say with a heavy sigh. I don't want anything bad to happen to either Jack or Joe, and I know with them both being associated with me, there's a strong possibility of that happening.

"No more talk about Pete or anyone else tonight."

My eyes search his face. "What do you want to do instead?" I ask, my voice low and seductive, because I know what I want.

"Oh, I can think of a few things." He's not the only one, but I'm glad we're both thinking in the same direction. "I need you, but after what happened tonight, I'm…"

I silence him with a kiss. A demanding, senseless kiss that should tell him that tonight isn't an issue for me so it shouldn't be one for him. I want us both to forget about earlier, and the only way for me to do that is to lose myself in him completely.

"Mmm, I like your way of thinking. I'm taking you to bed because I want you, and after, I want to have you in my arms as we both fall asleep."

"That, Detective, sounds like an excellent plan. One I'm totally on board with." His face lights up and, as I look at him, a sense of calmness spreads over me. There's no panic or fear. Only confidence and control. And as these thoughts sink in, I know I have a decision that I will need to make if we continue spending time together, but not even that has me frightened. Something is telling me that if we continue this relationship, not even my deepest, darkest secret will be able to come between us.

"Right, no more deep thoughts," he says, standing. Jack offers me a hand and pulls me to my feet, but doesn't stop there, and I squeal as he effortlessly throws me over his shoulder, slapping my arse. "Stop wriggling." His laughter echoes through the flat as he marches toward my bedroom. He unloads me to the bed and I giggle. "Now, that's a noise I could get used to hearing."

"What?" I ask, pushing myself up to the top of the bed.

"Giggling, laughing as though you haven't got a care in the world." He stands staring at me.

"When I'm with you, I don't." The words tumble from my lips without hesitation. I sit up as realisation hits me that I actually meant what I just said.

He unbuttons his shirt and removes it. "You're being very revealing tonight."

"What can I say?" My eyes are on him as he removes his suit trousers. "You bring out the best side of me."

"Glad to hear it." He lowers himself to the bed and crawls up toward me. His hands slide up my legs and heat rushes through me. With his eyes on mine, he grabs the waistband of my silk pyjamas and pulls them and my lace knickers down, before tossing them aside. He lifts his head and searches my face. I nod. His mouth curves, and with a glint in his eyes, he lowers his head. My eyes close and I groan as soon as his tongue connects with my clit.

CHAPTER THIRTY-EIGHT

Jack

PEOPLE COME into our lives for a reason. I'm a firm believer in that. Some stay with you for the ride. Others drop off along the way. I'm currently sitting at my desk and wondering what the hell I've done to have Maria in my life. Because the funny thing is, without her even realising it, she's powered her way into it and that's where I want her to stay.

I glance at my phone, internally debating if what I'm about to do is the right thing. *Fuck it.*

Me: I know you're a very busy lady but I'd like to take you for lunch.

Stupid! It might very well be, but I want to see her without sneaking around. Spending time with her at the flat is always incredible, but I want more. I need more.

I'm not sure what happened last night. Everything just seemed to click into place in my head. And it's not just the sex, which is hot. It's everything about her. She challenges me in ways I've never been challenged before. I see everything differently. My life for the last few years has really meant very little to me. My work has been my everything, but not now. Now, I want Maria to feel the same about me as I feel about her.

My life has a whole new direction.

My phone buzzes in my hand and I can only smile seeing her name flash on the screen.

Maria: Detective, you must be crazy.

Me: Crazy about you. Lunch?

Maria: I'd love to have lunch with you.

Me: Where?

I'm smiling because it was easier than I'd thought it would be getting her to agree to a lunch date.

Maria: How about my brother's restaurant? I have to see him today about funeral arrangements.

Me:Really?

That might not be the best idea she's had.

Maria: Yes. Really. For me it's the safest place to be. Somewhere Pete won't be.

Me: OK. I'll see you there at 1pm. But that means I won't get a goodbye kiss when I leave you.

Maria: I'm sure I can make it up to you later tonight.

I can already imagine the teasing expression that will be on her face as she typed out her last message. God, the things that woman does to me. All I want to do is be with her. To grab her hair, wrap it around my fist, and grind against her because I'm so, so turned on. And, right now, that is a huge problem.

I push back my chair and lower my head to the desk, giving myself a few minutes to breathe in an attempt to stop thinking about Maria and everything she makes me feel. But it's damn hard not to think about her when I have visions of her lying before me last night. I could only watch on as she fell apart over and over.

These thoughts are doing nothing to help my growing problem.

All I can see is her lying on my desk, legs spread and me taking control the same way I did last night.

"Fuck. Someone looks as though he's not getting much sleep." The deep voice of Craig carries through my office as the door swings open, banging against the wall. I lift my head and sigh. "Someone looks well and truly fucked."

"What do you want?" I ask as he takes a seat opposite me. At least now I no longer have a problem to deal with. I sit up and straighten my back.

"The victim in the hospital has come around. One of the nurses has said he's up for talking."

"Perfect. Take an officer with you when you go."

"What the hell?" He sits there studying me. "Why are you not coming with me to question him?"

"Because I'm going for lunch." *Shit.* Not what I was meant to tell him. "I have somewhere else I need to be. Someone that none of us have spoken with yet."

"I see. We'll get back to the somewhere you need to be in a minute," he says, leaning back in his chair. "This isn't good. You've already fallen for her, haven't you? Maria Fraser. Fuck."

"Craig…"

"Cut the crap. You shouldn't be doing this and you know it. Do you really want to put your career on the line? Everything you've worked so damn hard for? You get caught and you'll lose everything."

"Maybe, or I might get the woman and a conviction."

"Jack, you are my friend, and as a friend, I'm telling you this is all going to end in tears. Either with your job or your life."

"If it does end as badly as you think it will, see the positive. You'll get a promotion."

"Jack…"

"Don't. Whatever you're going to say, don't bother unless it's to do with the case." I stare at him for a long, drawn out moment. "If that's everything, you should get on. I have a few things I need to do before I leave the office."

He pushes his chair back and stands. "Just remember I've been there before when you've been hurt, and no doubt I'll be there again when this all turns sour." With that, he leaves the office, pulling the door closed behind him.

Deep down, I know he makes a very valid point. Yes, I stand to lose a lot, but I can't help the depths of the feelings I have for Maria. I know I should've walked away from her at the first signs I was starting to feel something for her. But now it's too late. There's no way I can walk away from her without causing myself more pain and grief.

It can't be done.

He didn't even ask where else I was going. I glance at the time. I have enough time to go and pay Collette a visit at the office. I'm just hoping when I get there, there is no sign of Pete or Maria.

Maria hasn't said anything to me about her, which makes me think she doesn't know about her and Tony, or the baby she's carrying. I'm hoping that I'm not going to have to break this news to her, but somehow, I think I will.

IN HINDSIGHT, I PROBABLY SHOULD'VE BROUGHT AN OFFICER with me and made this an official visit. But I want this off the record. I need to find out what she knows. I exit the lift and she's at her desk. She looks my way and smiles, her eyes roaming my body. There was a time I would've appreciated a woman's longing glance in my direction, but not anymore. The only woman I appreciate is meeting me for lunch.

"Miss Donnelly," I say, approaching her desk.

She stands and offers me her hand. "Yes, and you are?" She asks the question but she already knows who I am from the way she's shuffling from one foot to the other.

"Detective McKenzie. I'm investigating the death of Mr Fraser. I'd like to have a few moments of your time to ascertain your relationship with the deceased."

"I am rather busy, but okay." She sits back down at her desk, hitting some keys on the keyboard before turning her attention back to me. I'm not sure what Tony saw in her. She's pretty enough, but she's nothing compared to Maria. "What can I help you with?"

"What was your relationship with Mr Fraser?"

"He was my boss," she replies, looking anywhere but at me.

"I know that's not entirely true."

She looks at me, an almost shy smile on her face. Collette Donnelly is anything but shy; she's a woman who was more than happy to have an affair with a married man behind his wife's back. "What is it you want to know, Detective?"

"The truth."

She takes a moment, as though she's thinking about the facts she wants to give me. It would be in her best interest to just tell me the truth. "Tony and I were in a relationship. He was so happy when he found out he was going to become a dad. We both were."

"So, you are pregnant?" She nods. "Was he planning on leaving his wife?"

Her eyes dart around, again avoiding looking at me. I

already know the answer; Tony wasn't planning on leaving Maria. Why would he? "Well?"

"No, he wasn't!" she shouts. "He still wanted her, even though she couldn't or wouldn't give him the one thing he wanted. He wanted me and our child to play second fiddle to her. She was always going to be put first."

"Surely you must've realised that there would be a downside to getting into a relationship with Tony Fraser?"

"Yes, I knew what I was getting into, but I thought all that would change when he found out I was pregnant. He even came with me to the scan appointment. He was so happy when he saw the image on the screen. But even that day wasn't special enough for him to stay with me. He still went back to her."

"You sound very bitter."

"Of course I am. Wouldn't you be? He picked her over his unborn child. He hasn't even provided for either of us."

"Thank you for your time, Miss Donnelly. I am sorry for your loss," I say before turning around and walking back to the lift. As the doors open, I step inside and stare across to where Collette is sitting; she's still watching me.

I frown as I realise I might have a new suspect for the death of Tony Fraser. Although, after speaking to her, I'm not sure who she hates more, Tony or Maria?

Could Collette Donnelly be responsible for the murder of Tony Fraser?

CHAPTER THIRTY-NINE

Maria

"I THOUGHT I was meeting you later," Giovanni says as I enter the restaurant. "Where's Joe?" he asks, looking beyond me.

"Joe has dropped me off. He'll be back in an hour or so. We need to talk, and not just about the funeral," I say to my brother as he wraps me in his arms.

"Yes, but every damn time I see you there's too many ears listening," he whispers. "What about the villa? Do you still want to get away?" He releases his hold, only a little, and holds me at arm's length, "You look tired. Are you okay?"

"Yes, I'm fine."

He's still studying me. "You don't want to get away. Something or someone is keeping you here in Glasgow. Maria DeLuca, cosa hai fatto?"

The restaurant door opens behind me and I don't have to look back to see who it is. I feel his presence, but it's Giovanni's body tensing and his wide eyes that dart between me and who has just entered the restaurant that confirms it's Jack. "Sei una sciocca donna. Che diavolo hai preso in questa volta?"

"Giovanni, enough. Everything is fine."

Jack places his hand on my back. I turn and offer him a smile.

"This," Giovanni gestures between Jack and me. "Isn't safe for you. If Pete finds out, he'll kill you both."

"Giovanni, I'm hoping Pete will be behind bars soon enough," Jack tells my brother, who is now looking at me with disapproving eyes. "If you are not happy having us here for lunch, we can go somewhere else, but Maria thought this was the safest option and I'm kind of in agreement with her. I also have things I need to discuss about the case with you both."

"Of course. I'm not going to ask my sister to leave the family restaurant. But I do want to speak to you after, Detective."

"That's fine."

"I'll show you to your table," Giovanni says, almost grudgingly. We follow him through the restaurant to a secluded table in the corner, where there are no other diners. "Do you want the menu or…"

I butt in, "Just two specials and some water."

"Fine," Giovanni huffs, walking away mumbling in Italian. "La mia dannata sorella ci farà uccidere tutti."

"He's not happy, is he?" Jack reaches across the table, taking my hand, and suddenly I wish we were seated beside each other, because his arms around me would offer me comfort in what is a fucked up situation.

"He'll be fine. I was surprised when you texted."

"So was I. Are you okay? You look tired and pale," he says, and something in his voice has me asking myself the same question.

"Of course. I'm fine, or I was until you asked. Jack, what's wrong?" He's rubbing his thumbs over my hands and it's making me nervous.

"Collette Donnelly." Of course he would bring up her name; he's a detective, after all. And she's bound to come up during his investigation. But Collette's is a name that sends my head in a spin, making me dizzy. I hate her and I hate myself. She's carrying inside her body what I've longed for all these years. A baby. If only my life had been different, then I would've been a mother.

"What do you want to know?" I ask, looking him square in the eyes. I won't keep this from him.

"Did you know about her and Tony?"

"Not until recently. I had my suspicions that they had slept together, but…"

"Maria, why didn't you say something?"

"Say something about what?" Giovanni demands, putting down our water.

"Oh, Giovanni, sit down instead of looking at me like that," I tell him. He sits down beside me, looking at our joined hands. "I found out about their affair from James Stevenson. He didn't know about it until after Tony's death when Collette spoke to him to see if she and their baby were provided for."

"Merda santa! Quel bastardo."

"I can imagine what you've just said," Jack says with a scowl. "Maria, why didn't you tell me?"

"It's not something I want everyone knowing. She's having his baby. I presume you've spoken to her."

"Yes. I had to because one of the safes that was removed from your house had items in it for her. She doesn't know that, and they won't be given to her until after our investigation."

"What's in it?" I ask.

"There was a scan picture, but there's also details of a bank account in her name and title deeds for a house, also in her name."

"So he did provide for his child?" I look downward, not wanting to look either man in the eye. I've been so bloody stupid. "What does this mean?"

"I'm not sure. But I'll tell you this, she carries a lot of hatred toward Tony. He made it clear he would never leave you for her."

"If he did, life would've been so much easier." I say it without thinking. My brother puts his arm around my shoulder. I lean against him, still with my hands in Jack's. Giovanni knows, and it's only a matter of time before Jack finds out the type of woman I really am.

A waiter brings out our food. Giovanni releases me. "I'll let you eat." He kisses me on the head and leaves the table. I'm now alone with Jack, and as I look at him and the food on the table, I don't feel so hungry.

"Maria, is that all you've kept from me?"

"Yes," I lie. "I've not even told Lou that she's going to become an auntie. It's all she's wanted to hear from me."

"Can I ask a personal question?" he asks, eating some pasta. "Mmm, this is good."

"Of course it's good and, yes, ask."

"Why didn't you and Tony have children?"

"My reasons were selfish. Tony was desperate to become a dad. I wanted children, and I think I'd be a great mother. But I couldn't bring children into the world we were a part of. That would've been cruel. No child should have to grow up living the way Tony did. So the choice not to have kids was mine and mine alone."

"I'm sorry. For what it's worth, when you have children, you will be a great mum," he says as I move pasta around the plate. "This wasn't what I had in mind when I asked you for lunch."

"You have a job to do and I know these questions had to be asked."

"Right now, I wish I wasn't a detective because I don't want my job to come between us." I think I see sadness in his face at his very true words, but I could be mistaken. God, how I wish the same. "Is there a reason you're not eating?"

I look at the plate and I've hardly touched my lunch, whereas Jack is almost finished. "I'm not very hungry," I say. It's not a lie. I just feel a bit off today.

"What time do you plan on working to tonight?" he asks, changing the subject.

"I'm not sure. I might not even go into the club. Maybe just grab myself an early night, so that tomorrow I wake up feeling more normal."

"You should do that."

"That doesn't mean for you not to come over."

"If I can come over to yours, neither of us will get much sleep, and you look exhausted. So, I'll let you rest. But you've to take some paracetamol before going to bed and hopefully you'll get a good night's sleep."

"What about you? What will you do?" I ask him.

"I have some things to take care of at the station. A new lead to look at. Then a few reports to write up and then I'll take myself home for an early night."

I wonder about his new lead but don't ask, even though I want to. We carry on eating in silence, or rather, Jack does. I continue to play with my food. I know what my problem is. Since Tony's death, and even before it, I haven't been looking after myself properly. And with everything else going on, I just haven't put myself first.

I need that to change.

But in order to do that, I need to change everything around me. I thought with Tony dead, I wouldn't have to keep looking over my shoulder. How wrong was I? At the moment, I'm in an impossible situation and I don't know what to do.

I smile at Jack as he looks at me, worry lines etched on his forehead.

Footsteps come toward us and I look up, expecting to see my brother, but instead, find a very worried looking Joe. "Maria, we need to go," he says, and I look behind him because I'm certain something is wrong and, to me, that means someone has seen Jack and me together.

"Joe, what's wrong?" Jack asks.

"Nothing," he tells him, but the alarm bells are ringing loudly in my head.

Joe steps away from the table. "Give me a minute," I say to Jack. I walk towards Joe and I can see that something is very wrong. And if I can see it, so must Jack. "What's wrong?"

"It's McGovern. Jimmy McGovern wants to meet with you now." My heart sinks. I had hoped it wouldn't come to this. "I can't get a hold of Pete."

"I don't want Pete anywhere near a meeting with McGovern."

"I agree, but I'm thinking it's not wise for us to go into a meeting without back up."

Fuck. He's right. My eyes dart back to the table. "Maria, no. McGovern knows he's a cop. You take him with us and we're all dead."

"I know. What about Mark? I don't want to involve him, but I trust him."

"I'll call him now and tell him where to get us. I'll wait outside." I watch as he walks away with his phone to his ear.

This isn't how I thought my day would go.

I sigh, returning to the table but not sitting down. "Jack, I need to go. Something has come up and I need to deal with it."

His eyes search me and I know he's trying to figure out what the hell is going on. He's not the only one. "I'll call you later."

"Yes, and thank you for lunch." I step forward and kiss him before turning and walking straight into my brother.

"What's the hurry?"

"Giovanni, I have somewhere I need to be. You can have your chat with Jack now. But remember, he's a detective, so behave."

"You'd be the one best to remember that." I kiss him on the cheek and walk away, knowing he's right.

CHAPTER FORTY

Jack

"You and my sister?" Giovanni says, taking the seat Maria has just left. I sit in a daze, watching as she walks away.

"Yes, and I'd love to stay here and talk to you, but I think something is wrong," I tell him, standing.

"What do you mean?"

"I mean, I've just heard Joe mention Jimmy McGovern's name and that has me worried. Especially when she all but runs out of the restaurant."

"What the hell? What are you going to do?"

"Follow her and find out where she's going to meet him. Then watch on." He's out of the seat and following me as I walk toward the door.

"I want to come with you," he says as I open the door. Her car is just moving off.

"There's no time. I've already promised you I'll keep her safe, and I will. I'll call you later," I tell him, leaving him in the doorway.

Jumping in my car, I start the engine and wait because her car is stopped at a red light up ahead. The car is indicating left, so I have a few minutes of time. When the red light changes to green, I move away from the restaurant. I need to keep my distance. I'm hoping that Joe doesn't pick up on me tailing them, although I'm sure he will.

I call Craig. "Where are you?"

"Just leaving the hospital. Why where are you?" he asks.

"Following Maria's car."

"What the fuck?"

"Are you in the car on speaker?" I ask, knowing he took an officer with him.

"No, so talk."

That I'm glad to hear. "Look, we went for lunch, Joe came in, they spoke for a few minutes and Jimmy McGovern's name was mentioned, and she left with Joe. So, yes, I'm following her car across town."

"Okay. What do you need me to do?"

"Head back into the city and I'll call you when the car stops. Who did you take to the hospital with you?"

"Stacey. She was the only person not rushing out of the office."

That could work, depending on where Maria is meeting McGovern. "Okay, speak to you soon." I'm hoping it's somewhere public and not some rundown warehouse where he stores his shipments. I can send Craig and Stacey into a hotel or a restaurant; they can keep their distance but also Craig will make sure Maria is safe. And if he believes there is a problem, I know he'll intervene.

I hate driving in the city centre. Stopping and starting is no use to anyone in a hurry. All this congested traffic. It's about time the council did something about this. Put a ban on cars in the centre, leaving the roads a bit clearer for public transport and emergency services. That would make things so much easier.

I keep my eyes on her car that is now turning right, and I know they aren't meeting in some rundown warehouse. Keeping my distance and driving a little slower, I watch on as her car comes to a stop. She and Joe get out and he hands over the car keys to a waiting doorman. Mark is waiting on them.

At least she has Mark and Joe for this meeting. I feel helpless as they enter the hotel. I call Craig. "The Hilton Hotel."

"We'll be there in two minutes," he says, hanging up. I drive my car to the car park at the back of the building and park up in a space. There's no worse feeling in the world than how I feel right now. I have to sit out here not knowing what the hell is going on inside the hotel. Not sure if she's going to be okay with that bastard of a man.

Unlike Tony, Jimmy has spent time inside for crimes he's committed. His name hasn't been linked to any organised crime in the last eighteen months, and now that he seems to have re-surfaced, it has me wary.

Jimmy McGovern is a supplier of drugs, women, and guns. He takes no prisoners. Cross him once and consider yourself dead. An undercover investigation put him behind bars almost five years ago for human trafficking. I wasn't involved in that case but the reports I read were horrific. No woman should be put in that situation. He was drugging them and selling them on to the highest bidder.

He's kept his nose clean since he was released early on good behaviour. So why now? What is he planning and what does Maria have to do with him?

My phone rings and I answer it. "We're here. I've just handed my keys to the doorman. I presume you want us inside?" Craig asks.

"Yes. Pretend to be a couple. Have a few drinks. If they are in the bar, sit out of sight. Maria will recognise you and that might put her in danger."

"Will do." He ends the call and now there's nothing I can do but wait. And I'm not good at that.

CHAPTER FORTY-ONE

Maria

I FIX my hair nervously as we wait. "Maria, I need the confident woman here today, not someone who is nervous, because McGovern will use that to his advantage," Joe tells me. Mark sits at the table directly beside us, looking around. He's been very quiet today. He did mention to Joe that he thought Pete should be here with me for this meeting. I haven't told him what happened with Pete; he'd only tell Lou and she'd want to kill him.

"I know that, but I could really do without this."

"Why? What's wrong?" Joe asks, and I can hear his concern.

"I'm just feeling off."

"We'll get through this meeting as quickly as possible and hopefully that will be the end of your dealings with McGovern. After this, I'll take you home."

"Thank you," I say as a waiter brings over the pots of tea and coffee I ordered when we arrived. McGovern is already late and I'm starting to get a little pissed off. He wanted this meeting. The least he could do was show up on time.

"Mark, how are Lou and the kids doing?" I ask. I've not seen them in what feels like forever.

"They are both keeping her busy. Keeping her mind off everything. Although, I know she wants to see you."

"I want to see all of them. Why don't I have the girls one night next weekend and you two and go and do something together? Just the two of you. No kids. No Pete. No worries."

"You make that sound so easy," he says, forcing a smile.

"It is, and the girls couldn't be in safer hands than with Auntie Maria."

"I'll speak to Lou."

I spot McGovern entering the bar with two of his men. He stops, his eyes scanning the room. He smiles seeing me and walks toward us. I stand. "Gentlemen," I say as they approach. "Jimmy, it's good to see you, but didn't your mother teach you any manners? It's rude to keep a lady waiting," I say as he takes my hand.

"My apologies, Maria," he says, kissing my hand, and his wandering eyes skim over my body before lingering on my boobs. Typical man. He reminds me so much of Tony. He always assessed any woman he was introduced to. "I had a small problem that needed my attention."

We all sit down. "Would you like some drinks?" I ask.

"No, thank you."

"See, you do have manners. Now, what is it you wanted to speak to me about?" I ask, wanting to get straight to business.

"A woman after my own heart. No small talk."

A couple entering the bar grabs my attention for a split second. I turn quickly back to Jimmy, not wanting him to see where my attention wandered off to. Although, having seen Craig, I hope I manage to stay calm.

Bloody men in my life always wanting to rush in and save the day. Well, in Jack's case he's already done that and I suppose this is his way of making sure I'm okay. "Small talk isn't why you asked to meet with me.'

"No, it's not. I've been told you are now running your husband's businesses."

"Yes, most of them, although there are some aspects of his business I'm not interested in," I tell him before taking a drink of my tea, and now I wish I was drinking something a bit stronger.

"Yes, I can understand that. But, here's my position. I did a deal with Tony. We had a gentleman's agreement in place and I have already purchased the shipment he required," Jimmy tells me, leaning back in his chair, looking relaxed. His eyes focus on me, waiting for my reaction.

"Any agreement you had with Tony is now non-existent."

"Mrs Fraser, I don't think you understand. I'm holding you to your husband's word." I don't like how he's changed his way of speaking to me. "The shipment is ready for delivery and needs to be paid."

"I will not be held responsible for an agreement between you, especially when I have no interest in the shipment." I stand, trying to hold it together.

"I do like a feisty woman," Jimmy says, moving forward in his chair. Joe moves into place in front of me and Mark is now by my side. Craig and whoever he is with both have their eyes on our table. I hope he doesn't move or call Jack, because I know it wouldn't make this situation any better. "Mrs Fraser, this isn't up for debate. You're in charge of the Fraser empire so you'll have to handle this, or there will be consequences."

I push Joe gently aside and put my fists down firmly on the table. "I'm sorry, Mr McGovern. I won't be a pushover for you or anyone else," I say, leaning forward close to his ear. "I have no interest in your shipment of firearms, so I suggest you offload them to someone who actually wants them. Or, if you can't get rid of them, dump them in the Clyde, and that way we can ensure innocent people don't get hurt. Goodbye."

I turn to walk away, straightening my dress, but he grabs my arm. "I like you. You have fire and spirit, but that doesn't solve my problem."

"That's your problem, not mine." I pull my arm away and walk away with my head held high. I see his men stand from the corner of my eye, but Joe is standing in front of them. "Boys, leave it. Not here," Jimmy says.

I breathe a sigh of relief as I pass by the table Craig is sitting at. I try not to look at him as Joe falls in beside me. Mark is a few paces behind. Craig takes his phone and I already know who he's calling which must mean Jack is here or outside. "Just keep walking," says Joe. "You did good, but I don't think that'll be the last we hear from him."

"I know. That's what concerns me. We also have a small problem," I say quietly, hoping that Mark doesn't hear.

"Yes, I saw that. We were followed from the restaurant. Call him, just be discrete so Mark doesn't find out. Put his mind at ease. If you want to meet him, arrange somewhere from here. Maybe the club."

"Mark, are you okay?" I ask, stopping and turning back to him.

"Yes. I still think Pete should've been with you for this."

"I don't want that man anywhere near me."

"Why?"

"Because he tried to force himself on me at Exquisite."

"Oh."

At least he looks shocked. "Yes, oh. So I will be severing all ties in the coming weeks with him and, for the sake of your two girls, I think you need to do the same. He's a dangerous man, whereas you're a family man. And you should take care of them. We all have options to get out and you have one too. Grab it with both hands and don't look back."

"It's not so easy," he says heavily.

"It's only difficult if you make it that way."

"You don't get it." And as he says the words, I'm suddenly aware that I might not want to understand what he's saying.

"Talk to Lou. You both have to put the girls first. Yes, she might want to hang on to this world because it's all she's known and it's her last link to her family. If she does, you have to talk her around. I want all of you safe, even if that means you leave Glasgow, breaking all ties."

Mark nods as we step outside into the warm spring air. "Do you need me for anything else today?"

"No. Go home to your family." He kisses my cheek and walks away. I glance around, noting he's not walking in the direction of the car park. An attendant asks if we want our car collected and Joe tells him yes.

I stand outside and make the call. "What the hell do you think you're playing at?"

"Hold on," Jack says. "You're the one that dashed out on our lunch date to meet up with McGovern. I had to know you were okay."

"Well, I'm fine, and I'm sure Craig has already told you that."

"Craig told me that slimy bastard had his hands on you."

"Yes, he did, but I'm okay. Do you have time to swing by the flat?"

"Now?"

"Yes. I'm going there now."

"Okay. I'll be the car following you for the second time," he says and hangs up.

Bloody men. What is it with them? Our car is now in front of us, the passenger door opened. As I get in, I notice his car just at the exit of the car park.

So, he was here. He smiles and I can only shake my head in annoyance.

CHAPTER FORTY-TWO

Jack

"I'LL BE BACK in the office in an hour or so," I tell Craig.

"Fine. But I don't think you should say anything to her about how pissed McGovern was after she left."

"No, you're right. She doesn't need to know that. Do you think he will leave things as they are?"

"Come on. Even you know the answer to that. I don't know what the meeting was about because I wasn't that close to hear what was being said. Maybe she'll tell you but I'm not sure she will."

"I know. Hopefully I'll have more information when I'm back in the office. See you later." I end our call, still following her car through the city. This time, my journey isn't filled with so much worry about her, although I'm sure she'll have more than a few choice words with me. I want to know why she was meeting with McGovern, and I'm hoping she tells me the truth. At the moment, I have no reason to believe she's already lied to me, but this is huge.

McGovern is a big-time gangster, not some petty criminal hoping for a piece of the action.

Craig got a lot of information at the hospital. The victim was really talkative and stuck the knife into the DeLuca family. He's as certain as we are that the attack on him came from Giovanni. His attacker was Italian, he just doesn't know who it was. This is something I need to put to Maria and she's not going to like it that I'm running an investigation into her family.

I can understand why Giovanni ordered a hit on one of Pete's men, but I can't condone it. Not in my job.

Maria's car turns into the side street and stops. She and Joe get out. I park my car and get out too, and all I want to do is take her in my arms and ensure she is okay, but I can't do that, not here on the street where anyone can see.

"Joe," I say as I walk toward them.

"Afternoon, Jack."

"Joe, can you check everything is okay with both clubs tonight? I know it's not what you want…"

"Maria, it's fine. Don't worry about me, just make sure you get some rest, and if you need me, you call. It doesn't matter what time it is."

The hairs on the back of my neck stand. What's wrong? I look at her and she seems tired and a bit a pale. "And as for you…" She turns her attention to me. "I'll deal with you upstairs."

She marches away.

"Rather you than me." Joe smirks. "Be gentle with her. She's been feeling off today."

"What, since her meeting with McGovern?" I ask, full of concern and wondering if anything else happened that Craig hasn't told me about.

"No, she was feeling like this before. I think she's been overdoing it. She has so much on her plate."

"Noted. I'll make sure she's okay before I head back to the office."

"Can you send me a message when you leave?"

"Yes. I'd better head up."

"Good luck," Joe calls after me.

From the look on her face as she walked away from me, I think I'll need it. I enter the door, ensuring it closes firmly behind me, and walk up the spiral staircase. The front door is open, and as I enter, she's in the kitchen, putting on the kettle. "Maria…"

"Don't Maria me. Do you realise the danger you put me in having Craig and whoever that was in that hotel today? You're lucky Mark didn't see him."

"To be fair, I didn't realise he would be with you. When I heard McGovern's name, I jumped the gun. I panicked." She starts laughing. "What's so funny?" I ask.

"Do you want tea?"

"No. I can't stay long. I need to get back to the office."

"Okay." She makes a cup of tea, walks into the living area, and sits down, curling herself up. I sit down beside her and feel her head; she doesn't look well. "I'm fine, or I will be after a decent sleep."

"Will you tell me why you were meeting him?"

She turns and hesitates for a moment, deep in thought. "Because he and Tony had an agreement and he's planning on holding me accountable for a shipment."

"A shipment of what?" I ask.

"Guns."

"Fucking hell!" I jump to my feet and pace the room. "What the hell, Maria? I can't stand back and let this happen. You do know that?"

"I don't want it to either. You think I want to be responsible for innocent deaths across the city? I'm sure Craig told you I had words with him and I told him that I wouldn't be taking delivery of his shipment. But you know McGovern. I don't think he'll let me out of this deal."

I pace some more before sinking to the floor on my knees before her, taking her free hand in mine. "Let me help you."

"I'm not sure you can."

"Of course I can. I protect what's mine, and you are most certainly mine. Give me a few days to set something up that ensures he is caught in possession of the firearms."

"I'm not convinced."

"I promise I won't put you in harm's way. I'll find a way to do this without involving you. What about Pete?" I ask, thinking that I could end up putting away two criminals for the price of one if I set this up right.

"He's not been in touch. Mark said he should've been at today's meeting, but I couldn't have him there, not after everything. I know he wants the shipment. He told me so himself a few weeks ago."

"I promise you, everything will be okay."

"Funny, I actually believe you."

I take the cup of tea from her hand. "And so you should, because I mean it. Now, as much as I want to stay here and ensure you're okay, I need to get back to the office and deal with a few new developments."

"In Tony's case?"

"Not really, although we know everything we're dealing with is interconnected. So that brings me to what I need to tell you."

"And what's that?"

"We believe Giovanni ordered the hit on one of Pete's men. A revenge attack for Leo's death." I hate that I have to be the one to tell her, but it's better coming from me rather than someone else.

"I see. So what happens now?"

"If I don't have any concrete evidence then I can't seek a conviction. I want Pete behind bars. If Giovanni keeps his nose clean, then I have no reason to investigate him. Your brother wants to keep you safe. He wants you as far away from Pete as possible."

"If your investigation does take you straight to Giovanni, will you cut him a deal?"

"If, and it's a big if, then yes, I'll do whatever I can to help him."

"Thank you."

"Right, I'll go. Do you want me to come back later on and check on you?"

"No. I'm going to drink this, call Lou, then I'm going to bed to sleep off whatever this is that is lingering on me."

"As long as you're sure." I really wish I could stay here instead of going back into the office.

"Yes, I'm sure. Go before I pass on whatever this is."

"Nothing like share and share alike." I stand and lean down, kissing her head. "I'll call you later."

"Go away. I need rest."

"I'm away," I say, reluctantly walking away from her.

CHAPTER FORTY-THREE

Maria

I GRAB my phone and call Lou because, no doubt, Mark has already mentioned today's meeting and I don't want her to worry. It's bad enough hearing Jack's concern for my wellbeing.

"Hey, stranger," she says. "I've just been talking about you."

"Is that why my ears are burning?" I say, laughing.

"Yes. Mark tells me you want to take the girls one night next week."

"Yes. I'm missing them and it gives you a chance to spend some quality time together. You both need it."

"What about you, Maria? What do you need?"

"To rest, because I feel like crap. Then all I want is a normal life."

"You mean legitimate. No dodgy dealings."

"Yes, and I want Pete out of my life."

"Is he causing problems?"

"Nothing I can't handle." The intercom buzzes and I

walk over. Not even looking at it, I buzz him back in. What has he forgotten? He's only just left.

"Why don't we meet up for lunch during the week? I've not seen you in what feels like forever," she says.

"Yes, we should. Look, I need to go. I'll speak to you soon."

"Ti amo sorella."

I smile. "Anch'io ti amo." I end the call, putting my phone down on the table and walk over to the door. "What have you forgotten?" I ask, opening the door, expecting to see Jack. But, he's not who is standing in the doorway. All I want to do is slam the door closed, but I can't; his dirty boot is wedged against the bottom of the door, stopping me.

"Expecting someone else?" he says, smirking and pushing his way inside the flat. I watch on and visions of the other night fill my head, as he moves into the living area.

Two arseholes in one day. What the hell have I done to deserve this?

"Pete, what do you want?" I ask, following him into the living area.

"I heard you had a meeting with McGovern today and wanted to find out how it went."

"You already know how it went or you wouldn't be here." I lean against the chair and watch as he gets himself comfortable on the couch. *Looks like he plans on staying.* Why would he be here, especially after the other night? Unless he plans on finishing what he started at Exquisite. Chills run down my spine with that thought. Of course he must have that in his mind. A man like him is never going to be happy at the way events unfolded at the club. I don't have the strength or energy to put up with him today.

I look at where my phone is, and there's no way I can

grab it and call for someone to help without him knowing. I'm in trouble. Big trouble.

"I can help you," he says, putting his feet on the coffee table, sliding my phone farther away from me and crossing his legs.

"Everyone wants to help me today," I mutter.

"I'll take the shipment for you." I mull over his words and my conversation with Jack springs straight into my mind.

"I'd rather none of us was bringing a shipment of firearms into the city."

"In an ideal world, we wouldn't need them, but you've lived long enough in our world. You know how this goes. We need to protect ourselves and our families. And the money we make is good."

Unfortunately, I do. "Fine. Can we work out the details at a later date? I'm not feeling well and just want to get to bed."

"I'll stay and look after you," he says softly, his eyes drifting from my face down my body, and then I see it. The same old dirty smirk that he had on his face mere minutes ago. "Seeing as lover boy couldn't stay." I freeze in horror at his words. *He knows*. Panic sets in and all I want to do is run. "Neither of you are very discreet."

"Pete, just go."

"I'm going nowhere until I get what I want. You and the detective. Who'd have thought you'd put out for a man of the law? Tony will be turning in his grave. What have you told the detective about our businesses?"

"Nothing. What do you take me for?"

"I took you for a woman who had more sense than you're currently displaying. What about Tony?"

"What about him? He's been sleeping about for as long as I can remember, and what about Collette and his baby?" He doesn't flinch at what I've said. "How long have you known he was having an affair with her?"

"Since it started. He needed someone to talk to, especially when she told him about the baby. A baby that you refused to give him."

"Have any of you ever wondered why I didn't want a baby with him?" I yell. He stares at me, waiting for me to continue. "Because I didn't want to bring a child into this life we all lead. A child is innocent and pure."

"I remember when you were once pure." He stands. His eyes darken and I hate the expression on his face. It scares me. He steps toward me and I know I should back away instead of being a fool and standing up to him. "What is it about you, Maria? You always seem to pick the wrong men. Tony, and now the detective. Neither is any good to you dead." I gasp. "Don't worry. Your friend, and I use the term loosely, is still alive. No harm will come to him, yet."

"You mean if I give you what you want?"

"What I want is you by my side and in my bed night after night."

"Over my dead body," I say as he closes in on me.

"It wouldn't be the first time I've fucked a dead woman." He reaches out, tucking my hair behind my ear. I flinch from the small touch. Why does his statement come as no surprise to me? "But I don't want you dead, Maria. I want you very much alive. I can give you everything Tony couldn't, and in return, you'll give me the one thing you never gave him. An heir. Someone to carry on my family name." His rough fingers cross my face before touching my lips.

"What makes you think I even want children?" I say, shrugging his hand away from me.

"Because I've watched you with Lou's girls and there's

no doubt in my mind you want children. And what's more, I know you'll be an amazing mum to our children."

He's delusional. Fucking delusional. Not a hope in hell of that ever happening. I'd rather be dead than spend my life stuck with a murdering bastard like him. "Please go home," I say as he snakes his arm around my waist.

"I'm not going home until you come with me to where you truly belong," he says, pulling my body closer to his.

"I don't belong with you. Never have and I never will," I tell him through gritted teeth.

I'm not looking at him. I can't. Although, maybe I should've been when I feel the force of his hand slapping me across the face.

"Now look what you've made me do."

I push against him using all the strength I can muster, but it's not enough. His grip tightens around my waist and his other hand is digging deep into my shoulder.

"I love you. I don't want to hurt you, but when you resist and fight against me, you leave me no choice."

I laugh, because this situation is so totally fucked up. "Love? You don't know the meaning of the word."

"I do. I was prepared to wait. Give you time to grieve, but that bastard has been here every fucking night. You're not grieving. You're nothing but a fucking slapper."

I try again to pull out of his hold, but it's pointless trying as he grips on tighter. I have no energy to fight against him.

He leans forward and starts kissing his way around my neck. Bile rises in my throat and I have to force it to stay down. His dark eyes are watching me, waiting for me to make my move.

I won't make it yet. Not when he's expecting it. I'll let him think he's won. I close my eyes as his mouth works its way slowly up my neck until I feel his lips on mine. This isn't how I saw my day. All I saw was some painkillers and my bed.

With his mouth on mine, I know I have to let him think he's won, but it's proving harder for me to allow. His tongue slides along my lips, trying to force them open. With a deep breath, I part my lips and reluctantly kiss him back.

With my stomach churning and bile rising, I move my hands and glide them up his back. His grip loosens and I almost sigh with relief, but his kiss deepens and it's the last thing I want.

I open my eyes and he's so lost, so consumed by the kiss. I gather all the strength I have, and with a deep breath, I push his body away from mine, breaking all contact. He stumbles backward and I do what I've wanted to do for so long; I lift my foot and kick him hard in the balls.

He falls to the ground, moving the coffee table as he does, taking my phone farther away from me. I move quickly, but not fast enough because he grabs my ankles and pulls me to the floor. Trying to stop myself, I bang my head on the floor.

Shit.

Pain radiates through my head. Wriggling and still lashing out with my feet kicking against him, he doesn't move. Instead, he laughs as he lunges himself at me, his body now on top of me. I push against his chest, but all I get for my troubles is another slap in the face and a punch in my stomach. Tears fill my eyes and the pain… nothing stops the pain that is shooting through my body.

I close my eyes because we've been in this position before, only Jack was there to save me. All I see is darkness, and all I hear is his chilling laugh. The one I heard that fateful night in the cellar of the nightclub when I know he and Tony must've raped that poor young girl.

This is my punishment. For not being brave enough to attempt to save her. This is my fate. This is how I've chosen to live my life, and now I must pay the price.

CHAPTER FORTY-FOUR

Jack

I'VE TOSSED and turned for the past few hours and I'm not one hundred percent sure why. It's been a long day that I thought would be over by now. I switch on the bedside light and glance at my phone. Two a.m. and no messages or calls from Maria.

I can't get her out of my head. She looked so poorly when I left her this afternoon. I call her again. It rings out. I know she's probably sleeping, but I have this feeling deep in my gut that something is wrong. And that is what has been keeping me awake.

I stare at my phone in my hand, hesitating for a minute before I press call. It rings twice. "Jack, what's wrong?" Joe asks groggily.

"Have you heard from Maria since this afternoon?"

"No, why?"

"I'm not sure. I just don't have a good feeling. Something doesn't feel right. My gut hasn't let me down before."

"Okay, that'll do for me. I'll meet you at the flat," he says, and I can hear rustling in the background.

"Do you have a key?"

"Yes." He ends the call and I get out of bed, pulling on a pair of jeans and a t-shirt. I rush over to the cupboard and grab a pair of trainers and put them on before leaving my bedroom. Dashing down the stairs, I grab my car keys and leave the house. I'm at the bottom of the steps when I realise I've not set the alarm or locked the front door.

I take a deep breath and run back inside, setting the alarm before locking the front door. Opening the car, I'm trying to control my thoughts. None of them are good. I just can't shake the feeling that something is very wrong.

Five minutes; that's all it should take me at this time of the morning. Traffic will be quiet. I start the engine and speed off along the street, racing toward my destination. I know I might be over-reacting, but I'd rather know and see for myself that Maria is okay.

Traffic might be quieter, but the streets are still busy with clubbers heading home after a night out. It's funny, sometimes the city seems so much busier at night. Or maybe in the depths of the night, I tend to notice more.

As I drive along the road, there are people coming out of the club. I turn into the side street and Joe is just getting out of his car. He nods as I get out of my car and walk toward him. Neither of us say anything as he puts the key in and opens the main door. I'm glad he has a key because I can't remember the damn code she told me for the door. My heart starts pounding fast as I take the stairs.

The door to the flat is open. I turn and glance at Joe, who is now pulling a gun from the back of the waist of his trousers.

Bloody hell.

I don't think. I act, not waiting to see what Joe is going

to do. All my years of training are gone. I left them at the bottom of the staircase. Fear is controlling me. It's the one emotion I always tuck away. It's hidden in the depths of my soul, but not tonight.

I dash into the flat and freeze.

In my head, I'm trying to process the scene before me, but I can't. Joe quickly moves past me and is on the floor, lifting her head, but all I can focus on is all the blood. So much blood.

"She has a pulse, but it's weak," he says, his eyes filled with tears.

Relief fills me at his words. She's alive.

So many thoughts enter my head, but I need to re-focus on what we need to do. And right now, the most important thing is to get her the help she needs. "Let me take her," I say. "You call an ambulance and tell them I'm on the scene too."

He moves away and I take his place beside her on the floor. I take her in my arms and hold her, staring at her face that is now covered in bruises. Who would've done this to her?

"Pete! He's responsible for this." I lift my head, and even though Joe is talking on the phone, giving our location, he nods his head, agreeing with me.

I turn back to Maria because she needs me now. I have plenty of time to deal with Pete and I will deal with him, even if I have to kill him myself. "Maria, talk to me. I'm here. Everything will be okay." Tears trickle slowly down my face. I need her to be okay. She has to be. I rock her gently in my arms, repeatedly telling her that she'll be okay, that I'll look after her.

She groans. It's only a little, but it gives me hope. Something to hold on to and focus on. "I'm staying with you, forever."

This beautiful woman in my arms has already been through so much in her life, she has to come through this. But when my eyes glance down her body and see where the blood is coming from, I'm not sure she will recover. Why is there so much blood there?

"Jack, keep talking to her. I'm sure she can hear you. I'm going downstairs to let the paramedics up." I nod without looking at him.

Her skin is cold so I hold her a bit tighter, hoping that the warmth of my body will heat her. I bury my face against her and now I'm sobbing. *She has to be okay.* She's only just come into my life. We have to have more time together. I press a kiss on her soft, cool lips and she groans again. "I love you," I say quietly and I'm slightly shocked by my admission.

Footsteps and loud voices carry up the stairs and I know help is on the way. "Jack!" Joe places his hand on my shoulder. "Let them do their job. They'll look after her," he says, and he must sense my reluctance to leave her. But I stand and step back, watching them do what they have to do to save the life of the woman I love.

"How much fucking longer?" I say to Joe as we sit in this private waiting room.

"As long as it takes." I know he's right, but I'm so restless. I just need to know she's doing okay. I need a doctor to come and give us an update on what's wrong, and what they're going to do to fix her. "Jack, I should call Lou and Giovanni."

"You should. I know Maria would want them here."

"Yes, but what about you?" he asks.

"Giovanni knows about us but Lou doesn't, and let's

face it, she won't be happy. But I'm not leaving. Lou will just have to deal with it."

He nods and takes his phone from his pocket. I can hear him talking but I've already zoned his voice out.

The waiting room door opens and there stands Craig, his cold eyes set upon me, judging me. "Come in instead of standing there on display."

"I got a call. How is she?" he asks, sitting down beside me.

"We don't know anything yet."

"What about you?"

"Hanging in."

"Okay." He pauses for a second, his eyes now watching Joe. "I don't know what we can say that won't…"

"What? Result in me being suspended? Right now, I don't give a flying fuck. All I want to know is that Maria will pull through."

"Sorry," Craig says.

Joe ends his call and takes a seat opposite me. "Why would you get suspended? I called you because you are dealing with the investigation into the Fraser murder after I found her beaten up and lifeless body in her flat."

I lift my head and shake it. I don't want him to lie. Not for me.

"That'll work," Craig says, his eyes drifting across the room and back to me. "It will."

The door opens and a doctor enters and takes a seat. "Detective, you came in with Mrs Fraser?"

"Yes. How is she?"

"She's awake and responsive and asking for you." I'm not the only one sighing with relief. As I look at Joe, he's wiping away a tear from his eye.

"Can I see her?"

"Yes, I'll take you through. Although, I don't want her

being questioned right now. I'm sure she'll give a full statement when she gets some rest. And rest is what she needs."

The doctor stands and holds the door open for me. I look at Joe. "On you go. I'll see her next," he says.

I follow the doctor along the quiet corridor to the room she's in. He opens the door and I step inside. A nurse is cleaning her face and she's wincing in pain from the touch.

"Maria." Her name falls from my lips. She looks better but scared.

The nurse glances between us. "I'll come back and do this. Leave you two alone."

"Thank you," I say as the nurse leaves the room, closing the door behind her.

Neither of us speak as I walk toward her. I pull the chair from the side but she wriggles and pats the bed, making space for me to sit beside her. "I'm glad you're here," she says softly.

"Lou and Giovanni are both on their way."

"So I only have you to myself for a short time?"

"Afraid so, but I'll make it up to you. Maria, what happened?"

She moves her head and I can see the pain she's in. I hate that bastard. "I called Lou straight after you left. I was too busy talking to her that when the intercom buzzed, I didn't look to see who it was. I thought it was you, maybe you'd forgotten something. So I let him straight in, thinking it was you. It wasn't until I ended my call, opened the door and saw him filling the doorway I realised."

"Pete?"

"Yes."

"Maria, what did he do?" I ask, although I'm not sure I want to hear the details.

"He was so mad at me. He knows about us. Kept saying I was nothing but a whore for putting out for you.

He told me over and over he loved me, but at the same time he was slapping me and punching me in the stomach. He was on top of me and I closed my eyes just wanting it to be over, but he stopped after he removed my knickers."

My blood is boiling at her version of events.

"He held his hand in front of me and asked what was with all the blood. I couldn't tell him so he hit me again and again."

Tears run down her face and I take her hands I mine. "Stop if you want."

"No, I'm fine. The pain that was radiating through my body was unbearable and I couldn't move. He got up and kicked me in my stomach and just left me there, lying on the floor covered in blood."

"And the blood? What has the doctor said?"

"That I was pregnant. Around eight or nine weeks."

I watch on helplessly as she tells me. It was Tony's baby. A baby she vowed never to have with him, yet she was pregnant and didn't know.

"I'm sorry," I say.

"Don't be sorry. Tony's baby is the last thing in the world I wanted. I blame myself. If I had known I was pregnant, well, I wouldn't have been…"

She's babbling and rambling on, not making sense. "I'll issue an arrest warrant for Pete."

"Fine," she mutters, turning away from me.

"Maria, is there anything else you need to tell me?" She stares blankly toward the window and a feeling of unease spreads through my veins. "Maria!"

She turns back to me, tears filling her eyes. "It was me. No secrets."

She's making no sense. No sense at all. "What was you?" I ask. I let go of her hands and the sad look in her eyes tells me all I need to know. "All this time. You've been with me. I've slept in your bed night after night. Trusting you. And all this time you've lied to me."

"It's not like that!" she cries. I stand up and step away from the bed, running my hands through my hair. "I didn't pull the trigger."

"So you fucking hired someone to do it for you. That makes you as bad as he was."

Her crying turns to full on sobs and I know if I stay in this room a minute longer, I'll put my arms around her and I can't do that. Not now. Not knowing the truth.

"Jack, tell me you understand?" Her trembling voice pleads with me.

But I can't tell her what she wants to hear because there are so many ways Tony could've been dealt with. If only she had come to us first before taking the law into her own hands. I had so many lists of suspects, but Maria Fraser was never on my radar, even after Craig brought her up time and time again.

I'm a fool. Yet again.

Only this time around, the hurt is so much more painful than I could ever have imagined. "Jack, please. I need you. I need your help."

"No, you needed help before you decided to end Tony's life. I can't help you now," I say, moving toward the door. I take one final look at the woman I've fallen in love with, before opening the door and walking away.

"No, Jack, please!" she screams. Her cries haunt me as I walk away.

To be continued xx

BOOKS BY

KAREN FRANCES

The Captured Series

Family Ties a Captured Series Novella

He's Captured my Heart Book 1

He's Captured my Trust Book 2

He's Captured my Soul Book 3

She's Captured my Love Book 4

Captured by Our Addiction Book 5

A Beautiful Game Series

Playing the Field a Beautiful Game Novella

Playing the Game Book 1

Playing to Win Book 2

Saving the Game

Moving On a standalone

The Scripted Series

Scripted Reality Book 1

Scripted Love Book 2

Enemies of the City Series

Secrets and Lies Book 1

Love and Truth Book 2 coming soon

Past and Future Book 3 coming late 2019

ABOUT THE AUTHOR

Karen Frances is the author of twelve romance novels and two novellas.

She currently lives just outside Glasgow, Scotland, with her husband, five children and two dogs, although she does dream of living somewhere warm and sunny and by the sea. Her days are spent helping her husband run their family business. She spends some of her free time trying to keep fit and prepare healthy meals for her family, when their busy schedules allow them to all sit down at meal times together. The rest of her free time is spent plotting stories, writing and occasionally reading.

Karen writes stories that are both believable and full of life. More often than not she loves sending her readers on an emotional journey alongside her characters.

For more information
www.karenfrancesauthor.co.uk

ACKNOWLEDGMENTS

It's always hard trying to remember everyone I should thank when it comes to the end of the process, so this time around I'm keeping this short and sweet.

To my amazing team that help me bring my stories to life and publication, I'll always be grateful for all you do; Karen, Kari, Krissy, Suzie, Margaret, Pauline and Leah thank you all for everything you do.

A huge thank you to all the readers and bloggers who read my stories, taking time to review and recommend my books to others.

I'm extremely fortunate to be surrounded by a supportive family and friends and for that I'll always be thankful.

Printed in Great Britain
by Amazon